EZEKIOLA
AND THE
RISING
SONS

THE FOUNTAIN OF FIRE

2

LUCY KYAN

ISBN(eBook): 979-8-9855985-2-0
ISBN (Paperback): 979-8-9855985-3-7

This is a work of fiction. The characters, names, incidents, places, and dialogue are products of the author's imagination, and are not to be construed as real.

Leone Potere Press—Pompano Beach, FL

Title Production by The Book Whisperer

Cover design by Jane Dixon-Smith

For all the souls living on this planet;
and for the ones guiding them.

"In order for the light to shine so brightly, the darkness must be present."

— Sir Francis Bacon

Chapter 1

Reviving the warrior

In the Black Mountains of Circa, the Emerald's training ground painted a sobering portrait of fighters unable to make an ounce of progress with Ezekiola. He stood motionless in their midst, bearing a faraway gaze of utter despair. Breathing heavily, wearing only breeches, sweat poured down his body, magnifying fresh bruises.

"Let me guess; he's asking for another break?" Igor asked, his heavy accent dripping with sarcasm as one of his men approached. It was Yossan, one of his top Emerald warriors, assigned to supervise Ezekiola's training, distinguishable from his smooth, golden-brown skin. Unlike their trainee, Yossan's body bore no bruises. Nor sweat, but he had a scowl on his face and shook his head.

"This is not working," Yossan said.

"Did you try the last technique I showed you?"

"Yes, it didn't work either," Yossan answered curtly.

Igor stood up, scratched his head, and spat sideways, a tic he never managed to eliminate.

"It's been nothing but failures with him!" he exclaimed,

baffled. "How could this boy have absolutely no fighting skills? Wasn't he a skilled warrior, serving the Sons of the Night Sky as Zeke?" he asked.

Yossan remained quiet instead, knowing well that after a month of trials, no answer would satisfy his superior.

Training was something Ezekiola had never done before. Perhaps if it had been regular training, he could have handled it. But training on volcanic grounds in some dark, misty mountains gave him a sense of landing in purgatory. A layer of black film caused by toxic fumes covered his bare skin, and waves of heat from unpredictable winds were only part of the ordeal. There were instances he could barely see what was in front of him. Other times, his skin would literally peel off because he suddenly walked into a pocket of blazing hot air. Almost everything here irritated his skin, including the black soap.

It was a far cry from the summer he expected to have, one where he would spend time with his friends, visit his family, and above all, see more of Leanne. He had so many questions for her—about her life, how she lived on Planet Blue, what she thought of Circa, and especially, what she thought of their unbreakable bond. Instead, right after his link was sealed with her, he was shuffled back and forth between his teachers and Headmaster Nomi Antares. He barely saw his friends, and quickly had to say goodbye to Leanne before being sent off to the Emerald training camp. The most they had shared was one long walk in the Black Forest, the memory of which he carried with him like a scent, one he wished would never wash off.

After the first few days, Ezekiola realized the Emeralds had skipped his preliminary training altogether. Only later, did he understand why. It wasn't just his fine build that gave the impression he was a proficient fighter. It had to do with the fact that Ezekiola had merged with the body of his twin, Zeke. Initially, as this was new to them, the Emeralds were curious to see if Ezekiola would have organically acquired Zeke's fighting abilities, with the hopes that some minimal knowledge would have unconsciously transferred from Zeke to him. After a few training sessions, when it was obvious this wasn't the case, the Emeralds pulled out their manuals to apply revival techniques usually used to pull warriors out of amnesia. They did this to warriors who lost their memories in battle, those in a state of shock, or when minds were hit by oblivion, often caused by repeated crossovers into other worlds. With Ezekiola, the Emeralds had one goal in mind: revive the warrior in him by awakening Zeke's memories on how to fight. With the High Council's approval, they tried their standard revival techniques.

But when those techniques didn't work, the leader of the Emeralds, Igor Sanza, stepped in. Igor was the latest elected leader of the Emeralds, with a penchant for overstepping his authority just to prove himself. This trait of his was not surprising. Igor's past was known to his warriors. He grew up with an errant half-brother who was so deviant, he ended up serving the Sons of the Night Sky or SONS, as they were called. Igor's life from that point on became a continuous effort to be righteous, all to show himself to be the opposite of his half-sibling. Bearing such a family scar, Igor was excessively vigilant and distrustful of everything, including his own warriors. In a hush environment, Igor thought it wise to move in a more innovative direction with Ezekiola. He pulled out ancient handbooks and brought in his special scholars, asking them to apply untried formulas, even creating new ones on the spot. There was much more Igor was going after. Indeed, he believed that a dormant

Zeke, having served the SONS, knew more, and had answers to many of his questions. He was sure of it. With Ezekiola under his custodianship and his warriors taking his orders, Igor used this opportunity to push boundaries and delve deeper into his experiment. He didn't just order his warriors to fight in strange formations—the Emeralds used sound and subjected Ezekiola to extreme heat and diets, making him wonder if they had all gone temporarily mad. Igor believed Zeke's memories lay dormant somewhere in Ezekiola, and all they had to do was awaken them.

To Igor, Ezekiola was a far cry from what he had been told about him by the great Count, Meredus of Loggia. In fact, he was warned against pitting his best Emeralds against him, in fear that the magnitude of his strikes could possibly outweigh theirs, considering he had linked with the sacred Fountain of Fire. Linking with this sacred element magnified by a hundred-fold the powers of the Emeralds, giving them a force that can be wielded to any desired end.

How wrong he was. What extraordinary powers? The boy couldn't fight! And after a month of monopolizing his best warriors and watching Ezekiola's poor performance, Igor simply couldn't bring himself to believe that this particular Emerald Belt student had tapped into the Fountain of Fire. His warriors didn't believe it either. And those who held an ounce of belief that this novice somehow had linked with the sacred fire, were slowly converting to the camp of non-believers. There was just no evidence. No one ever saw what happened between Ezekiola and Zeke. Some warriors even harbored doubts that perhaps it was Zeke who dominated Ezekiola, acting as a spy, meanwhile serving the SONS. After all, it was Zeke's body in front of them, not Ezekiola's. Being naturally suspicious of everything, Igor couldn't eliminate such a possibility. But before confronting the Count, or worse, contradicting him, Igor had to be sure. And then, there was something else percolating in Igor's mind. The Count was the wielder of the great planetary rod under his custodianship. Igor wanted to ask for its use but knew his request would have to come only after exhausting every avenue.

"Did he ask you to stop?" Igor asked.

Yossan nodded. "He can't breathe right," he said.

"Then put him closer to the fumes. Maybe the heat will make him recall," Igor commanded.

"He hasn't mastered temperature. He'll collapse," Yossan stated the inevitable. He saw this happening often with apprentices who were not yet ready for this type of extreme training.

"Hasn't mastered temperature, you say? Or hasn't mastered his mind? Ezekiola is either expert at fooling us or there's been a grave mistake, Yossan," Igor stated and headed towards the circular center where they held demonstrative training. Training zones were scattered all over the borders of the mountain, and different rounds took place in selected areas. The one where Ezekiola stood was used for simple unarmed combat, aimed at grip strength, and pulling strength. Further out, training grounds were used for testing power and explosiveness. On the inside of the mountains, halls were reserved for striking and weapon training, and where it was said to be the pit of the mountain was dedicated to the Emerald Robe's ultimate training—the one with their belts. This was where body and mind were tested to their fullest capacity, where warriors had to show mastery over their belts by becoming one with them and manipulating them to their desired end. Often, the first indication would come when warriors learn to create friction by firing up their belts. Only then could they start to exit Circa, traveling to other worlds.

Igor mumbled a few words to some of his crew. Ezekiola locked eyes with him from a distance and, using his telepathic abilities, quickly read his mind. It was the same thought that permeated the rest of the warriors he had been training with: they doubted him. Observing from his vantage point on a platform, Ezekiola scanned the warriors. The age gap was astounding. Since Cypress School hadn't produced Emerald Belt students for many years, Emeralds had to seek help from outside. On one end, there were warriors tall and slim, who looked older from behind, only because of their long white hair, carefully tied in the back, yet their faces bore no sign of aging. On the other end, a handful stood with such imposing physiognomy and symbols adorning their dark skins that volumes could be written on them by decipherers. Some only observed and never spoke, and others spoke tongues between themselves that Ezekiola had never heard before. There were even a few oddball Emeralds whose skin shone a blueish tint under the sunlight. Ezekiola had done a double take when he first saw that. What kind of group was this? Where did they all come from? There seemed to be an inner ranking system among them too, that Ezekiola hadn't quite figured out. But one thing he noticed with certainty—the warriors who interacted with him did so half-heartedly, as if he was a temporary experiment to be dealt with. Except for Yossan. Ezekiola wondered why he hadn't been able to read through Yossan. The man barely spoke, despite being the one who was supervising him. Either he thought nothing or was good at concealing his thoughts.

"Ezekiola," Igor spoke out. "Or Zeke? Which one is it actually? Should we start calling you Zeke?" Igor asked, having reached the end of his patience. Ezekiola remained quiet. He could see through all of Igor's thoughts.

"You're the one who tapped into the Fountain of Fire, traveled to Planet Blue, found a wondrous lady to link with, and are on your way to getting our whole universe back on track. Isn't that so? You, the fountain reviver, can now do

ANYTHING! So where is the warrior Zeke that you say you've dominated and where are his skills?" he asked, side glancing at his men, noting perceptible nods.

Sensing the impasse, Ezekiola, too, was at the end of his tether. Truth was, he never felt anything remotely close to what he had the last time he held his belt when it was on fire. That's when he lifted his twin Zeke into the air, merging with him. Ever since that episode, holding his Emerald Belt was like holding any other mundane piece of cloth. No heat, no fire, no power. Did it just fade away? He caught himself more than once thinking whether what had transpired in the last months of his life was real or not. He wanted to learn more about the Fountain of Fire, but the Emeralds were teaching him none of that. He was in the Emerald's camp only because he placed trust in his headmaster Nomi and the Count, believing that what they were doing was right. But often, he wondered if it hadn't all been a grave mistake.

His answer to Igor came out plain and simple: "I told you before, I'm not Zeke and I have none of his skills," Ezekiola said.

"You're wrong!" Igor burst out, his eyes growing a shade darker. "Apparently, you're so skilled, you're supposed to teach us!"

Staring into Igor's fiery eyes, he saw flaming darts about to shoot out. Ezekiola stood motionless, not knowing what to say or do any more. Truth was, he didn't remember a thing about Zeke, nor had he carried over knowledge that Zeke possessed in his life. As far as he knew, he was Ezekiola, with his own mind as it was before. It would take numerous years for him to get to where the Emeralds wanted him to be. Ezekiola was tempted to walk out and end the pathetic spectacle Igor was putting on. Yet it was during this moment that something told him not to move. He stood calmly in the middle of the circular training ground, while the Emeralds observed him like they would a statue in an empty room, where that extra time might get them to forge different opinions about him. They could perceive a faint character of his, like a thin ray of sun cutting diagonally across a room. Ezekiola resisted the temptation to just walk away. He knew that power of decision rested with him, not Igor. With all he had gone through with the Emeralds, especially their leader, added to Nomi's and the Count's expectations, he was not going to be the one to walk away. He held his ground.

Igor picked up on the invisible message. "Training is over," he announced abruptly. "Yossan, come with me. Give this to the High Council and call for an urgent assembly. Ask for the Count to be present." He slipped a letter sealed with the insignia of the Emeralds. Yossan knew this had to do with Ezekiola, as if Igor had tested something one last time, and it confirmed a prior decision he had already made. He just hoped it was a positive one but didn't have a good feeling judging from Igor's tone.

The meeting venue was the White Hall located in the heart of the Limestone Mountains, the largest room for holding official assemblies. It wasn't just every member or representative of the clans that were there, Yossan along with several senior Emeralds, who were training with Ezekiola, were asked to be present. The meeting commenced more brusquely than anticipated, with the commander of the Emeralds, Igor Sanza, addressing the Council first:

"The threat of war looms over us. Circa's veil no longer holds, recently penetrated by the SONS, there is word that our missing Emeralds are still alive, kept prisoners somewhere, that our sacred books are changing hands in a black market, and amongst us is a boy, Ezekiola Astrid, who we've been told has tapped into the Fountain of Fire, with zero recollection about his twin, Zeke, with whom he merged. Zeke, as you all know, served as a high-ranking member of the SONS. He now lies dormant in Ezekiola. We tried on our end to simply revive his warrior memories, which the Council approved of. We have been unsuccessful at this. As Emeralds, we can only work with warriors with simple amnesia. Our manuals are not designed for cases like Ezekiola." Igor paused and scanned the room to garner all the attention for what he was going to say next.

"The High Council has the means to achieve the awakening of all of Zeke's memories. Having tried and failed, we ask now for the Council to approve the revival of his memories with the use of the sacred planetary rod wielded by our great Count present among us today." Igor motioned in the direction of the Count who was sitting among them, stunning several members who had never before heard such a request. The Count however, seated next to Headmaster Nomi, had wisely anticipated this moment. He responded:

"If your standard techniques haven't worked on reviving his fighting skills, have you thought of asking the Council to authorise the Caspol Dance?"

"The Caspol Dance has been banned for many years now, and we will not bring forbidden rituals back into our world." Igor too, had prepared himself for this battle of wits.

"In that case, perhaps you can request making an exception to the rules," the Count parried. "The intention two warriors put in their belts before they begin the Caspol Dance draws out selective memories only. It's safer and will allow only for limited recall. If you try this with Ezekiola, he will easily remember fighting skills without digging further into the life of Zeke." The Count hoped that Igor would be open to such a possibility, considering the exceptional circumstances they were in.

"I will set no precedence, especially for someone who has served the SONS, nor revive an ancient dance that was blackened and tarnished by what the SONS made of it. We ask that you use the powerful rod under your governship instead. It is the only solution we see at present. In fact, it may give us more than just reviving fighter skills. We can find out where the SONS are stationed, what their plans are, where they are hiding our missing warriors, and where they keep the Emeralds' sacred stolen books. Those manuscripts must return to their source. They represent a far greater danger if the writings are deciphered on the sacred Fountain of Fire!"

"For all we know, those Emerald warriors could all be dead." Someone in the crowd interrupted the discourse, breaking the steam building in the room.

"Or alive!" Igor continued, maintaining his momentum. "This boy has all the answers we need. Don't be fooled by his innocence. Remember, he was a full-fledged warrior of the SONS, able to manipulate elements, travel in and out different worlds, even one like ours! That's how he penetrated our so-called veiled planet. This is no child we're handling."

"Igor," the Count spoke firmly this time, "this is Ezekiola we speak of. He does not live Zeke's life. You know well what the staff will do. It doesn't do selective memory; the staff is all powerful, it revives the whole. If he gains access to Zeke's life entirely, the knowledge of it will torment him."

"But it will not kill him. He will work through it."

"Reviving all of Zeke's memories in him will be far more damaging than we may think. It will arrest Ezekiola's progress and any movement forward. What good would that do?"

"The outcome will be for the greater good. Use your staff and everything is solved here," Igor insisted.

"It is out of the question to awaken such memories! His darkest deeds will come to life, and he will remember everything he has done as Zeke. The guilt will be too much to bear, and just that will be enough to cripple him. It will halt his evolution, worse yet, make him regress. He might go searching for his past and get lost in that, too. His sanity will be at stake. This will not be for the greater good. That is not how we measure these things here. There will be more harm done than good. Right now, his life is at stake, for the SONS will surely come for him. It is crucial Ezekiola learns how to fight and wield his belt as quickly as possible. That is all we ask for. You know very well the safest way for him to be a full-fledged warrior without going through all the years of training is through the Caspol Dance."

"We will not use the Caspol Dance! It is evil in its roots, and we will not bring such things back to life. Our principles stand and we will not waver on this," Igor argued, irrespective of his rank in the hierarchy of the Council, overstepping as much his authority as his tenacious opinions, no matter who the interlocutor was.

"I don't ask such exceptions lightly. Like you said, our veil has thinned, and we have Sons of the Night Sky roaming in and out of our planet. You know well how innovative they can get, what they can do. Ezekiola needs to be ready and to protect himself, otherwise all our collective efforts to preserve and tap into fountain's power as a whole will go up in flames."

"Then so be it. We stand at odds. I will not monopolize my warriors to waste time reviving selective memories. Nor will I waste my warriors' time trying to teach him quickly either. We've wasted enough time and we're too little in number. Already our Emeralds must stand guard in so many restricted zones and other key lines on our planet that cross over into other worlds. If Ezekiola wants to truly become an Emerald

Robe, he'll have to start like any other apprentice with theory first at his school. I'm sending him home."

As brusquely as the meeting started, it ended with Igor's and the Count's words hanging in the air. With too much disparity and lacking majority, there was no consensus. No decisions were made.

The Count exited quickly, motioning Nomi to follow him. Something unprecedented happened for which he had not planned. An idea sprouted in his mind like an abandoned seed on forsaken land. It begged to be watered. It was something too wild to cross anyone's mind but his. And he was about to nourish something desolate into life, taking Nomi along with him once more. Someone the Count never thought he'd see again was about to receive an unexpected visit.

Chapter 2

Cruel Summer

The Brown Robes had much to be proud of when it came to their domain. Nature endowed them with the needed esthetics. Somehow, there were more types of trees, shrubs, and flowers packed on their grounds than anywhere else at the Cypress School. Their territory reached far and wide, and every summer the glory of their lands was magnified through impeccable landscaping. During the school year, no one except for Brown Robes were allowed on the grounds. As summer neared, many Brown Robes headed home. But over time, the upkeep of such a vast land became problematic. So, the Brown Robes devised a way to get maintenance done by making an exception to their restrictive rule, allowing any student on their grounds, and it was on a first come first serve basis.

At the beginning of every summer, like ants coming out of a hill, students aspiring to become Brown Robes poured onto the front porch of the Ye Ole' Brown Lodge to put their name down for volunteer work. It was a prime opportunity to get a glimpse of the grounds, and perhaps even show some of their worthiness. Labor varied from polishing wood, printing books, to gardening and refurbishing wall tapestries. The task force was usually assigned by a summer committee of Brown Robe members. This year, Borghis opted to be on the committee. And he brought with him some novelty, a new policy he proposed: mandatory communal work. Up until then, work was attributed to brown belt volunteers only, but now it would extend to students who had mandatory communal service to carry out. For those who offended school rules in a severe manner, it gave them the opportunity to take responsibility for their acts, a payback of sorts.

On a cloudy afternoon, one student with a red belt tied around his waist stood handling a wheelbarrow filled with earth, which he then tipped sideways. Thankfully, Atlas thought, this was his last day. For a whole month, he had toiled on the lands of the Brown Robes, his prescribed work. It all had to do with the items he had stolen from their lodge on graduation day the previous year, including the little black book—Borghis's diary—which he had conveniently handed over to his sister, Helva. Indeed, on that fateful graduation day, Atlas, along with his friends Nohlan and Ezekiola, were supposed to escort Nohlan to the Brown Robe's lodge to pick up some extra clothes. Atlas however, had gone a step further, rummaging through the books belonging to the Brown Robes, including Borghis's diary. After flipping through it and discovering just how madly in love Borghis was with his sister Helva, Atlas stole the diary. Later, this diary was given to his sister in exchange for a favor. Now he was paying the price for that action.

Atlas and Borghis barely spoke that summer. That much Atlas could handle. What he couldn't abide was the relationship that had developed between Borghis and Helva. It made his emotions tilt and spill over, just like the earth in his wheelbarrow. When his sister had graciously returned Borghis's journal, the two had spent more time together than ever, strolling in the Black Forest, disappearing for hours at a time. Naturally, Atlas's relationship with Helva had turned sour. Despite his warnings to stay away from Borghis, his sister did the opposite. And what little peace Atlas could find that summer vanished the moment Nohlan came into the picture. As soon as word got out about Atlas's communal work, Nohlan was first to put his name down as a volunteer. And with his insider's knowledge of where Atlas was to work, he immediately opted for gardening work. For Nohlan, these were high times. With Ezekiola gone training in an Emerald camp, he was happily planning to spend all summer next to his other friend. But for Atlas, it was nothing short of a cruel twist. With manual work that strained his muscles each day, remaining in the same spot for long periods of time, and too little time to read his favorite books, it was a recipe for some form of torture. Surprisingly though, there was some spark to his day. Orgali, Nohlan's and Borghis's little sister, loved tagging along after Atlas, doing her bit of work and play. She would make quirky comments and left art installations on the landscape, which brought laughter to his day.

Atlas dumped a fresh bundle of earth around the neck of the last tree on his list. There had been about fifty of them, tied with ribbon strips to indicate which ones needed mulching. Nohlan usually handled the stirring of the earth while Atlas would move the trolley around. He opted to do it that way, since it created some physical movement. Nohlan had just left to get his tools. They were almost done. He was patting away the last pile of earth in the shape of a mountain when Borghis surprised him with a visit.

"What's this?" He looked at the earth mound covering several inches of the trunk.

"It's a pile of earth," Atlas responded from his crouched

position. Somehow, he didn't like the visuals of being so low in Borghis's presence.

"I know it's a pile of earth. How many did you cover *this* way?" Borghis asked, pointing to the tree.

"Well, all of them on the list," Atlas answered matter-of-factly. "And what do you mean by *this* way?" he asked in turn.

Borghis didn't answer and looked around to take note of the surrounding trees, a crease forming between his brows. There were hefty mounds of earth around the neck of trees, as if they had lusciously cascaded down from above, topped by some of Orgali's artwork, composed of colorful stones, branches and leaves to make a collage of either happy, sad, or angry faces. The shipshape landscape of the Brown Robes suddenly looked like a children's playground. It didn't help that Orgali was hopscotching with her friends not too far away.

"Well, what's wrong?" Atlas asked, standing up.

Borghis turned back and asked: "Why is there mulch heaped up around all of these tree trunks?" pointing in several directions where Atlas had worked.

"What do you mean? That's what I was supposed to do," Atlas answered, a puzzled look on his face.

"You were supposed to spread the mulch over the roots as a layer, not a mountain."

"Well, what's the matter with that? Layer, mountain, it's all the same. It's earth. Trees need earth," Atlas said plainly.

"No, you're suffocating the tree this way," Borghis replied firmly.

"Well, the rain will flatten it out," Atlas said.

"On the contrary. Your craft of stacking deep mulch will block oxygen and water from getting into the soil to reach the roots. You were told to have the mulch circle the tree, like a ring, and it should extend at least three feet from the trunk. You had to keep it clear of the trunk," Borghis explained. Taking a garden trowel, he went down on his knees and shoveled away the earth to keep it clear from the trunk by several inches. He then took the shovel and tossed three quarters of unnecessary earth onto the side.

"You were given simple instructions to only add enough mulch to keep the layer three to four inches deep. You put at least ten inches on all these trees, turning them into eventual volcanoes!"

"That's not what I was told!" Atlas protested. "Nohlan simply said to cover the trees with a pile of earth. And this is not a volcano!"

"Well, you should have known better. You'll have to restart your work," Borghis expressed his verdict in a surprisingly cool manner.

"What? This is insane! I've spent weeks doing this and now you tell me?" Atlas's chest suddenly tightened. Another day in this field, and he was sure to collapse.

Borghis shook his head. "Your job has to be redone. What you did Atlas is build volcanoes around trees, so much that my sister thinks of it as a play yard," Borghis said.

"Oh! So, this is what it's about? You don't like Orgali hanging around me? Your silent treatment didn't quite work out the way you planned?"

Borghis's gaze sharpened as he took a step closer, towering over Atlas. "Your work is wrong, Atlas, like some of your past acts. It's as simple as that. I suggest you stop arguing and do it the proper way, especially if you want to start your classes on time and not still be toiling on our grounds when fall comes around."

He left without another word, like a cat who had cornered his prey but chose not to kill it. Borghis's words hung in the air, and as Atlas watched him head back to the lodge, he took to the shovel to let out his fury, digging up a heavy load of earth and tossing it in the air. As the clouds grew darker, Nohlan was heading back when he caught sight of his friend shoveling earth skywards.

"What are you doing? You're supposed to mound the earth around the tree, as on the ground, not sprinkle it in the air!" Nohlan said, perplexed.

"REALLY Nohlan?! You mind giving me precise instructions on how this thing should be done?" Atlas shot back, sweat pouring down his forehead.

"What's the matter with you? A minute ago, you were laughing with my sister, and now you're like an erupting volcano!"

The volcano word was too much for Atlas to bear. He flung the shovel to the ground, took off his dirt filled tunic, dropped it on the ground as well, and headed shirtless into the woods.

Nohlan felt a few droplets of rain on his face as he stood baffled. He looked towards the lodge and saw Borghis watching them both from the gallery. Borghis motioned him to come over. What now? Nohlan wondered.

"What did you tell Atlas to do, exactly?" Borghis asked, hands on his hips.

"To do gardening work, which, by the way, I participated in completing," Nohlan added proudly.

"The one thing I asked you, Nohlan, was to guide Atlas to do a fraction of our landscaping and you failed."

"I asked him to do what you told me. How is that failing?" Nohlan asked, confused.

Borghis pointed toward the trees with earth mounted around them. "Is that what you call successful mulching?" he asked.

Nohlan looked dumbfounded, then saw Orgali from afar gathering back the decorations she had planted in the mounds of earth as the raindrops turned into light drizzle. "Oh, that's all right. Orgali's just having fun. She likes it when the earth is mounded high to plant her rocks and stuff. It shows better, looks nicer too."

"No Nohlan. That's your friend not knowing the basic principles of adding soil the right way. You better go back and help Atlas do all the fifty trees on your list properly this time." As he was about to say something else, he spotted Keenan heading his way. Keenan was walking faster than usual, as if restraining himself from running. Keenan motioned Borghis to come down from the porch.

"I have to go, Nohlan. Just fix those grounds with Atlas and put them in decent shape."

Borghis stepped down to join Keenan.

"The Forest Stewardship Council wants to have a word with you now," Keenan said.

"About what?" Borghis asked.

"They didn't say." A look of distress crossed Keenan's face. "Since this new senior, Falco Rasspan, has been elected as their head, he's been sending out strange requests. Just yesterday, he asked me to compile a list of sporadic doors I've gone through since I've graduated to the Brown Robe level. I don't even remember what I ate last week, and he's asking me to pull up an entire year's time travels through sporadic doors."

"Why did they ask you for that?" Borghis's brows furrowed.

"I don't know. When I asked the reason behind it, they said it's a new protocol and they have the right to request it. You'd think they would be busy counting trees, but I feel they're on some quest, mapping things out."

"He'll probably ask me to provide the same thing," Borghis reasoned. Keenan stopped him in his tracks for a moment.

"Just watch yourself with Falco. He's an older member, very fond of rules, and now that he's head of the Forest Stewardship Council, things have changed in there," Keenan warned. "Don't forget, he was one of the few who wanted us expelled indefinitely after he heard of our escapade on Planet Blue."

"So, I heard," Borghis agreed. "Maybe he's upset we didn't take him along to save Ezekiola and the boys," Borghis mused.

"Maybe. I heard he takes pride in his staff, holding the greatest record of entries into other worlds. But we're the only ones who entered Planet Blue. So that might surely eat him up, that we've done something he's never done before," Keenan added thoughtfully.

The Forest Council was headquartered in the heart of the Black Forest. They called it the Sanctuary. Their cabin was a large rectangular bunker with no esthetics surrounding it save for a few original boulders said to be some of the oldest rocks on Circa. The Council took pride in their austerity and minimalistic decor, inside and out. The members of the council were senior Brown Robes, with the latest novelty being their newly elected head: Falco Rasspan.

As Borghis and Keenan made their way to the cabin, the light shower turned into heavy rain. With no landscaping done whatsoever around the headquarters, the trees closest to the bunker hunched over it, creating a cocoon effect. The oldest tree among them had some form of growth on it, spread out in heavy black lumps on separate branches. In the past, Borghis had warned the council about this, suggested trimming, and possible removal of the tree, but evidently nothing was being done about it. And with its disorderly branches intertwining with others, the lumpy growth had easily spread onto other healthy trees. Branches too weak to withstand the heavy lumps had fallen off, and now lay sprawled on the ground with new forms of fungi growing on them. There was an eerie look to the place. As he approached the Sanctuary, Borghis suddenly imagined he was going into a bat cave.

Entering the Sanctuary, Borghis and Keenan had to cross a long, narrow vestibule that had one lone bench and nothing else. The walls were thick, and the place was a maze. There were no doors to the rooms in the Sanctuary, for it reflected things as they are in nature, all in open air. Falco was standing in front of a large rectangular table, with the council members serving as his backdrop. It was an interesting set up, Borghis noted. There were a few other Brown Robes, with papers in hand, as if they were the administrative clerks of the day. It was quite a large number, considering the request to have a 'quick' word with him. Borghis's eyes quickly shifted to the rectangular table located in a back room, far behind. A drape covered it with some shape underneath he couldn't quite make out.

"Hello Borghis, we're so glad you could make it under this rain," Falco greeted him. A shallow smile flickered on his face. His natural silver hair had been slicked back, unevenly covering bald spots, giving him a distinctly cool air.

Borghis nodded in his direction and at the rest of the group, while Keenan waited next to him.

"You asked to see me?"

"Yes. We thank you, Brother Keenan, for escorting your friend and bringing him to our grounds," Falco motioned Keenan towards the exit door, clearly dismissing him.

"It's pouring rain outside," Borghis interjected.

"There are rain tents set up for that purpose on our grounds. He may wait under one of those," Falco answered.

"Can't he just wait in the vestibule?" Borghis suggested.

"This is a private affair, and as you well know, there are no doors to our Sanctuary. Everything is in the open. The walls here are like the trees in a forest, as thick as they may be, they have ears."

Falco gave another one of his smiles, and Borghis wasn't

sure if it was the smile or the statement that made his blood pump faster.

"I thought we're all brothers here," Borghis ventured, still uncertain which direction their conversation was going.

"Yes, aren't we?" Falco agreed. "And some falcon brothers have to keep greater watch on those who deviate," he said, a fleeting smile sliding across his face. Falcons were, of course, the emblematic symbol of the Brown Robes, representing their brotherhood. Borghis quickly realized he wasn't in for a friendly exchange. He changed tactics.

"Well, you heard right, Keenan. Thank you for escorting me to the Sanctuary and enjoy your stay under the tents outside," he said. Keenan exited, shutting hard the entrance door behind him. It suddenly dawned on Borghis that there were others standing in the room.

"And how come they're staying?" he motioned to the other Brown Robes not part of the Committee.

"Oh, but we're all brothers here," Falco repeated what Borghis had said a moment ago with such poise, Borghis would have rammed his face with his staff had he been holding it.

"Come follow me," Falco said without giving another chance for Borghis to protest. He led everyone into the back room with an arched entryway towards a large rectangular table, the one Borghis had spotted when he arrived. A drape covered several items on the table. Falco theatrically lifted it, exposing several wooden staffs, each ornamented in different designs.

"Do you know what these are?" he asked, and walked around opposite Borghis, his fingers slowly caressing the edge of the table.

"They look like staffs," Borghis answered the obvious. He had seen many staffs as a Brown Robe but had never seen those. The carvings on them were exquisite.

"Yes, but these are not just any staffs," Falco said, and pointed towards one of them, making a clicking sound with his forefinger as the nail on it was an inch longer than the rest. "They are the sacred staffs that are under the custodianship of the Forest Council," he said with a hint of pride.

Borghis had read about them somewhere in his studies. From what he could remember, they were much like artifacts, to his knowledge never used, emblematic more than anything else.

"So why did you ask to see me?" Borghis was still unsure what this was all about.

"Ah yes. Of course," Falco nodded; his measured pace was getting under Borghis's skin. "Do you remember how many sacred staffs there are?"

"From memory, I recall there being six," Borghis answered. He glanced at the staffs and made a quick eye count. There were five. So, this is what it's about, he realized.

"As you can see, we only have five staffs. The Exit Staff is missing," Falco's mouth curved somewhat differently this time. Borghis stood still as a rock, seeing for the first-time what Falco was mapping out. Keenan's intuition had been right.

Falco continued: "You see Borghis, you were the last to enter a sporadic door, according to the testimony given by our falcon members. And not just any door, but into a world that hadn't been entered in ages," he said and paused purposely, gazing deep into Borghis's eyes.

"What are you implying? That I took this Exit Staff and not my personal one?"

"Perhaps the only way you could have ensured your way back from Planet Blue, a world that we haven't entered nor exited in a very long time, was to steal the Exit Staff and take it with you, a crime under the Forest Governance Act."

"So, you think I was unable to use my own staff?"

"Your personal staff would never have made it back to Circa." Falco quickly replied.

"You really think, with all that I have learned as a Brown Robe, I was unable to do this?"

"Your knowledge is limited," Falco affirmed.

"My knowledge is based on our falcon statement: Worlds and Mansions hold no veil over the falcon's eye. My eyes and staff knew where to go, what to do, and how to get back. You insult as much our falcon legacy as my personal evolution with what you're implying."

"You've become a falcon who has transgressed."

"Transgressed? Am I being investigated for something here?" Borghis asked, still maintaining his cool.

"Hmm," Falco mused, a malevolent yet amused look flashed in his eyes. He sat down at the head of the grand table and motioned a member of his council to come closer, whispering something in his ear. A Brown Robe appeared from the room next-door, holding several staffs in hand, then handed a specific one to Falco. Borghis's jaw dropped when he recognized his personal staff in Falco's hands.

"What are you doing with my staff?"

"You broke rules, endangering lives, and the consequence to that is your staff has been officially confiscated, along with the others who followed your lead."

"What?! You can't do this! We had to save Ezekiola and his friends and bring them back. We didn't harm anyone with our staffs!"

Falco continued, as if he'd never been interrupted. "A decision will be rendered on what we'll do to you and your likes, and whether you will continue your education at Cypress School. Until this decision is rendered, your staffs will remain in our custody. Next time, think twice before venturing to places you shouldn't go. And I'm not talking about your escapades with your lady in the Black Forest that seem to inhibit your senses and govern so much of your time." Falco's eyes narrowed, his words sharp as knives, piercing a deeper place than expected. He then hammered home his next words: "Devious boys like you will learn obedience under my governance."

Borghis was just short of jumping on Falco.

"You've lost your mind! This is wrong and I'm bringing this to Nomi."

"Oh, I should mention, he signed this decision."

Borghis was speechless. He hadn't seen this coming. His heart pumped hard, the veins on his temples and throat were visibly bulging, and it took all but his last ounce of willpower to restrain himself in the face of Falco's words. There were too many witnesses to start a fight. Regardless, he had never been a good fighter, and his best arm had always been his staff as they usually are for Brown Robes. It had become an extension of him, as staffs often do, a part of him, now held by Falco. For the first time, the thought crossed his mind that he should take warrior classes to deal with the likes of Falco.

"That'll conclude our business for today. You're dismissed for now." Falco stood up abruptly and left.

Borghis stood motionless. The creep had the audacity to dismiss him just as he had Keenan. He waited a moment before turning to head out. Borghis wanted to punch one of the walls on his way out, but thought better of it. They were too thick, and the impact on his knuckle would be greater than the thrill of letting go a jab. He'll have to find another way to shake Falco's words off of him and to get his staff back.

The rain was heavy by the time Borghis stepped out. It was refreshing to see his friend who was still waiting for him, his outfit drenched as there were several large holes in the tent making it a futile shelter. The image of his friend drenched made Borghis even more furious at Falco.

"Did they ask you the number of sporadic doors you went through?" Keenan asked, not showing any expression of anger from staying out in the rain.

"Oh no, Falco is aiming for the gold! He's accusing me of stealing the Exit Staff that's gone missing. AND he confiscated all of our staffs!"

"What?! Doesn't he need the headmaster's consent to do this?"

"Well apparently, he got Nomi to agree to this! I just can't believe it!" Borghis blurted out, his emotions flaring. He turned back, glaring at the Sanctuary one last time. "I hope that sick damned tree falls on them," he said.

"Don't worry about getting our staffs back. We'll talk to Nomi and see what this is about," Keenan answered coolly. It always impressed Borghis how his friend would remain level-headed in the face of difficult situations like these.

"What I'm more curious about is this Exit Staff. Isn't it one of their sacred staffs that they don't even use? Those staffs are like decors. Do you think Falco is making this up just to accuse you?" Keenan asked.

"I don't think he's making it up. It looks legitimate. We didn't take it. Obviously. Who would even steal an Exit Staff?"

"Actually, the question is *why* would someone steal it? Again, what's the Exit staff for? To ensure your way out from a world less traveled, or one that's highly dangerous." Keenan said pensively, taking a short pause. "And if they just discovered this missing, it means someone's about to take a trip into a doomed land."

Chapter 3

Far from home

"What do you mean you were originally from Circa?!" Leanne asked, flabbergasted.

While she paced back and forth like a wildcat, Leanne's parents attempted to explain to her for the third time some of their family history. They were in a small dorm reserved for their stay at Circa. At first, their intention was to trickle information down in small doses, not revealing too much at once to their daughter. Yet every bit of information seemed as shocking as the next, prompting Leanne to ask more questions, forcing her parents to spill everything at once in a disorderly mishmash.

"So, you're both telling me we've been on the wrong planet all this time?"

"No, we were exactly where we needed to be. Like we said, we were part of a group that took the decision to go to Planet Blue to help create a link between our planets once again, in the hope of reviving the Fountain of Fire. You had to be born on Planet Blue and carry its essence for us to accomplish this. And because you were born there, and linked with someone from Circa, you fulfilled part of a great plan, but we're just at the beginning of it," her mother explained.

"Are there others like you from Circa?" Leanne asked, wide-eyed. Her parents remained quiet for a while, exchanging looks.

"Yes, there are a few. Their identities are hidden however," her father answered.

"And what happens now? What's next?" Leanne asked.

"Again, like we told you, your mother and I will be traveling back and forth; we need to have a presence back home so as not to arouse suspicion. There are things we also need to do and settle before making any permanent changes for ourselves."

"You two are going back, but what about me, and my school, and my friends?" Leanne frowned.

"For your own safety, you'll be staying here. After reviving the Fountain of Fire, we cannot take the chances of you and Ezekiola being so far apart, at least until the Emeralds figure how to train him in using this power. Your seal protects you two here on Circa, but nowhere else. After speaking with the Count, the decision is for you to stay here and attend Cypress School. This way, you can continue your education. It's a form of boarding school, see it as that. We are in talks with the headmaster of the school, Nomi Antares, as to what type of training will be best for you. You'll get a customized curriculum. You'll be staying in the Ladies' division."

"So, I'm not going back home?" Leanne asked in disbelief. One part of her was scared, another partly pleased.

"No, not yet. Everyone back home thinks you've just gone missing. Circa is better protected than our planet because of its veil and the Emerald warriors. You'll find the Emeralds stationed all over. They're guarding the school as well."

"Speaking of Emeralds, where's Ezekiola? I've barely seen

him," she suddenly included him in their conversation, as that too, had to be computed into this phenomenal equation.

"He's gone training," her father answered quickly.

"Where?"

"In a camp with the Emeralds."

"For how long?"

"We don't know."

Leanne sighed. Every answer given by her parents seemed to agitate her further.

"And that shouldn't be your concern," her mother swiftly added. 'Make sure your head is wrapped up with studies here, Leanne. I don't want your attention to slip away.' Her mother paused, glancing at her husband. "And there's one more thing. Your father and I think it's best you keep a small but safe distance from Ezekiola, temporarily for now."

"Keep a *small but safe distance* from Ezekiola?" Leanne repeated. "Do you hear yourselves? You just said a moment ago you didn't want us so far apart, and now you ask for a small safe distance?" Leanne was bewildered.

"We're not saying he's bad. It has to do with the forces he's wielding. Something like this hasn't happened in ages, Leanne! Everyone here is trying to sort themselves out and figure what the next step should be, and how to help this boy manage what is happening. Think about it, he merged with his twin, something they never saw coming! No one knew when the Fountain of Fire would be revived, and now everyone's caught up on how to handle what has unraveled so quickly, the Emeralds included. This is not something to be taken lightly. So, all we ask is for you to just stay away from him, for now."

Leanne threw her hands up in the air and stormed out of the room. She can't go back home. She can't see Ezekiola, or even see her friends, all for what? None of their answers satisfied her. She felt like a prisoner on another planet. As she walked away from her parents, she recalled her time with Ezekiola in the Black Forest. It was the second-best moment she had with him, the first one being when they sealed their link. As they were on a long walk together in the forest, she questioned him about his telepathic abilities. It fascinated her that he was able to do that. They played mind games. She'd asked him to guess what she was thinking. He said it wasn't guessing; he could access her thoughts as if he was thinking them himself. After a few tries, the thought of kissing him popped out of nowhere in her mind. She blushed and politely asked him not to read her mind anymore. He smiled and promised not to. She wondered what he remembered from that fateful night when he confronted his twin. He said he only recalled the fight and feeling fire in his hands and body. He couldn't remember the rest. He asked her the same, and she only recalled running into the woods and after that, everything going blank.

She dreamt of him, although she never told him about it. Neither did she tell him about his twin Zeke showing up in her dreams, too. She would even get strange impressions of Zeke in the middle of the day out of nowhere. She didn't understand why that happened. The only explanation she found was that she had also merged with Zeke in Madame Camille's shop on that auspicious day, and she had touched his essence. Could it be a side effect of merging? She often wondered about that.

During their walk, she had to remind herself it was Ezekiola who was next to her, not Zeke, and it was those ocean blue eyes staring back at her from time to time, not those black beads that sent shivers down her spine. Still, she hadn't quite adjusted to him. At times, she struggled to remain neutral when looking into his eyes, where all sorts of emotions would rise in her. She imagined what it must be like for Ezekiola to find himself in that situation. She yearned to learn more about this

Fountain of Fire they spoke of, and how to wield its power. Some of it scared her. As far as she knew, he was half aware of what exactly happened. And now her parents were asking her to keep a small, safe distance, whatever that meant. None of it sat well with her, and her conversation with her parents left her in a gloomy state.

All that changed when Helva and Daria came into the picture. Once her parents left and she settled in at the Ladies' division, the girls decided to give Leanne some tours. As sullen as she was about being far from home, she realized she couldn't have asked for a greater excursion than being on another planet, practically living outdoors among giant trees, with secret portals scattered all around, and Gemins roaming in and out of a mystical forest. Leanne called it magical. Helva and Daria, who had taken Leanne under their wings by now, laughed at her interpretation. But when she told them about the animals that roamed Planet Blue, they proclaimed those creatures magical.

"Lions!? You've seen lions?" Daria asked, eyes wide open. "We consider them fantastic creatures. We can only dream of them!"

"Yes, but we don't get to touch them. They're dangerous, and they sure can kill you," Leanne explained. In their quest to explore animals on other planets, Daria had taken several books out of the library. She quickly shuffled through the encyclopedias and found the feline division. She would land on a page, and the girls would be absorbed for half an hour examining the drawings and the writings.

"Look! There it is," Leanne pointed at a picture of a lion sketched out just as it looked on her planet. They read some more, flipped pages, observed additional feline sketches, some of which made their jaws drop.

"Wow! What is that? I've never seen anything like it

before," Leanne said as she stared at a white furred animal with a black mane, three times larger than the lion she was familiar with in her world. Helva read the text beneath the portrait of the massive being.

"It says here that the Solevs are large nocturnal cats whose dwellings vary from mineral rich landscapes to abundant wild fauna that can provide nourishment for their survival. Although many planets can provide the needed diet for Solevs to survive, the light on most planets is not conducive to their circadian rhythms, their evolution and longevity solely reliant upon darkness and time spent sleeping. The Solevs do not survive on planets where light is present for more than three hours."

"It's interesting that they can't survive because of light. Have you ever seen a Solev?" Leanne was fascinated. Both girls shook their heads.

"We have a lot more than three hours of light here on Circa," Helva said, flipping to the next page to see if there was another sketch of a Solev.

"It's still amazing that your smaller felines live up to a hundred years on your planet,' said Leanne. 'Little cats on our planet barely survive past fifteen."

"Oh!" Daria gasped. "That's so sad! How is it that they have such a short lifespan?" Daria asked, looking at Helva for an answer. Helva shrugged. Having never studied animals on Planet Blue, she didn't know the reason for the short lives of those animals.

"You're so lucky you have animals living this long here. Maybe we should bring a few into our world," Leanne said, smiling.

"And you're lucky to have the variety you do. We don't have half of the animals you have on Planet Blue," Helva added. Indeed, Leanne realized that although animals survived much longer on Circa, the wildlife was more spectacular and diverse on her planet.

"Still, I'm amazed you have these books here. How come there's all this information on other planets? We have no such thing. We barely know what's outside of our world."

"Many of the planets are veiled. Also, the Brown Robes contribute to the research and work in nature. They go in and out of portals into different worlds and keep track of evolution. They experiment as well, with plants and animals. When a project is approved, they can plant something on another planet, which is simply discovered as something new in their world. They keep records of everything and turn them into books," Helva answered, showing the book in her hand. Her dream is to do just that one day, when she becomes a Brown Robe.

The girls toured Cypress School and its surrounding areas. Helva and Daria held many sessions explaining the school system, flooding Leanne with information on the Brown Belts, Red Belts, Emerald Belts, Blue Belts, not to mention the White and Silver ones, known as healers, astrologists, and universal librarians, then moved onto describing the Robes, explaining how graduation worked, and what role they each played on their planet, all of which made Leanne's head buzz. Despite that, she remained attentive. She asked many questions about the belts, especially the Emerald one, in hopes that their conversation would lead the girls to reveal more about someone she was longing to hear about.

When Nohlan and Atlas finally finished their landscaping job that summer, Helva and Daria scheduled a visit to the boy's division of Cypress School. Nohlan and Atlas tagged along, enriching Leanne's visit. Atlas especially was glad to have some reconciliation with Helva with everything that had happened with Borghis. Helva described how portals worked, being careful not to disclose too much since Nohlan was present. Their recent incident had taught her a lesson. She had inadvertently put them all in danger, her brother too, and now regretted part of her decision. Then again, had she not risked what she did at Ezekiola's request, he would not have tapped into the Fountain of Fire, nor would he have had Leanne by their side.

For the occasion on that same night of their visit, they stayed out late in the Black Forest. They were having lively discussions around a fire pit that Nohlan prepared and who was feeding it kindling. Nohlan enjoyed lavishly layering the fire, turning what was supposed to be a small-sized bonfire into a mighty blazing beacon that could light up a city. And just for fun, he used his instrument, a special horn that Brown Belt students possessed, to raise the fire still, thrilling his friends.

"Wow, Nohlan, this is incredible! Is that sound raising the fire?" Leanne asked.

"Yes! And watch this!" Nohlan said. He upped his performance and sent off high-pitched tones that made the fire rise even higher, with miniature blasts emanating from it. Leanne was at first dazzled by the flames until something darker surfaced from her memories related to fire and her eyes betrayed her. Helva was quick to spot the shift in Leanne's expression.

"Nohlan, tone it down a little," she said abruptly.

"Oh, come on! We only get to do this in summertime," he pleaded.

"I'm serious, take the fire down. We're going to get the Forest Stewards on our case again. That Falco Rasspan is not a fan of ours."

"He can't do anything. He's just the new little ruler of the forest, big deal."

"Yes, he can, and he just—" Helva held back saying what

had just transpired. Borghis was fuming from what Falco did, confiscating staffs; she had never seen him so flustered. She didn't dare bring it up since he specifically asked her not to tell anyone until he resolved his situation.

"Just bring the fire down now," she repeated.

Nohlan sighed and did as he was told. A strange silence permeated the air, as if fun, like the fire, had been stamped out. They sat quietly for a moment. Then the inevitable topic came up.

"So do any of you know when Ezekiola is coming back?" Helva asked, looking at her brother Atlas first, and then at Nohlan. It was the question Leanne was hoping would be asked. Finally.

"He's still with the Emeralds, training in their mystery camp," Atlas said, casting a furtive look at Leanne.

"How long will he be there?" Helva persisted.

"He told us this was a summer thing; he should be heading back when summer's over," Atlas answered.

"I thought he was going there to do some training a few weeks at most. Just enough time to test the Fountain of Fire in him, that's what I heard," Nohlan said in turn. "Did you feel the Fountain of Fire?" he innocently asked Leanne who had remained quiet.

Leanne shook her head. "He's the one who tapped into it, not me." They all looked at her, as if Leanne was the last person to find out what they all knew.

"What is it?" she asked, noting their looks.

"You created a link with Ezekiola, so you as much as he can tap into it," Helva stated.

"Me?" Leanne's eyebrows shot up. Maybe that's why her parents didn't want her to leave Circa. The risk was too great to have her separated and far away from Ezekiola on another planet. If the power of the fountain started acting up in her, it would be quite a crisis to handle. "I don't even know what it is exactly. How can I even tap into it? Is it like real fire?"

Helva explained: "It's an element, just like fire, and—"

"Or more like air," Nohlan interrupted.

"Right, like air, but an invisible one that—"

"Like air!" Nohlan cut Helva off again. This time though, her expression stiffened. "Do you mind Nohlan? I'm trying to explain something here."

"Sorry, it's just that I want to make it easy for her to understand."

"Thanks Nohlan," Leanne gave him a smile and turned her attention back to Helva.

"You can tap into it only when the right components are in place. From what we understand, it's magnetic in essence. So, like a magnet, there has to be a receiving and a sending end, a positive and negative polarity, emitting their respective charges on each end. Circa has been trying to link with Planet Blue for a while now. There are other planets we've linked with, and the only way we were able to tap into the Fountain of Fire is if someone here was able to link with someone on Planet Blue. You and Ezekiola were the first to achieve that."

"But I didn't feel anything. Ezekiola was the one who felt it and did something with it, not me." Leanne's protest was followed by an awkward silence.

"I think they're looking into training us about this subject. They won't have any choice," Helva said quietly, as if she had tapped some insider information about what was going behind closed doors. "I hear there might be new mandatory classes starting this fall; one of them may be called the Cosmic Fire."

"What does this fire do?" Leanne asked.

"Our knowledge is limited. It's something the Emeralds are familiar with. It's in their sacred manuals, and there were only two copies of those volumes. The first copy was burned, and the second stolen. I don't think anyone thought tapping into the fountain would happen this quickly. And I think they were caught off guard by what the powers of the fountain did to Ezekiola. It made him fuse with a twin brother. Can you imagine that?"

"So, what kind of powers are these exactly?" Atlas asked.

"We don't know about the exact powers, but essentially it gives freedom from limitations and power to do incredible things," Helva answered.

"Hold on Helva, you're making it sound like it's nothing big, keeping it too simple and mundane," Nohlan interjected. "The Fountain of Fire, I hear, has all sorts of amazing potential and can-do mind-blowing things!" Nohlan's face suddenly lit up: "like becoming invisible, manifesting a body when you want to, living without food or water, restoring anything back to health, even recalling things back to life."

"Oh, come on Nohlan! You're adding more to it like the bonfire you just boosted and had to tamp down," Atlas interrupted.

"No, he's not exaggerating. We've heard about this too, although we've never seen it happen," Daria said, catching Atlas's attention.

"Look at it this way, some things can be done for sure—the power to shift in and out of this world and the next like the Emeralds do here on Circa. You won't need anything to transport you," Nohlan said, garnering his friend's attention. "Telepathy is another one, like the Blue Robes. Omnipresence —being in several places at once, again like the Blue Robes; access to reason and logic, like the Red Belts."

"So, it's almost like being a brown, emerald, red, blue— name the robes—all of them at once." Atlas summed it up in his own language.

"Right!" Daria said laughing, fond of how Atlas's mind

simplified things. "Except the Fountain of Fire will enable this for all of us, not just a few."

Helva picked up the thread. "That's why the SONS want it for themselves only. It would give an equal amount of power to others if they accessed it, making everyone on par with them. The power of the fountain is the heritage of all, not just a selected few. They can't accept that. It naturally breaks down barriers, and the only way to keep those barriers up is to prevent others from accessing it. The SONS know what they could do with such powers under their control. But the ingenious part of the fountain is that for it to maintain its integrity, a dozen planets must bond. This way, the slightest contention would drive away unity. Unity is what it thrives on. That's why the original link was broken on purpose. Several planets veiled themselves, Circa included, and went into hiding, so to speak. The SONS have been trying to link in various ways but haven't been successful with Planet Blue," Helva stated.

"So that's why Zeke was sent after Ezekiola, to prevent this?" Atlas asked the question.

"Zeke was sent after Ezekiola, not just to prevent but to kill him," Helva added. "In fact, Zeke knew about the Fountain of Fire when he saw Leanne, and thought by killing his twin, he could easily replace him. But Leanne created a link with Ezekiola, not Zeke."

"Is Zeke alive in him?" Leanne asked, anxious as to what they thought about that. They stared at her, the question having crossed all their minds ever since Ezekiola was in his twin's body, but no one had dared to ask. A shuffling sound was heard in the woods. Momentarily, they were distracted, but the question was so intriguing, they paid no further attention to the background noise.

"Well, we were told by Nomi that it's our friend as we know him, not Zeke. Not to be fooled by his appearances. I mean then again, they look the same. We saw them both standing in front of us. They're almost spitting images of each other," Nohlan said.

"I wouldn't be so sure. Something's changed in him since he merged with his twin. Sometimes when I look at him, I feel unsettled," Atlas cut in. Leanne didn't dare say it aloud, but she had felt that, too.

"Well, Nomi also asked us to be 'attentive,' which I see as being careful," Nohlan then admitted. "So, to answer Leanne's question here, it's possible parts of Zeke overflowed into him."

"What do the ladies say in your division?" Atlas asked Daria.

"Well, rumors are flying now that we have a rogue amongst us, and we're supposed to be cordial towards it, no questions asked. But we ignore the gossip though," Daria added.

"I don't think we should completely ignore what's being said. I think we should all be cautious and speak to one another if we notice anything. We don't know exactly what the Fountain of Fire does, right? Nobody here does. Who knows if he could be dangerous? I think that's why he was sent away to the Emeralds, so they test him to see if Ezekiola can reintegrate back into school, if he won't pose a danger to us," Atlas's thoughts were flowing out unfiltered.

"I thought he was sent away for his preliminary training," Nohlan said, confused.

"It can't just be training. There's more to this. That's why we were told to be careful with him. That's why they have Emeralds stationed everywhere now in the Black Forest and in the vicinity of the school. Open your eyes, Nohlan. The Emeralds are not just here to close portals!"

So that's why I'm asked to keep a small safe distance, Leanne thought to herself, connecting strange pieces of the puzzle. She listened attentively as Atlas's concerns prompted more discussion in the group.

With the fire cracking loudly and the night noise, no one heard the small shuffling sounds that came every now and then behind a close-by tree. There, sitting with his back against the trunk, Ezekiola was about to surprise his friends with a happy visit after finally being let out of the Emerald camp. When he heard his friends talking about him and his twin Zeke, especially in front of Leanne, he froze and listened carefully. Twice he wanted to get up and interject, to cut off the conversation. But he stayed put and continued to listen. He heard every word behind that tree, all the talk of how dangerous someone like him could be, the threat he posed, followed by speculations of his terrifying powers, going as far as how he could even kill. He stayed in place, still as stone until the discussion had died out, until they all left, and he stayed longer still, heavy with his own thoughts, until the last flame of the bonfire died out at dawn.

Chapter 4

The Caves of Agiri

It was a long walk to his destination. With every stride, the hooded man moved forward without stopping, as if an invisible army was marching before him, clearing a pathway. He strode ahead of his apprentices who trailed behind carrying large bundles over their shoulders. His face, veiled with a black shroud just beneath his eyes, was further hidden by the darkness consuming the caves. Only his dark eyes were visible, with two distinct patches on his right temple. Normally, he would send his messengers to do these tasks, but this time, he wanted to be present. Never before had he walked the long stretch of what formed the great caves of the planet Agiri. For this occasion, however, he would have walked through any infernal pit if he had to.

He knew Agiri only through the stories told by his brethren. Indeed, the many members of the Sons of the Night Sky regularly transacted with the underground Mystics. Here, there was no opportunity to walk through clear meadows and open fields. In this world, the inhabitants' only way to survive was to live in caves, for the poisonous rays of the sun of Agiri could kill anyone who was exposed to them. Inside the caves, the darkness was profound. An underground maze of countless floors spiraled deep into the ground. Torches were lit at different intervals but cast minimal light into the habitats of the living who over time developed and learned to thrive on a peculiar commerce—bartering and exchanging the goods of the dead. But lately, something else was percolating here. Something that reached the ears of the SONS and made every neighboring world of Agiri suspicious of them. Their latest novelty—the business of reviving the dead. Astonishing as it sounded, the Agiri Mystics had somehow developed the skills to revive deceased bodies. Living constantly in caves, most died young on a planet of such extremes. And now, ingeniously, the Mystics were also able to use the fresh bodies of slaves from other worlds where there was greater longevity and substitute them with deceased souls. It was no surprise then that the slave trade here had increased by tenfold. Skilled slaves were sold for profit, while the others lost their lives in the swaps. To ensure the success of this transaction, all that was required was something belonging to the deceased: a garment they had worn, a remnant of their body. With so little, the Mystics enigmatically performed this new wonder. How was it possible? The revered teachings on how to bring the deceased back to life were knowledge hidden from most worlds. Whether the Mystics did this through unraveling ancient mysteries or by the discovery of a new formula remained unknown.

The hooded man was curious. But this was not the reason for his visit today. He observed the skulls hung in various stalls, emitting eerie tinkles as a passerby brushed against them. Indeed, the caves were adorned with the bones of the once living. The air was thick with putrid smells strong enough to stir just about any being's insides, mainly rising from the bodies of those who should have died but were being kept alive instead. Vases were displayed filled with what appeared to be a black fluid. Chimes made of nails clinked away with every draft of nauseating air. Anything could be found here that necromancers might need—formulas in vials, dried organs, hairs, feathers, poisonous nocturnal birds, snakes, two-legged reptiles, some alive in cages rattling and squeaking away in various corners.

Dakor, the hooded man walked past it all. This wasn't the section he had come for. There was something more important he planned to transact. He noted the small ebony figures, talismans in human form with large heads portraying the Agiri sun. It was the most cherished thing in their world, decked at every little opening of the cave, they supposedly protect the inhabitants from the outside world. And yet, it was known that there was one individual who had developed immunity to the rays of the Agiri sun. She made a name for herself, expanding her knowledge about the power of the sun and harnessing it. Dakor was heading straight to her.

Rikka was sharpening her needle when Dakor arrived with his crew. Her face was a canvas of spots, and her eyes had an opaque film over them. With no iris or pupil in view, murky clouds of gray-blue had taken over what was once perhaps a translucid azure. A natural effect from being exposed to the Agiri sun. She didn't stop to look up. She dipped her needle into a small flask, continuing her work. It perplexed Dakor how she could even see. A few drops dripped as she tested it on herself, instantly piercing a hole in her skin, making her bleed. She didn't react. All the cavities on her hands and arms bore testimony to her skill. Here, she was known as a Venoma Weaver, skilled in the art of cultivating organisms grown by the poisonous rays of her world's sun. As the only one to have grown immune to the sun's rays, she became highly innovative and for many years sold things that the SONS were after—such as a sophisticated poison. She needed one last component to complete the latest request from them.

Dakor took off his veil and quickly glanced around the working space. Measuring tools and several books with open pages were laid out across a wing-shaped organism on her table. She handled it with extreme care, as she would a newborn child. The order dominating her working space contrasted heavily with the excessive clutter and filth of her dwelling. Her living space would have appeared freshly looted if it wasn't for the accumulated debris, insects, and aged dusty webs visible in every corner. Dakor circled closer to her, observing her creation. In the past, she had delivered ably for them, and was well paid for it. Something about this new product however made him apprehensive, aside from the hefty price she was asking.

"How potent is this?" he asked, staring as the droplets she had just tested on her skin were gently deposited on the organism she was manipulating.

"Potent enough," Rikka answered. It wasn't the first time she dealt with questions. No one understood the mechanism of what their sun could do, and she enjoyed keeping her buyers in the dark. "Did you bring what I asked for?" she asked.

"Can it kill?" Dakor asked without answering her question. Rikka stopped and gazed at him with what looked like blind eyes.

"It shouldn't, but could," she said, snickering.

"I said I want him alive, not dead. Your produce sounds risky," he warned.

"What you asked for is risky. And risk has a price. Pricey to make, pricey to risk. This boomerang you see in front of me needs to bring the one you seek to the edge of death. It is the only way it will execute what you want."

"Explain how, and remember, your life hangs in the

balance," he said towering over her, staring into her murky eyes. The SONS had never had this product made. Of all the poisonous weapons Rikka had presented to them following their latest demand, the organism in the shape of a boomerang was the one that Dakor's superiors had agreed upon. Yet he remained hesitant. The whole mechanism and how it worked did not sit well with him.

"Do you think you can threaten me? You forget that death is what we thrive on here. You walked through our caves. You saw how we're flourishing. We remain alive no matter what happens. Kill me now, and I will be revived!" Her eerie laughter reverberated in the room as she playfully manipulated the organism in front of her.

"Indeed, I have noticed it seems so in your world. And what of this new commerce of yours, of reviving the dead? How did you come across this?" Dakor asked suspiciously.

"I have no knowledge of it. That remains in the domain of the Mystics. I'm just a mere Venoma Weaver," she said with what Dakor adjudged false humility, concealing something. He could tell she knew more, and he didn't like that one bit.

"Oh, so you think this new wonder your Mystics are practicing will enable you to live, to be revived, no matter what?" Dakor mused. With a swift movement of his hands, a circular abyss opened in mid-air right before Rikka's eyes. She gasped, surprised to see an image. A horrid scene emerged showing her his intentions. To drill the image further into her mind, Dakor came close to her ears and spelled it out.

"Not so. Not if I shred you to pieces that will be hard to find. They can't revive you then," he whispered. Rikka stood up, and rapidly broke away from the vision that Dakor infused her with. She stared at him with her opaque eyes. With time and experience, she had discerned to recognize real threats that could be carried out. There was no uncertainty in Dakor's voice. He stood back, a glimmer of satisfaction detectible in his eyes. His words had hit their desired target.

"Sit down, and convince me this will work," he commanded.

Rikka obeyed reluctantly. The faster she did this, the faster they will exit, she told herself.

"This boomerang you see is like a mushroom and a flower at the same time, grown and nurtured from the venomous darts of the Agiri sun. The boomerang becomes violet from taking in the poisonous rays of our sun. Like the mushrooms here that burst violet dust upon touch, it's the shade it gives off. The boomerang would erupt on the body of its targeted host, sending a violet effervescence like the smell of flowers that bloom. Except, this is the boomerang's bloom. Poisonous and deadly in a high dose. It enters through olfactory nerves first, then is absorbed by the skin, and the essence enters the brain." Rikka paused, noting Dakor's attention shifting to the boomerang, weighing its potential.

"Now, for the results you wish for, a distinct recollection must be brought to the host about his past, something that governs his emotions, more than his mind. It's what works best. Once he recalls, the boomerang must be executed from a master thrower, once without fail, into the opening of the cavity of the neck. The host will forget almost everything and recall only that which the boomerang carries as essence. The scent is all powerful, affecting the brain. If it is his past you want to revive, then that and only that will remain. The result should be irreversible. Where are his goods?" she asked.

"Should be irreversible?" Dakor repeated her statement. "You've never sold this to us in the past. How could you be so sure?"

"Everything else I have sold in the past worked, didn't it?" Rikka said with certainty, exuding a hint of pride.

"Dump the bags," Dakor ordered his men after a moment of reflection.

The apprentices dumped the content of their sacks onto the floor. Pieces of fabric, carvings, tools, a leather pouch, small books, icons of a child, another of a mother, dark trousers, several shirts, and a burnt belt came out. They were all goods that belonged to Dakor's most promising apprentice: Zeke. Rikka selected the burnt belt. Closing her eyes, she reached out and touched it.

"OH!" she cried in pain, quickly crouching in a fetal position, startling the apprentices who stood back. Rikka's head turned into different directions, momentarily absorbed by a vision, while Dakor observed following her gaze. It looked like Rikka was watching something in empty space, every one of her reactions giving legitimacy to the invisible scene she was witnessing. Her eyes widened suddenly; a terrifying look crossed her face. Then she shut her eyes again. She was breathing heavily as she held the black belt, and abruptly fell to her knees, depleted. She let the belt drop from her hands. In an exhausted state, she finally plucked a small strand of material from the burnt end of the belt. She went back to her working station, and carefully laid the threaded bits on the table next to the organism.

"Wait outside, I'll have it ready for you. Make sure you stick to the slave I chose; this girl is a lance warrior in her world with exceptional skills. Boomerangs in Agiri don't grow in abundance like mushrooms. I had to step under the sun many times to make your product. You will only have one chance. She's waiting for you in the pit. The gatekeeper will lead you to her."

"This better work, your life depends on it," Dakor cautioned, and threw a sack of coins in her direction. "And don't tell me this was difficult for you. You're immune to it. To all of this," he said and headed out.

"Aren't you, too?" Her words echoed but were ignored.

Dakor and his men made their way into the pit led by a stocky gatekeeper with a morose face. The precious jewel was in Dakor's hands. It felt light yet sturdy. Like a mushroom and a flower at the same time, Rikka's words reverberated in his mind. He contoured the shape with his fingers. The boomerang's skin was soft. He followed the gatekeeper deeper into darkness, a small torch emitting a meek light. They descended endless spiraling stairs. Often, he had to rely on his hearing more than sight to follow. Many times, he lost track of the light as clouds of black air filled the gap separating him and the gatekeeper. At one point, he heard metal clinking of keys and figured they had arrived. Even with the gatekeeper's lit torch, blackness engulfed the room, and he could barely adjust to the dim view of what looked like corpses up against a wall. He realized they were in the section where the skilled slaves were held, chained to the wall. The gatekeeper headed towards a specific slave; the one Rikka had picked for him. Dakor realized they were lance warriors, all of them, apparently coming from a world she transacted with, a world where female eyesight, agile bodies, and hunting skills were far more developed than theirs. The gatekeeper had told him they were all sisters from the same clan.

"No, wait," Dakor stopped the gatekeeper. "I want to see them myself," he suddenly said.

"Our venerable Venoma Weaver has already picked one for you. She's over there," he said, pointing in a direction where he was headed. Dakor couldn't see a thing unless the torch was literally in a slave's face.

"I don't care which one she picked," Dakor responded abruptly. "I want to pick the slave myself. Bring me somewhere where I can test their skills."

"Our venerable Venoma Weaver tested each in the abyss of the pit, one fell and died. We already lost a slave," the gatekeeper answered. The abyss was in the heart of the caves, like a big swallowing mouth waiting to devour whatever comes its way. No bridges were built, and unwanted corpses not to be revived were dumped in this large deep hole. Criminals were often condemned to such deaths, losing their life in the pit.

"I said I want to test them myself," Dakor insisted, and grabbed the torch from the gatekeeper's hands. He moved closer to each slave and observed their faces first, then arms, and then the rest of the bodies. Their eyes struck him the most. They were bigger, their pupils were far larger, abundant with white lashes that reflected light into their eyes. He counted seven of them. He asked to see them all.

The gatekeeper sighed, twiddling around with his keys to unshackle one at a time. They were brought to the edge of the abyss. Each took their turn, a ticket to freedom that Dakor promised: to perform with precision, for their life depended on it. He took his time to observe from afar on an elevated platform. Even in that darkness, devoid of light, every one of them was proficient in the art of throwing with a lance; their precision was remarkable. In utter darkness, they always hit their target. But there was one who refused to play the game. She threw anything that was given to her into the abyss instead. She wouldn't throw herself in, however, Dakor remarked. He watched her stand her ground. This unexpected defiance frustrated him. He immediately went to confront her.

"Do you know what will happen to you if you stay here?" he asked, edging closer to her.

She didn't answer, although her gaze shifted to the two marks on the side of his temple. They were triangles whose edges didn't touch.

"Here are your choices," Dakor said, taking his time, his

dark eyes holding her gaze. She could feel his breath on her, and with him being this close, she observed the black lining around his eyes.

"Either they will throw you into the abyss like a criminal, or they will sell your body to the Mystics. They're performing quite the art, I hear. Imagine losing your body to another soul," he said, taking a pause. "Or you can do as I ask, and you may gain your freedom in my lands."

She remained still as a rock, as if he had never spoken. A true warrior, whose spirit can never be broken. But Dakor recognized these spirits and enjoyed the interplay, wanting more than anything to penetrate the impenetrable. It was a great skill of his. Once tamed; these kinds produced the greatest apprentices. The SONS had produced many this year, none he was satisfied with so far as the head of his warriors. Something more was needed for what was coming. The right cards had to align, and he had one great desire that needed to be consummated above all others. And this scheme he was devising was far more personal to him. Without even seeing her perform, he chose her, the defiant one. He whispered one last thing, audible only to her ears. He smiled; his words having roused her spirit. In time, and to her greatest chagrin, Dakor's intuition would prove right.

"Practice starts tomorrow," were the last words he spoke.

Chapter 5

Salt and the Sea

Gespar collected the salts from the Loghian Sea, right below where he lived. The fog was at its height at dawn and the descent from the steep cliff demanded his full attention. Despite his sleepless nights, the morning breeze kept him alert. The fog thickened as he descended the cliff, and by the time Gespar reached the shoreline, he couldn't see a thing. He took a few steps closer to the openings in the seafloor where he harvested salt. The sensation of small rocks beneath his feet that contoured each opening told him he stood in the right place.

Working through the haze with visibility at its worst gave Gespar a strange sort of comfort. Besides, he only had one eye left. The left one had a patch over it. The smog made his past, present and future matter not. It was all vapor that dissolved in the air. Time here, too, was short. It was one of the reasons why he had escaped to this planet. Daylight vanished after three hours, turning the remaining ten hours into darkness. The obscure planet of Voronar was known for this. With so little light in this world, it was the perfect place for interminable sleep, a leisure which Gespar still couldn't partake of. Nevertheless, he liked walking to the shore of the sea, just to try to stand at the exact spot where land, water, and air met. There was a special place at this juncture, where it was neither wet nor dry. A delicate in between space. He only found out about this because it was the last thing he read when randomly opening to a page of the Kama, the sacred books, right before he buried them in forsaken lands. He tried hard again this morning to find that in-between space. Gespar's hands hovered over the sand, then over the water, gently swaying them back and forth, barely touching the surface. It was either wet or dry. He could not determine where the spot was, where it was neither. It remained a mystery.

With strong, skilled hands, Gespar gathered the salt amassed through each opening in the seafloor. This activity could only be done by hand. The salt came from brine. The relatively cool evenings and soft warm days on Voronar formed a thermal shock, so that with each morning, wind gathered the salt near the edge of the sea where he collected it. This salt contained an excessive amount of minerals, one of which was magnesium. For those able to access it, Voronar's salt allowed minimal sustenance of life on its planet, otherwise starved of sunlight. Shoveling salt, putting it in large bags and bringing each bag, one by one up the hill using ropes and barrels, was not for the faint of heart. Gespar had to do this over a dozen times, just to have enough to sell at the market. It was back-breaking work, but plump as he was, Gespar had the heavy physique to manage it. Yet with each physical movement, a closer look at the definition of his body would tell a different story. His frame, although now thick as a block of marble, seemed to conceal an unknown past.

Gespar didn't need much to get by in life. Just his craftsmanship for salt making. His lodging wasn't much either, a small cabin where a cot lay on the right side. Besides, this time of year, he slept outdoors to watch the stars fade into darkness as he closed his right eye. Once he climbed back up the hill, Gespar organized his bags, lining them perfectly side by side and never in odd bunches. Order was a remnant of a skill he couldn't leave behind. Looking up, he spotted his cat from afar heading towards him. Something dangled in her mouth. As she came closer, he saw it was a large hare she had caught for his evening meal.

"Andiya, you clever girl," he said, stroking her thick neck.

He went into his cabin and took out a wooden bowl. He refilled a smaller one with a generous amount of salt he had just harvested. He broke lettuce grown in his garden into pieces and poured some oil over it. Only a few droplets came out. That too had to be stocked up along with other essentials he needed. He made a mental note to buy it at the market tomorrow. As he mixed his lettuce, a peculiar spiraling sound outdoors caught his attention. It was different from the usual sounds of nature. He stopped for a moment, not sure if he heard right, then a few moments later, he heard it again. He glanced at the door, then to his cat who didn't move. Her ears weren't twitching either. He found this curious. Since Andiya didn't move, he decided to ignore it. It was only when he heard it a third time that caution suggested to step outside to investigate. He exited and looked around the vicinity of his cabin, then stared into the deep woods. It was pitch dark. A torch was lit close to his cabin as usual, next to his outdoor cot. His salt barrels were in place, as he had left them. His bags and cart were well-stationed, and his horse was resting in his usual spot with no sign of agitation. He remained outdoors for a short while, to see if the strange sound would repeat. He didn't hear it. He went back to continue preparing his meal, but his attention kept shifting to the door. Gespar looked at Andiya again, who lay resting next to a chair, calm as the tranquil sea. He trusted her, so he brushed it off. Old reflex, he told himself, from a past life. After the meal, he went outside and laid down to enter his most undesired part of the day. Every night Gespar slept, he died in his waking life, and came alive elsewhere. Comfort was hard to find. His dreams were remnants of a past to which the glowing stars above could testify. But they too, will burst and die one day, he thought, while drifting into sleep. They'll go back to their source. Everything made will be dissolved. Will something new take its place? He slept with those strange thoughts in his mind.

In the morning, Gespar gathered his cart, prepared his horse, and headed into the city. His cat always accompanied him. She had to. Andiya was his only means of protection in such lands. Thieves and outcasts were only part of his problem. There was the grave danger of his salt being devoured in one shot by a wild pack of animals. Hunger was rampant in these lands. With such little light, no produce flourished to its potential. And the salt Gespar harvested was one of the few minerals that miraculously sustained the living. In fact, it made them fatter. His plumpness was no accident, as he enjoyed the fruits of his own labor. But it wasn't just the animals who devoured them. The giants salted everything. With such weak tastebuds, they poured it generously onto their food, but more so, to keep themselves alive. The thirteen-foot beings, known as Golas, thrived on Voronar. The mineral kingdom on this planet was what they needed to sustain their complex bodies. The lack of light helped them conserve their energies too, as they spent less time living and more time asleep. It took a minimal effort to stay alive.

There were few like Gespar who sold their stock at the market, mostly outlaws who found their way to Voronar, called Kozi, getting by selling what they could on this barren planet, some barely surviving. They were naturally identified because of their smaller size. As usual, dozens of Kozis would show up, clamoring for the best spots. He quarreled his way to the stall masters—the larger Golas—to negotiate a spot, avoiding as best he could the whips and batons that would fall on Kozis to keep order. Being a regular and having a special product wasn't enough to guarantee a spot. Gespar had to give half his earnings at the end of the day to the stall masters to continue selling here; it was just short of slavery. As he was setting up the produce in his stall, crazy Yolsha, an old beggar who stole from time to time, passed him by. Her face, decrepit as a dried mushroom, bore crater marks that resembled erupted but dormant volcanos. It was rumored she had been a prophetess in her long ago past, but war and strife brought her to another state of mind. She held remnants of her gifts however, and from time to time, she would utter follies that were true. With time however, it became harder to discern. Today again, wrapped in cloth that barely held itself onto her bony body, she was yelling her usual nonsenses to stall merchants, Gespar being her focus that day:

"Your salt is a damnation! You extend the lives of the Golas by giving it to them. Let them die instead. Can't you see that they're taking everything from us? You filthy slave!" She slapped the surface of the bag Gespar had just untied, sending a good chunk of salt flying in the air.

"Move away!" Gespar shoved her hard enough for her to land several feet away, cracking something in the midst. She stood up, limping this time. She came closer, as if she had never fallen.

"Kozis like you will pay a dear price. I know what's on your head, Gespar," she hissed his name, pointing a finger at him. Gespar stiffened at hearing her say his name. No one knew his real name here, yet from time to time she would utter it. He glared at her and caught the delight in her eyes. "You will die burning in the dark pits of hell, blind this time! May your other eye get ripped out of its socket and your pain be excruciating!" Gespar broke his gaze from her, and continued the setup of his stall, this time, taking out his whip and untying Andiya so she could take care of her.

"Come closer, and you will become her meal. I haven't fed her this morning," he said and continued untying the third bag, then placed his cart underneath a tent to shade his horse.

Yolsha slowly backed away as Andiya came closer, but her rambling continued.

"Oh, they're coming for you. Did you hear the call last night? Did you, boy?" Gespar stopped again. He glanced at her, weighing her words, wondering if this was all part of her foolish talk. It was not uncommon for outcasts coming from other worlds to tell stories from where they come from, which Gespar routinely dismissed as preposterous. Many would bring back rumors. the last one he heard was the surreal claim of the wondrous Fountain of Fire coming alive. It was all foolish talk. He trusted no one on this planet. But that's not what Yolsha was talking about. She was referring to a sound. And he had heard something the night before. Yolsha's eyes narrowed as if she had her answer.

"Ha! So, you have heard. They're coming for you, and they will rid us all from your wretched presence!"

Andiya jumped on her, lifting a paw, heavily scratching her right arm. She fell again, bleeding, yet letting out a disturbingly high-pitched laugh. The sound of her laughter quickly drowned when the ground beneath them reverberated. Gespar called Andiya back to him. He turned his back and focused on the incoming traffic heading his way. Hordes of Golas were rushing in their direction. The stall masters had opened the gates of the market. With each one of their steps, miniature tremors were felt, shaking stalls, animals, and produce alike. They tossed one another out of the way, in their attempts to be first to snatch quality goods. It would be common for Andiya to fend off eager Golas who cut lines, ones who didn't wait their turn to buy. She had to, otherwise, Golas would fight between themselves, and the outcome was always worse. Several would get knocked down, wrecking many stalls in the process. This happened to Gespar, and he had also witnessed stalls falling apart this way. Gespar had trained Andiya well, for despite their size and build, Golas were afraid of cats. For the rest of the day, Gespar focused on his task and sold all his produce. And as much as he ignored his interlude with Yolsha that morning, a small yet imperceptible wavelength of her words came to haunt him by the end of his labor.

After dark, Gespar headed to the local inn. He sat at the very end, where Kozis, like himself, had to sit and ordered his usual double pint. Their chairs were smaller, located closer to the dumps, swarming with clouds of flies. It was the lesser's lot on this planet. Golas, being numerous, tall, and strong, held the privileges. At night, they sipped their drinks served to them in massive caldrons. Drunkenness helped them sleep, knocking them out after several consumptions. It was their favorite time of day, wasting themselves in idle talks and slander, biddings, and cat fights located in a pit at the center of the inn, some making spectacles of torture out of stray cats with no master. By the time Gespar was done with his second drink, the inn had transformed itself into an abyss of chaos. He was sipping quietly, with Andiya waiting by his side when someone his size walked in. Probably another outlaw going for a drink. Of the many seats available, he curiously came and sat next to Gespar.

"I'll have what he's having," the stranger said. At the sound of his voice, Gespar's ears pricked up. He recognized it, but from where? Never one to engage in conversations, Gespar was tempted to look, but held himself back. At this hour, fights can break out over a mere glance. He had his whip and knife under his cloak but didn't want to fight. He was too tired. He hurried to finish his drink when the stranger next to him spoke once more.

"Have the rumors reached your ears yet?" he asked.

Again, that voice, Gespar now couldn't help it and looked up at him. The stranger was looking straight ahead; his face was hidden under his hood. Unsure of who this person was, Gespar's body remained stiff, on high alert.

"What do you want?" he asked sternly.

"Do you enjoy wasting away in such lands, Gespar, living to feed the giants, becoming lesser and lesser every day?" the stranger asked instead.

Gespar was in shock at hearing this stranger say his name. Who was he? What was he doing here? How did he find him? Was he alone? Were there others waiting for him outside? They both remained quiet for a period. Gespar was still in a daze, his mind stuck in a chamber where thoughts battled viciously. An answer finally emerged.

"How I live concerns no one."

"You have skills that are needed elsewhere. Not in these lands," the stranger's tone hardened. Gespar's chest tightened. He continued to push back down whatever was rising in his throat. Whoever this stranger was, he seemed to know him.

"Don't come to me for skills, those are no longer my ways," he replied. Gespar's mind started playing out possible exit strategies in case something was about to happen. Unbelievably, Andiya was sleeping at his foot.

"Ways fluctuate and change. Maybe you can make something new of your life, perhaps an admirable one this time?" the stranger suggested. As if sensing his tenseness, and noticing Gespar's gaze shifting to the back door, he then added: "I come not in war if that's your concern." Gespar reflected on that tone of voice again, and with experience on his side, he knew the stranger's statement to be true. His shoulders relaxed slightly. Curious to see where this conversation was going and what the stranger's purpose was, he decided to carry on.

"You place blind faith in those who cannot serve," Gespar added.

"Faith is not blind, but merely an idea that needs to be proven. It seems you lack challenge amongst your kind here, too," he said, quickly glancing at several Golas who were hyped up over the cat fight.

"I won't exit Voronar, if that's what you're asking."

"So, he will come here then, but you have to bring him back."

"Bring who back?"

"The one who ignited the fountain."

Gespar's face lit, quickly overshadowed by something else. "That cannot be. Those are only rumors."

"This is no rumor. The Fountain of Fire has come alive and the one who has ignited it will be sent to you. I have tried other ways. If you don't teach him, none of us will make it out of this. And maybe then you will find that space you are looking for."

"What space?" he asked cautiously.

"The space where land, water, and air meet, where it is neither wet nor dry. The in-between sacred space you know of but have never found. Weren't you trying again this morning?"

Gespar looked visibly shaken. No one had ever penetrated his intimate thoughts this way. Whoever this stranger was, he seemed to read him all too well, all too deeply. As if the stranger had already received his answer, he continued.

"Perhaps your hands may do work that will lead you to that space, where you'll find your answer," he said. "I know what you did with the sacred books. That is in your honor. But you know as well as I do that they will find the books eventually if you don't retrieve them. It will end up in their hands. It is only a matter of time. Besides, you're not safe here." He took a small pause to drink, giving Gespar the time to absorb what he said. "I have something for you. A remnant of your past that will be of use. I won't come again. The decision rests upon you." With that, he slid a small pouch towards Gespar, and that's when he spotted the insignia on his cuffs. A large 'M' that stood for Meredus of Loggia. Gespar's heart seemed to stop. He followed the Count with his eyes as he gracefully stood up and disappeared out the door.

That night, Gespar didn't sleep. His thoughts brought him to places he never dared to go. He kept himself awake, in fear of where his dreams might take him. Gravity seemed to weigh upon him, compressing his body. He rose from his cot and walked over to the edge of the cliff, thinking the air and space will alleviate the pressure. The waters had spirit tonight, edging back and forth with appetite. He stared long at the waves crashing onto massive rocks with passion. A sense of relief came to him, to know that he wasn't the only one being pounded on by such a fluid yet invisible force.

He went back and laid down, staring up at the sky. The clouds gathered, and he felt the first drops of rain. After a few moments, it was coming down in thick heavy droplets, then a gush of rain. He didn't go inside. He didn't move but let the water crash onto his body like those waters that crashed onto the rocks below. It washed him, his face, hands, and body. Would it wash away the rest? He held onto the pouch the Count gave him and opened it for the first time. He laid out a long thin cloth across the ground where it, too, could be washed. Gespar closed his only eye, and next to him, laid a dark dusty belt, brightening closer to a green with each drop of water that came pouring down on it. By morning, it had turned emerald.

Chapter 6

The Exit Staff

The rest of the summer pressed hard on Borghis's shoulders. Barely a day after Falco's surprise maneuver of confiscating his staff, along with those of his friends Keenan and Gordi, Borghis called for an emergency meeting, he could not let such things pass. His coolness, once his trademark, vanished quickly, replaced by violent urges he never knew existed. Borghis took over the astronomy room in the Ye Ole' Brown Lodge, reserving it indefinitely, swearing no one was to leave the room until they came up with a decent plan. The three of them were sitting tight, avoiding everyone, and when not quarreling, they planned, sometimes in contemplation while staring at the mesmerizing walls that portrayed a myriad of constellations. After many hours, they still couldn't get past the first item on the list: Headmaster Nomi Antares.

"We should leave this room NOW and talk to Nomi! We are wasting our time like this! Master Falco probably had a chance to see him already and has prepared him!" Gordi proposed.

"*Master* Falco?" Borghis's eyes bulged out of their sockets.

"Gordi, don't you call that thing a master. He's anything but!" he protested and stood up to once again walk in circles.

"Well, in all fairness, he did earn the title because of his record travels," Gordi responded, turning his head, trying to follow Borghis's movements.

"I don't care how many times he's travelled. I can't even call that plucked bird a falcon brother, let alone a master!" Borghis was taking a deep breath and trying to calm himself down by looking at the stars on the walls. This proved an unsuccessful endeavor since his exchange with Falco. None of the serene constellations depicted in the astronomy room provided a sense of quietude.

"Let's say Nomi had agreed," Keenan said, "we can't just walk into the headmaster's quarters and blatantly condemn him for his decision." His was a more rational angle. "Are you sure that Falco wasn't lying about Nomi having agreed to taking our staffs?" he asked, attempting once again to retrace the events.

"Keenan has a good point. We haven't even seen any real evidence that Nomi signed away this decision," Gordi added helpfully.

"Trust me, Falco was not lying. That wretched rattler had almost a dozen Brown Robes in the room during his planned demonstration. They couldn't all be in on a lie. He had everything calculated and was several steps ahead of us." Borghis's gaze suddenly narrowed, as if the stars on the walls had just drawn up a new constellation of Falco in front of him. "I'm going to smash that viper into pieces when I get my staff back."

"Don't waste your effort. A snake only needs to be knocked once on the head to be terminated," Keenan said.

"So, what do we do?" Gordi asked, more of a plea than a request for a solution.

"Isn't there a logbook for the Brown Robes' artifacts, to

keep a record of their displacements?" Keenan asked out of the blue.

"Yes, I took it out already," Borghis answered. Indeed, he thought about it as soon as he had left Falco's bat cave. "I hid it in my dorm so no one can tamper with it."

"You were quick! Did you look at the history of where the Exit Staff has been?" Keenan asked, surprised.

"I ... um, just glanced at the last page to see where it was moved last time," Borghis replied, his mind still on Falco.

"You only glanced at the last page? What did it say?" Keenan asked, anticipation in his eyes.

"I can't recall, so it was probably nothing important," Borghis sighed, and sank back in his chair. "It doesn't matter anyway, the Exit Staff is gone, and he's blaming me for it!" he said, pressing the heels of his hands into his eyes, shaking his head.

"Yes, it does matter!" Keenan retorted, standing up. "Borghis, you are not thinking straight. Go take a walk and get that logbook out of your room, now! I want to see it. We all need to take a break anyway. It's not just the last page we need to see in that thing. If we're being accused of anything, we need to dig every little thing out there, trace the whole history, and put it in Falco's face. In fact, I want to see where every single one of their sacred staffs has been for the last year. He wants to play this game, we'll play it. For him to succeed in confiscating our staffs and accusing us of stealing his precious Exit Staff, I will not give him an easy exit!" Keenan said. Borghis nodded, suddenly encouraged by the determination in his friend's voice.

Borghis walked to his dorm but upon arrival, halted abruptly, his breath catching in his chest. What's this? Someone was sleeping in his bed. His eyes widened as he scanned his room to see if anyone else was there. He edged closer, unsure if the person was asleep. He couldn't make out the face. Whoever it was, was well bundled up underneath his covers. He waited a few moments to glimpse the motion of a breathing chest. But there was no movement. Was that something dead lying in his bed? It would be the last thing he would be able to handle. He approached, slowly lifted the covers, and sighed when he realized it was just a bundle of cloth rolled up in the shape of a tall body. Was this a prank? Curious, he gave it a push, and when it didn't move, he lifted it, feeling something hard in the middle. He unrolled the bundle slowly at first, then accelerated the movement, but stopped when he saw something brown fly into the air. It hit the wall and fell on the floor with a hard clunk. With one knee on his mattress, he bent over to look. His heart stopped. Even on the floor, in the dim dark corner of the wall, there was no mistaking what it was. Just the handle of that object was ornamented in every beautiful shade of sapphire stones he had ever seen. He heard a noise, and in a shocking instant, the reflex in his arm drove his next move, shoving that thing underneath his bed.

"Gmonin, Gdafta, Gnight!"

Borghis jerked upright, uncharacteristically shouting, whether in surprise or fright, he didn't know. For some reason, he instinctively stood up rigid, with his hands clasped behind his back. The intruder was Ariad, his favorite Gemin, who had surprised him.

"How ya doin, Borgh?" she asked playfully, always enjoying calling him such, with a twinkle in her eyes. The juxtaposition of Ariad's tender presence and his anxiety made it harder for him to hide his expression.

"I'm fine, how are you Ariad?" he asked mechanically, although he never said it that way. He wondered how unnatural he sounded.

"Whatya hidin' der, Borgh?" she asked, her head tilted to the side.

"I'm hiding nothing, just doing my bed," Borghis answered immediately. Realizing his hands were held tight behind his back, he quickly released them, awkwardly putting them on his hips. "Shouldn't you be out tending to the bruxes at this time? They need trimming, the branches are all over the place," he said with a little more authority than usual. He wanted her out of his room.

"Ya, ya, da bruxes will be done in time. Bopen already is on it. Ya said yur not hidin' nothin', but was dat brown and blue-green ting I see over der?" Ariad asked, pointing to the floor.

Borghis had shoved the bejeweled rod so fast underneath his bed that its edge stuck out diagonally. A remarkable third of what appeared to be a wooden stick was exposed next to his feet. In his nervousness, he hadn't seen any of it, while Ariad had been staring at it the whole time. He stood stock still, unable to move.

"Dat thing over der, see!" she reiterated, pointing. Borghis's heartbeat accelerated, his cheeks flushed, and added to the morning's anxiety, he could barely come up with a plausible answer. While shuffling ideas in his mind, Ariad's sudden laughter stopped him short.

"Tought ya should be happy, Borgh, I got ya the Exit Staff!" she shouted ecstatically, displaying the widest grin he had ever seen on her. "Yur going on a grrreat mission, to save Circa!" Borghis's blood drained from his face.

"What?!" he blurted out, his head spinning. "You... you... stole the Exit Staff?" He slowly reached underneath his bed and delicately pulled out the sacred artifact.

"Nay, nay, now, now, we only steal plants, flowers, seeds, and shrubs. An sumtimes, frogs. I did not steal anytin, I'm on orders here! I was asked to give ya dis, too." She handed him a piece of paper.

Borghis' face remained drained of life when he grabbed the

note from Ariad. He turned the letter around, only to discover an 'M' on the well-sealed envelope, the insignia of Count Meredus of Loggia. What on Circa's moons was this? With shaky hands, he opened and read:

"A fair servant calls upon bare falcons,
In wanderer's land to travel and tread.
Guide and deliver the ignited flame,
To the navigator, soundless and blue.
Then can the two cross the bridge,
The laborers' task be fulfilled.
M."

Borghis stared at Ariad, not knowing what to say. Was she making all this up? Or was there something more going on here? As numbness filling his brain, Ariad broke the silence.

"Nomi gave me da letter, yu can go talk to him!" Ariad's next statement brought Borghis's mind to a complete standstill. But he was told that Headmaster Nomi had signed the letter of Falco confiscating his staff. What's going on here?

"Ariad, tell me the truth. How did you get the staff?" he asked. Borghis could only handle and solve one thing at a time. If Falco found out where his precious staff was right now...

"Oh, dat's of no concern to ya! We don never ever say how we take tings," Ariad responded defiantly.

"Borghis, I think I have a better idea on how to go about this with Nomi," Keenan suddenly barged into his room, with Gordi fast on his heels. They both stopped dead in their tracks when they saw Borghis, standing across from Ariad, holding what appeared to be an extravagantly jeweled staff in one hand, and an open letter in the other.

"Time to tend to da bruxes!" Ariad said merrily, finding the perfect time to exit.

"It's not what it looks like, she..., she took it," was all Borghis managed to say under the sharp gaze of his two friends.

"What the hell are you doing, Borghis? Did you hide this in your room, too?" Keenan asked, his chest heaving slightly.

"Don't ask questions, just read this. It's from the Count." Borghis immediately handed over the letter to Keenan who read it quickly. A look of relief came over Borghis when he spotted a spark of comprehension on Keenan's face.

"Let me see!" Gordi snatched the letter and quickly read it.

"Oh, now we're in deep," Keenan said, looking pensive. "So, this is the Exit Staff," he said, touching it for the first time. Borghis nodded. "The letter was delivered with the staff?"

"Ariad gave it to me, saying Nomi gave it to her. She said the headmaster knows, and I should go talk to him," Borghis answered, catching Keenan's eye.

"Nomi gave her the letter?!" Keenan asked.

A satisfactory sigh slipped out of Gordi. "Ha! I knew we should have spoken to him. We wasted all that time in the astronomy room worrying."

"This means Nomi's in on this. That's why he signed the confiscation, so they won't suspect you or us any longer for what's coming. They are planning something. The Count's message is not clear. It refers to travel, delivering something, crossing a bridge, but that's it. No specifics."

"Let's go see Nomi now!" Gordi exclaimed.

"Hold on! I can't just walk around with this thing. Where do I put the staff?" Borghis asked, scanning the room. For once, he cursed the minimalism of the Brown Robes. His dorm, squeaky clean, lacked any clutter in which to hide an exquisite staff.

"Put it back in the bed. Put a sign up on your door, do not disturb. Nobody dares go into your room anyway," Keenan said.

With no time to think of any other hiding option, the boys

buried the staff in Borghis's bed, just as Ariad had done. Then, they made their way to the headmaster.

Their talk with Nomi left Borghis terrified. Ariad had not been lying. As they walked out of the headmaster's quarters, Borghis felt the weight of Circa resting on his shoulders for what he was being asked to do.

Chapter 7

Peace and Chaos

Leanne enjoyed most of her evenings with her new friends. They weren't hard to get along with. It was also refreshing to meet and spend time with Ezekiola's friends, Atlas and Nohlan. With Ezekiola still away in camp, it seemed it was the most she could do to pass the time. But she brooded over the conversation they had by the bonfire the other night, replaying in her mind some of what was said, in part confirming her mother's reservations of Ezekiola, in part creating new ones about this new element they all spoke about – the Fountain of Fire. It sounded so fantastic. She witnessed some things for sure, but not feeling the power of this sacred fire put her in a state of uncertainty about the whole thing. She wondered how Ezekiola fared in his training with the Emeralds, how much more time he would spend in camp, and if he had again felt the power of the Fountain of Fire. She hated not knowing.

It wasn't quite dawn yet, and she couldn't go back to sleep. Instead of sitting in her new plain room that needed a desperate makeover, she decided to go for a quiet stroll to pick flowers in the woods. In the Black Forest, Helva had explained, there were *sojas*, a type of a yellow flower that bloomed immediately after being plucked. Something which Leanne had dubbed as magic. She had seen a duo of them in Helva's and Daria's rooms. The essence of the flowers would last several months, turning any space into a perfumed haven. Since the ladies had rummaged through their division, almost all the sojas were gone. They would have to wait a full year cycle for their next growth. Leanne decided to cross over to the boy's division and get some there. Thankfully, the boys did not pluck sojas as much, preferring the musk scent of pines and cypress leaves instead. She wanted a hoard of them in her bedroom, especially if she was to stay in this new home of hers—for now. So, there should be plenty for her to pluck. After having been taken on so many gracious tours of the Black Forest, she already knew how to navigate through it. She had even walked through the restricted zone where she had met that little boy, Virgil. As she retraced her steps, she was amazed at how much her circumstances had changed since then.

Helva had indicated in which zones the sojas grew. They were often found in abundance close to a nasty family of bushes called bruxes. She headed in that specific direction and found a stock of them off the main path. She stood still for a moment, evaluating her position. It was a dubious spot. The bruxes were chaotic, each of their branches adorned with needle sharp spikes every few inches, all sticking out, ready to go to battle as if guarding the gates to a castle. None of their branches had been trimmed, but the bright yellow sojas stood lovely in their midst, ever so tempting to Leanne's eyes. She decided to go for it. She walked delicately at first, looking left and right to avoid scratching her legs. Then when one knee got scraped, she jump-skipped over the other bruxes, rushing through them like she'd just caught fire, scrapping her skin on both legs and arms, as if speed would lessen the damage. She came out completely scratched.

"Damn it!" she cursed under her breath. She blamed those Gemins. She learned that they were part keepers of forests and did much of the trimming. Indeed, she had seen one snapping away at bruxes in this area not long ago. Next time, she will take those clippers from their hands and do it herself, clearing out all the paths leading to the sojas in this forest. She finally got close to a soja, her prize, and plucked it. She waited in eagerness for the flower to bloom. It didn't. Disappointed, she tossed it on the ground and plucked another one. It didn't bloom either. What's wrong with them? Their petals remained closed. She frowned; she better not have scraped her arms and legs for nothing. Her skin had already started to burn in areas where it had been scratched. Frustrated, she tossed the second flower on the ground, and in her third attempt, aimed towards a larger soja through another set of bruxes, plucking it quickly.

"How are you enjoying Circa?" His voice startled her, sending a burst of butterflies swirling into her stomach. She jumped around to see him standing on the other side of the bruxes, wearing dark clothes, no belt, with a smile hovering on his face. Like a mirage, she momentarily wondered if he wasn't a fabrication of her mind. She hadn't heard him approach at all.

"You're back!" she said, caught in a strange moment. She wasn't prepared for this. Everyone had convinced her that she wouldn't see Ezekiola until school started, yet here he was, standing not too far away. Her eyes needed to adjust it seemed, as she didn't recall his cheeks being so hollow, nor his eyes such a deeper shade of blue.

"Yes, they let me go," he said, his eyes quickly glancing at the soja she held in one hand. He noted that it was plucked unevenly, the stem too short. He spied two others scattered on the ground.

"And you're up early!" she managed, unsure of what to say on the spur of the moment.

"I can say the same about you," he said, smiling. "I couldn't go back to sleep. Blame it on training I guess."

Leanne was partly astonished, partly confused, scanning his face, his shoulders, and arms, then back to his face. The obvious hit her. "You...you've lost a lot of ... umm..." she said motioning to his body.

A gentle nod in his head confirmed what she was saying, but he didn't add any comment to it. She wondered what happened, then realized she should have said and pointed out anything else but that.

"So, you like plucking flowers in high danger zones?" he said with teasing eyes, glancing at her scratched arms and knees with crisscrossing lines of blood.

"Oh yes, well, Helva said that these are sojas, and they bloom once plucked, but these ones are refusing to right now. I think I may have plucked them prematurely, or maybe this is the wrong flower," she said looking down at them with a little guilt. There was so much more to say and speak about besides these flowers, as her gaze shifted back to his arms and shoulders. Underneath his garments, his body appeared shrunken. Thoughts began percolating in her head again.

Ezekiola let out a soft chuckle and moved slowly through the bruxes, managing to avoid every single one of their invasive branches. Leanne watched his steps, bewildered at how he managed to avoid a single scratch. He came closer and took the plucked sojas from her left hand.

"What you have in your hand is a soja. And what Helva said was true; sojas do bloom once plucked," he said taking a short pause, "but never alone," he added. He bent down to pick up the other flowers Leanne had tossed on the ground. He hesitated for a moment, wondering if Leanne would be able to handle the effect of three, or if he should just start with two, but he was tempted to give her a real buzz and opted to bunch all the sojas together.

"It takes another one of its kind to generate the bloom because their proximity releases an enzyme which stimulates a reaction to one another, enabling them to open their petals, like this," he said. He gave the cluster of flowers a little shake, bringing them close so their scent caressed her nose. He kept his gaze on her in anticipation of her reaction. Leanne was momentarily immersed in those eyes, vibrating with intensity. She was pulled into his presence; into whatever force he was exuding. Now that he stood closer, she could see a hint of sorrow in his eyes, and something else, something she couldn't put her finger on, because it lay concealed deep within. Before figuring it out, the powerful effervescence of the sojas pulled her out of her daze as every ounce of her being was immersed in the heady fragrance, making her dizzy.

"Wow!" she exclaimed, taking a step back. She was breathing deeply, as if unable to get enough air. She was shocked by the sojas potency.

"This is really some—" she sneezed midway in her sentence, "I never thought that—" and sneezed again, and again and again. By the fifth sneeze, an uncontrollable frenzy of laughter overcame her, and Leanne was nowhere close to getting a grip on herself. Her eyes teared up and her head spun. When the sneezing stopped, she was able to get a few words out. "It never crossed my mind to put them together, so simple really," Leanne said, giggling. Her head was spinning as Ezekiola watched.

"This is like a flower onion," she said, with watery eyes. "Can you get drunk on this scent?" she asked, provoking laughter from Ezekiola whose eyes were now tearing as well. "I'm serious, everything around me seems like it's shining more, like it's all the more vivid," Leanne said as she spun around to look at the surrounding vegetation and up at the sky. She knew too much perfume could cause dizziness, but this was altogether another sensation.

"If you're not used to it, I'd say yes, it could temporarily affect your senses," he said, watching her turn in circles to test to see how far the smell traveled. She turned around, observing him a few steps away.

She looked again at his sunken cheeks, and she had to know.

"How come you lost so much weight?" she asked suddenly.

Ezekiola momentarily looked down, kicked at a few pebbles, then shifted his gaze into the woods. A pensive look crossed his face. "The Emeralds have, I would say, interesting training methods," he finally answered, bringing his attention back to Leanne.

"Are they starving you?" Leanne asked, more directly this time, taking a break from swinging the flowers back and forth beneath her nose.

"Not quite. They put me on diets meant for warriors who have amnesia."

Leanne frowned. She'd never heard of any such diet. He read her face and continued:

"It's what they do to withdraw or bring back memories of Emerald warriors. In my case, they wanted to sidestep regular training, withdraw some of Zeke's memories, specifically his warrior skills. Apparently, he was some well-ranked warrior who excelled in certain areas," Ezekiola answered, carefully watching Leanne's reaction to every one of his words, hoping he wasn't saying too much. The last thing he wanted was to drive her away because of this baseless assumption that he had remnants of Zeke who served the SONS still in him. Already, he wasn't fond of what his friends had said the night before, planting ideas in her mind about him being dangerous, a possible menace of some kind. It was something he would have to undo. Meanwhile, he had to be vigilant.

"Were they able to pull out Zeke's memories on fighting?" she asked, curious.

He shook his head. "None of it. I think I'm their worst apprentice. The Emerald leader probably hates me. In fact, he's the one who sent me back. I don't think we'll be seeing each other for a while," he said with a sigh of relief.

"Do you think it's possible that you will remember one day?" she asked. Ezekiola noticed the added interest in Leanne's expression. He mused over her last question.

"Maybe," he shrugged, not knowing how the mechanics of such a thing could work out.

"Did you wonder if it's possible to remember anything else from his life?" Leanne was on a role. But Ezekiola hadn't planned on answering these types of questions, especially so early in the morning. The sun had not even risen. But he couldn't ignore her concern either.

"I honestly don't know. I'm just me, as I know myself to be," he said, wishing he could give a better answer.

"I'm just wondering why the Emeralds tried to retrieve memories. Do they think you carry over shades of Zeke in you?" she asked, another question that caught Ezekiola off guard. With Leanne being so candid, whether under the effect of the flower or not, he had to give some response.

"I think they originally thought that, but nothing came out of my training. They tried all sorts of weird stuff, even went overboard with some of their techniques. I don't think they've dealt with something like this before. They looked like a bunch of amateurs experimenting on me. And in the end, they were disappointed." Silence hung in the air between them, then a question suddenly sparked in his mind.

"Would you still stay here, no matter my shade?" he dared to ask.

Leanne was taken aback. This was unexpected. Momentarily, she remained quiet. Truth was, it had crossed her mind once before, but she didn't dare feed those thoughts, worried where they might lead her. He was looking at her intensely, waiting for a response, as if his world's weight dangled on that one answer. Then he sensed it. The hesitation.

"I guess I would, I mean I'm here, right?" Leanne answered. He nodded, contemplating his predicament, and the uncertainty that surrounded it. No one seemed sure of anything where he was concerned. He couldn't blame them either, especially not Leanne. He chastised himself for asking such a thing from her. She was just getting to know him, had just switched her home planet for Circa. How could he demand more?

"Well, look at the bright side! You're back, and you can now eat anything you want," Leanne said, her smile, shifting the topic. He noticed and decided to go along. Enough brooding over Zeke. He smiled, and a thought popped into his mind.

"Have you been to the White Mountains, close to the outdoor amphitheater by the sea?"

"You have an amphitheater by the sea?" Leanne asked, surprised.

"Yes, if you want, I'd like to show it to you, and if we're fast enough, we can catch the sunrise there. It's a fun climb, that's if you're not afraid of heights," he said, with a mischievous look in his eyes.

Leanne's eyes lit up. "Yes!"

"I just need to stop by my dorm quickly to get my belt, you can come along," he said. That was now one of his rules, never to venture out anywhere with Leanne without his belt.

They left, and for the first time, Ezekiola's heart stirred in a place where it had space, void of the heavy load that was weighing on it. They exited the bruxes, Ezekiola helping her to come out unscathed. Her presence made the walk back to his dorm altogether a new experience, as if the trees, plants, and flowers rearranged themselves, vibrating with a different hue. For the first time, he was glad to be back. Some peace after chaos. He vowed to himself not to be parted from her again, whatever it took.

As they arrived at his dorm, Ezekiola was shocked to see a small crowd gathered in his living space.

"What's going on here?" Ezekiola asked.

"Pack your stuff, we're leaving!" Borghis blurted, bypassing any formal salutation.

"What?" Ezekiola was dumbfounded. Early that morning, he had left a quiet room, and now it was a full house, with Borghis and his brown chums, Gordi, and Keenan, circling his bed, dumping loads of clothes in his travel bag, as if readying for some long trek in the horizon. It didn't help that Borghis was holding Ezekiola's Emerald Belt in his hands at that moment.

"Give me my belt," Ezekiola demanded, stretching out a bony arm, like a frail branch sticking out of a sapling. He was still uncertain what this intrusion was about. Leanne instantly retreated, positioning herself near the door.

"What happened to you?" Keenan asked concerned, noticing his friend's skeletal frame. Ezekiola didn't answer, his gaze still fixed on Borghis.

"We're taking your belt too, don't worry," Borghis continued packing, as if his answer sufficed.

"Borghis, stop. All of you, get out of my room. I'm not going anywhere!" Ezekiola's face flushed, accentuating further his sunken cheeks.

"Yes, you are," Borghis answered with determination in his voice.

"Borghis, drop everything you have in your hands, and leave. This is my last warning to you," Ezekiola reiterated, this time, his eyes darkened. Keenan and Gordi stood quietly behind, not having yet adjusted to this new Ezekiola. Borghis, however, carried on with zeal.

"Things haven't been so dandy since you've been gone, and we have instructions to follow." Borghis held his stance.

"Things haven't been so dandy for me either," Ezekiola came close and tried unsuccessfully to grab his belt back from Borghis's hands who pulled it away in a swift move. "And don't talk to me about instructions. Give me back my belt I said!"

"I don't think you're understanding the situation here," Borghis said, changing his tone, coming face to face with Ezekiola, still a head taller than him. But as frail as Ezekiola seemed, Borghis still held an ounce of caution in him, noticing something new in Ezekiola's countenance—a lack of fear. "We have been asked to escort you somewhere, and the stakes are high, unusually high," he emphasized.

"Stakes or no stakes, I'm not leaving. And you're getting out," Ezekiola said, finally yanking his belt back from Borghis's hands.

"You're coming. We have no choice!" he shouted this time.

"Is that right? You think you're going to force me?" Ezekiola's tone hardened.

"Calm down, Ezekiola, we're not here to fight," Gordi said suddenly, taking it upon himself to calm the heat in the room. In a swift move, he went to grab Ezekiola's wrist, the one that held the belt, a gesture perhaps meant to be nurturing, yet in that instance, it was anything but the right thing to do. On reflex, Ezekiola jerked his wrist away, slamming his forearm against Gordi's face, then pushed Borghis as he was closing in on the space between them, slamming him into Keenan with an unprecedented force. Both Borghis and Keenan hit the wall in the cramped corner of the room, tumbling over one another.

"Calm down I said!" Gordi pulled Ezekiola back, grabbing him from the chest, surprised at how frail he was. Ezekiola lurched backwards, ramming Gordi into the dresser. Gordi growled as his hips painfully hit the edge. Meanwhile, Borghis and Keenan lifted themselves up, and attempted to get a hold of Ezekiola. The four tossed each other back and forth, propelling a "STOP IT!" from Leanne, who could not bear to stand by and watch the conflict escalate. The commotion in the room coming so early in the morning was enough to spur interest outdoors. Soon enough, Atlas and Nohlan dashed into the dorm.

"HEY!" Nohlan yelled, "Let him go!"

"Stay out of this, Nohlan!" Borghis blurted out, getting himself in a better position to tackle Ezekiola. Both Nohlan and Atlas lunged forth, while Atlas tried to hide his shock at seeing his friend's chest and arms, now exposed in a ripped shirt.

"ENOUGH!" It was the voice of Helva. Looking for Leanne, she strode in, and that effected a dead stop. They froze, all of them breathing heavily. It amazed Leanne how the sound of a voice can be so commanding. Ezekiola lay on the floor, in a corner, with a shredded shirt, never having let go of his belt. He cast his eyes on the floor, unable to look up, in this awkward turn of events, when all he wanted to do was see the sunrise on the top of a mountain. He stood up and ran a hand through his ruffled curls in a vain attempt to straighten up.

"What's the matter with all of you?" Helva demanded. Her presence was acting as a neutralizing force.

"He needs to come with us. We have somewhere to take him," Borghis replied. With Helva in the room, Borghis' stance shifted. "It's coming from the headmaster and the Count," he said, hoping they would grasp the gravity of the situation.

"I don't care who it's coming from," Ezekiola shot back, surprising everyone.

"Well, I do!" Borghis said, looking hard at Ezekiola. "As we speak, we've been stripped of many things, trying to save your throat! We're paying a price for consequences that should never have been ours to pay in the first place. Just so you know, we just got our staffs confiscated by a new FOREST RAT who wants to prove his superiority and devotion to strict rules. And now, we're in a worse position than ever before with what we just pledged to do. Guess for who? You!"

"Borghis, not like this! He just got back. Give him a moment," Helva said firmly. Something in her voice made it clear there was no arguing with her.

"What happened to you, Zek?" Atlas asked, taking his chance to connect with his friend.

"Nothing that concerns you," Ezekiola replied. He snatched a clean shirt from the bundle on his bed, removing the torn one.

"Whoa! We haven't seen you for weeks, and that's the greeting we get?" Atlas reacted, never one to hold back. Upon hearing Atlas talk like this, Ezekiola decided he would not hold back either.

"You want greetings? Maybe that's what you get from someone you call dangerous, or what were the exact words again? Oh, someone who can *pose a danger*. And maybe you two should go back to making more bonfires during your evenings, it sure fuels great discussions," he said. A stunned look appeared on the faces of Nohlan and Atlas.

"Come Leanne, let's get out of here," he said. Leanne cast a glance at Helva, who motioned her to leave, dispatching her, while she handled the other boys. A ladies' team effort. Leanne followed suit, somewhat baffled, exiting with Ezekiola, and casting a troubled look behind her, as if she was escaping a burning house with people in it.

With the two gone, the heat still palpable in the room, a perplexed Atlas, so behind on news, had to ask: "Who's this new forest rat?"

Chapter 8

Message in a Garden

The sun had already risen when Ezekiola stormed out of the dorm with Leanne. The turn of events that morning not only left him disappointed but disturbed. What Borghis uttered before he stepped out still echoed in his ears: "*It's coming from the Headmaster and the Count.*" What were they all brewing for him now? Was it true? Ezekiola blurted out that he didn't care, but in truth, nothing could've troubled him more. He was power walking in the Black Forest, not realizing he was several steps ahead of Leanne, pounding every one of his strides into the ground as if headed towards some damned destination. Leanne had been following quietly, curiously keeping a safe distance in hopes that the extra space would allow him to simmer down. On occasion, she was about to say something or simply turn back, but then thought better of it. It was one of those odd moments where silence was king. They were deep into the woods, coming close to the amphitheater when Ezekiola let out a disheartened exhalation.

"What the hell is this?" he muttered under his breath. The

iron gates to the amphitheater had a lock on them. The doors had never been barred during summertime. As most students were away at that time, they were always left open for visitors to enter.

"I can't believe it," he said, shaking his head. He looked closely at an unfamiliar oversized iron deadbolt. He flipped the lock and saw an elegant carving of a bird covering the full back of it.

Leanne came close and examined it as well. "It looks like an eagle," she said.

"Oh, this is no eagle. It's a falcon, the emblem of the Brown Robes, who for some reason decided to place a lock here," he said, slamming the lock against the door. He backed away, running his hands through his hair, looking at the surrounding area to find another opening. When he saw no other entry point, he yanked away at the lock, trying to push his way through the doors using the might of his shoulders on the improbable chance that they would somehow open the gate. Thoughts of Borghis and his friends came to him as he furiously pounded away.

"There's got to be a way in!" he shouted. After a few tries with his upper body, his legs took the shift, one at a time, attempting to ram through the gates, letting a little more of his fury out with each try.

Watching Ezekiola become more and more exacerbated, Leanne's mood for adventure, for mountain climbing, suddenly vanished. Just by the way he was kicking the doors, she reckoned he would need a whole afternoon to simmer down from this misadventure.

"Ezekiola, please stop! The sun's already up, and maybe today's not the best day to climb a mountain," she said. He gazed at her in disbelief, but more so in desperation.

"What do you mean? We're here, sunrise or not, don't you

want to go up the mountain? I know there's a way from the other side, it's a steeper climb, but it's doable," he said.

"How about we just continue walking instead? It's nice here in the forest. But let's walk slowly this time," she emphasized her last words, swallowing hard, anticipating his reaction.

Ezekiola stilled for a moment. He backed away from the amphitheater doors, backed away from the spectacular sunrise he had missed and the view he wanted to treat Leanne to. With his back against the locked doors, he slipped onto the ground and sat crumpled. He sighed deeply. The day had defeated him.

"Sorry about all this. Nothing turned out as planned," he said, his eyes reflecting that touch of sorrow they held when she had first seen him that morning.

"Don't be sorry. You really didn't plan anything. Your suggestion to see the amphitheater, the sunrise, the mountains, and even the hassle in your room, they were all unplanned," Leanne said. "I would've reacted the same. No, worse for the room part. Anyone putting their hands on my clothes would feel my wrath. You gave them a few warnings, which I found nice of you."

Ezekiola let out a small chuckle. Leanne came closer and was about to sit down next to him when she heard something in the far distance. She turned around and saw a small crowd walking in their direction.

"Is that Nohlan's older brother heading back over with his friends?" Leanne asked.

"What?!" Ezekiola exclaimed and stood up. He looked in the same direction. His nerves twitched, and his blood started pumping fast. Indeed, Brown Robes were heading their way.

"They better not come closer, I'm in no mood to see them. If Borghis thinks quantity will make a difference, he's mistaken," Ezekiola said, readying himself. As they approached, however, Ezekiola noticed it wasn't Borghis at all, but someone else at the head of the triangle formation. In fact, he did not recognize anyone. Their robes, although brown, had a distinct line contouring the edges and multilayered designs, some brimming with jewels. A few of them were holding thick stacks of documents in their hands. Ezekiola was curious.

"Young man," he heard the leader of the pack say from afar. "I hope you were not attempting to enter the amphitheater of the Black Forest. It is henceforth restricted from entry."

Ezekiola was surprised. Who was this person waltzing about telling him he can't enter the amphitheater? He and Leanne stared as the Brown Robe drew closer to greet them, accompanied by an impressive entourage. The tone of his voice however put Ezekiola on guard.

"Since when is it restricted to enter here? These doors are never locked," Ezekiola said, testing the newcomers' grounds. He glanced quickly at the faces of the crew to see if he could recognize anyone, but no one looked familiar.

"Don't be brash with me, boy! Weren't you the one who took Latin last cycle?" he asked.

The oddball question caught Ezekiola off guard. "Yes, I did," he answered, perplexed at how he came about this information. "What does that have to do with this?" he asked, puzzled.

The man let out a wolflike yelp. It ricocheted through the forest, contagious enough to affect his crew who laughed in unison with him. "Well then, you should know better: *Ignorantia juris non excusant.* The ignorance of rules is not a valid excuse, something highly expected from ones who revel knowing such languages as Latin, and, who also take delight in reading other people's minds I should add," he said, sending Ezekiola an unexpected shockwave. Of all the happenings that morning, these were the last words he imagined he would hear.

Ezekiola's hands began to twitch. He balled them up in fists, then relaxed them.

"Really? And which rule have I ignored?" Ezekiola asked, his eyes narrowing.

"The one all students at Cypress School should be aware of, and evidently are not. A failed duty attributable to your headmaster, of course," he said without hesitation.

"The Amphitheatre is a part of the school," Ezekiola ventured. "How does this rule apply?"

"Ah, but it's on forest grounds, under the governance of the Forest Steward Council," he stated. Ezekiola noticed the pleasure in his voice.

"And I will also add, many other rules have changed." He sniffed the air, catching a sweet scent. He recognized the flowery smell. His intuitive compass made him rest his gaze on Leanne. It made her instantly shudder. Ezekiola caught a glimpse of something enticing in the man's expression as he stared at her. He took his time studying her, his probing eyes moving along her features, sending shivers down her spine. He clicked his tongue.

"Ladies such as yourself must also know that there will no longer be plucking of sojas, as they are now classified as vanishing floras," he said ruefully. "They are now under my protection, as they are precious and rare. Like your kind, my lady Leanne. We provide a haven for those like you. We look forward to your visit to our Sanctuary. I made sure this was part of your curriculum, as you will soon find out. I will personally ensure you an enriching visit," he said with a smile. His invitation turned Leanne's cheeks hot as if struck by a violent fever.

Upon hearing him speak, something new and noxious came pulsating through Ezekiola's nerves. It was not enough that he boasted about new rules, *he was summoning Leanne to his Sanctuary.* This elevated Ezekiola's fury to another level.

He swallowed hard and remained calm, nonetheless. Oddly, it was at this very moment that something dawned on him. Borghis did not overreact in his dorm that morning. No, not at all. Here he was, the nemesis Borghis was up against, the forest rat, the one who took away his staff, and those of his friends. He was sure of it. A sudden comprehension washed over him.

Meanwhile, Leanne's heart was palpitating at a rate she could not control, and something about this man's presence sent her thoughts into paralysis. As if sensing her discomfort, Ezekiola drew closer to her, gently placing his arm around her waist for the first time, facing the strangers, grinning in their faces.

"Thank you for those insightful words. May we ask to whom are we speaking?"

"This is Master Falco Rasspan, our new elected head of the Forest Governance Council," answered the consort on his right. Falco smiled, but to his dismay, Ezekiola also smiled. For some reason, Falco didn't like that. As a reflex, he raised his chin up and spoke.

"You'll be seeing much more of me as we guard our forestry dominion and keep out the intrusion and filth that have lately soaked our grounds. Something I'm sure you're aware of," Falco said, staring hard at Ezekiola. They held each other's gaze for a moment, just as two beasts would before fighting for territorial grounds. With a nod, Falco then shifted his attention to his crew. They continued their procession, walking away into the woods.

As soon as they were out of sight, Leanne, whose breath was stuck in her upper chest, finally released with a whoosh. She turned to Ezekiola and asked: "Tell me, does your belt turn into a whip?"

"I believe so," he answered, catching her eye. "Why, would

you like me to whip him for you?" he asked, bemused, prompting a loud giggle from Leanne.

"Who was that? There is no way I'm visiting that man at that Sanctity or whatever it is he called it!" she said, all fired up from the exchange. "Did you happen to read his mind? What was he thinking?" she asked.

"No, I didn't need to. His kind doesn't scrutinize or filter their words. He says what he thinks."

"Is it normal that you have rules like these here?" she asked.

He shook his head. "Most of us run on unwritten rules. We never had a need to formalize them. I'll have to ask and see what this is all about. It just doesn't feel right."

"I don't know why, but for some reason I kept thinking that maybe this is the forest rat Borghis spoke about. What do you think?" she asked.

Ezekiola smiled, knowing well she caught on. "Oh yes! That's exactly what I think," he answered.

"Well then that's it. You have to go see your headmaster now," she blurted out.

Her statement stopped Ezekiola in his tracks, forcing him to face the inevitable moment he had brushed off earlier. What will he do? Follow orders again? He took a few steps in one direction, then paced back retracing his steps, finding himself in a small thinking space. What if they all wanted him to go back to that Emerald camp? He will just say no to that. But why would Borghis need to be involved? That didn't make sense. And apparently the Count is sending this request. What for? He couldn't wrap his head around what this could possibly be.

"Fine. I'll go see Nomi. But I'd like you to come with me," he said, surprising Leanne.

"Me? But this is a personal matter. Why should I be there?" she asked.

"Because everything that's happening to me is because of you," he said catching her off guard. "And every decision I make has you included in it," he added, leaving her mouth agape. Leanne couldn't quite think of anything to say to counter the sincerity of his words. Something stirred deep inside her. She wasn't used to seeing this kind of vulnerability in the boy with the green belt. With so many exceptional things happening in her own life, she could not deny him.

"Alright, I'll come. But if the headmaster asks me to leave, you understand that I will go," she said, squaring her shoulders a little. He nodded. It was good enough for him, though he'd make sure not to give Nomi the chance to do that.

They made their way to the headmaster's quarters. As they approached, Ezekiola could see from the outside window that Professor Balthazar was in Nomi's office, in deep conversation with him. Ezekiola gave Leanne a curious look, took a deep breath, and knocked. Nomi stood up and opened the door. At the sight of them, something delightful touched his face.

"Ah! Ezekiola! And Leanne! Great timing. Come on inside, come Leanne, meet Professor Balthazar," he said, inviting both to take a seat.

"Hello Professor," Ezekiola addressed Balthazar with a nod.

"I see you are back from camp," Balthazar said, running a close eye over Ezekiola's body, tracing some of the visible bruises. "And I can see the Emeralds clearly haven't dealt with apprentices in ages," he said. Leanne quickly exchanged a few pleasantries with the two men and learned that Professor Balthazar seemed to know a lot more about her than she expected.

"Well, I'm glad that you came now because a moment ago, Borghis was here," Nomi said, getting down to serious news. "He told me what happened earlier this morning," Nomi stated. Upon hearing that, Ezekiola squirmed a little in his seat, wondering what kind of story Borghis had relayed to their headmaster. This irked him a little, but then he thought of the forest rat, and sympathized, feeling less bitter towards Borghis.

"I'm sorry about this morning. I was not prepared to see him in my room so early, especially not to take orders. I just got back from training camp," Ezekiola said.

"That's alright. He's under a lot of strain right now, and we have, umm, things we have to resolve collectively," Nomi said, looking at the far side of his room towards a pile of papers mounted on his desk. Ezekiola recognized a similar pile he had just seen the Forest Council members hold in their hands. Were they bringing them here to Nomi? he wondered.

"I'm asking Borghis to do something that places him in a dire position. He's accepted to carry out an act, but it cannot be done without your consent," Nomi said. He stood up, fishing amongst a pile of papers stashed in a corner of his bureau. He came back with a large scroll. As he unfurled it, they saw it was a map. Nomi placed it on a midsize table, unfolding the edges carefully. Ezekiola had seen this layout before. His memory didn't fail him, and he suddenly recalled seeing this same image in the astronomy room with its circular dome in the Brown Robe's lodge. It was the layout of all the planets and constellations. Nomi's fingers traced over several planets. He circled Circa, then Planet Blue which was in proximity, displaying them to his audience.

"This is where we are," he said. He then moved his fingers to the far-right side of the map and pointed to a barely perceptible round sphere.

"This is Haack, where we want you to go. It's a dead mass, a moon long abandoned by its host planet. It's a misty terrain, too dark and barren to sustain life, except for those living things whose evolution has been arrested. Here, there is no growth, and no contact takes place with other evolved beings. Entry onto the moon is possible, but because of its lack of evolution, getting out is hard. That's why no one dares to cross through these lands in fear of being stuck. And this is where we are asking you to go, not to stay, but to traverse through. For this mission, it's the best avenue to use to get to a destination without leaving a trace for anyone to follow. It's a bridge to somewhere we want you to go. Once you cross it, someone will be expecting you on the other side. That's why Borghis has been given the Exit Staff to use as it ensures a way out of Haack," he explained.

Leanne, Ezekiola and Balthazar looked at the map. Ezekiola could see that Balthazar had something brewing in his mind. Later, he might find out what it was.

"Will the Emeralds escort us?" Ezekiola asked.

"Unfortunately, no. The Emerald warriors leave a trace, like animals leave a scent when crossing a path. It's easily detectible by the SONS. Also, the Emeralds are not aware of this plan, and it's important we do not disclose it to them. At least, not yet," Nomi answered, leaving to Ezekiola's imagination the reason behind this secrecy.

"Here, I have a letter for you. It's from the Count. Your instructions will be found in it. He specifically asked you to read it in the garden," Nomi said, his face a mix of hope and anticipation as to what Ezekiola would decide.

Ezekiola took the letter and stepped out into the garden. For some reason, he found himself at the exact spot where he had first met Meredus of Loggia. He opened the letter. Only a few words were written at the very top. He glanced at the back of the letter. It was an empty page. He reread the words on the front. Was this really the instruction? It sounded awfully mundane. He looked around to see if anyone was looking, making sure he was alone. He hesitated for a moment, wondering if this wasn't a little silly. Finally, he decided to follow through on the letter's instruction. He closed his eyes, gathering his thoughts, aiming them in a specific direction. After a few moments of holding his mind steady with intensity, a strange sensation overcame him. His body warmed up, and he found his mind sharing a greater space, one without boundaries. In this larger vista, his mind suddenly found its target and merged with something that was waiting for him. He recognized that signature. It was the Count's mind. He sensed his presence, and even with his eyes closed, he could see him, wearing his blue robe shimmering with green, and those deep blue eyes. Then he heard him speak. Although he knew this was in his mind, Ezekiola could have sworn it was as clear as if the Count was present with him in the garden. He remained still, listening to what the Count had to say, then took his turn to speak. Their exchange lasted a few moments. When it was over, Ezekiola opened his eyes.

He looked around. He was alone in the garden, the letter still in his hand. He stared back at the words as they were written: *Close your eyes and share my mind.* Whoever thought Blue Robes can speak and read minds so far away from one another? Ezekiola smiled, partly in awe that he was able to do such a thing as mind-reading and getting messages from afar. He smiled also because the Count answered one of his questions. He could bring anyone along. Now he couldn't wait to put his so-called friends to the test.

Chapter 9

The Blue Navigator

Borghis was not happy. For one, the horde of people Ezekiola was gathering to chaperone him on this voyage made Borghis very nervous. Like a military strategist preparing for battle, Ezekiola first chose Helva to accompany him, which completely took Borghis by surprise. Her intuition was priceless he claimed, and unlike Borghis who had his staff confiscated, she had hers and could use it. After all, she was the one who helped him enter Planet Blue to confront his twin Zeke. Upon hearing Helva was going on this journey, Daria asked if she could come along as well. That was perfect because it was exactly what Ezekiola needed to convince Leanne to partake in the expedition. He absolutely wanted her to be close, believing her proximity would enable him to tap into the Fountain of Fire and protect everyone if needed. As anticipated, Leanne said yes to him in a heartbeat.

Upon learning that all three ladies were coming, Borghis couldn't see himself carrying this mission out alone without help. Both Keenan and Gordi's presence now became indispensable to safely guard the traveling crew. And once Atlas and

Nohlan found out about the travel party through their respective siblings, they couldn't just stand back and do nothing. This was precisely what Ezekiola wanted. He never asked his best friends to be part of this journey, but if they had remained silent, it would have spoken volumes to him. Atlas saw through his friend's scheme and the position they were trapped in. He was reluctant to go on such a trip. The last time they journeyed outside Circa to Planet Blue, it was almost a disaster. Unfortunately for him, Nohlan was hell bent on joining in the adventure. In a show of loyalty and audacity, especially in the aftermath of their recent exchange, both Nohlan and Atlas came forward and asked to accompany Ezekiola, provoking a barely perceptible smile on his lips.

As the numbers of the traveling party grew, other things unsettled Borghis. His wish to rid himself of the Exit Staff kept being postponed, all because their departure date kept getting pushed back. To his great disappointment, Helva was behind this. While no specific date was assigned by the headmaster for this mission, except to be done 'soon,' she absolutely wanted to set their travel date during the full moons of Circa, a cycle that was set to take place only in a week's time. Helva argued that the gravitational pull of Circa's moons impacted greatly the entry and exit points into other worlds, same as tidal forces impact waters. It was safer this way, she said, to minimize unpleasant surprises. To Borghis' astonishment, his brother Nohlan agreed. Borghis thought Helva was turning this into some planned summer escapade. With that extra time now in their hands, Professor Balthazar suddenly got involved. He was adamant about getting Borghis and Ezekiola on board to run a Herculean trial of his—the catching of the doe in the astrological sign of Cancer. If they were to embark on such a journey, it was crucial they refreshed their memories on an important lesson. And Balthazar would not take no for an answer.

"The catching of the female deer? Why do I even need to do this? What does it have to do with my mission?" a distraught Borghis asked Professor Balthazar. "I'm a Brown Robe, I've passed this test a long time ago, I don't need to do it again!"

"Do you know of any Brown Robe who has traveled to Haack and back, planting seeds, tending to a dying plant kingdom, or handling whatever animal is left alive in those fog-ridden hazy deadlands?" Balthazar asked in reply.

"I don't know, maybe?" Borghis turned to Keenan and Gordi, whose heads confirmed a solid no. Keenan had even searched their library and found scarce information on Haack.

"Do you know for sure if this Exit Staff will work on Haack?" Professor Balthazar pressed Borghis further with another question. Borghis shook his head.

"That's right. NO. If anything goes wrong, and you're stuck, your only way out will be your inner compass. This Herculean trial of catching of the doe is aimed at exactly that—should your Exit Staff fail, you will still know what is best to do. You cannot solely rely upon external devices such as a staff, even if it's the best Circa has. If you do not know how this inner compass works, and how to awaken your ears to that internal voice, you will fail. The consequences this time, however, are far greater since you have the lives of your friends in your hands."

"How long is this going to take?" Borghis finally asked, conceding.

"We begin today. Meet me at the Herculean dome at sunset, both of you!" Balthazar commanded.

Balthazar programmed several trials, switching around landscapes to make them dark and misty, preparing Borghis and Ezekiola for what Haack would look like. At the start of every mission, he would repeat the instructions specific to the trial: "The mission is simple: catch the doe. It represents your inner compass."

Every day, Borghis and Ezekiola took turns, while their friends watched from a bird's-eye view outside the dome. It was always fun for observers, but not so for the participants. Some landscapes were so terribly hazy, they could barely see a few feet away.

"Make me go blind why don't you!" Borghis barked at the professor, outraged at the scarce visibility available in one of the settings. He had even waved his hands in front of him, stunned that he couldn't see them though they were mere inches away.

Balthazar then readjusted landscapes, enhancing sound this time. Nature sounds, such as the rushing of leaves, that far from soothing was so loud it became a far greater distraction than the lack of visibility. The cumulative noise was so terrifying, both Borghis and Ezekiola had aborted on instinct believing a hurricane was underway.

"Are you trying to blow our heads right off? How do you want us to find a female deer in this setting?" Borghis whined, to which Balthazar retorted: "That's exactly how it is, learn to find the doe in the clamor and noise." When Borghis and Ezekiola finally saw the doe, it was in a blink. One moment they saw her, the next she was gone. She was like an impression. Brief but fleeting.

Days later, after having gone through a dozen trials, Ezekiola realized that catching the doe could not be done using his normal faculties—his instincts, his mind, or even his eyes. When he grew comfortable not seeing in this way, he searched for another way to find the doe. He relied on something that has no rulebook, that no one can teach, but which can only be discovered by following its abstract, elusive guidance. He applied this new method. And that's when he caught the doe. It astonished him. Earlier on, the notion had come to him on how best to catch the doe using this very method, but he never followed it. For Borghis, it took him twice as long to catch the doe. But in the end, he did it. He also caught on.

Balthazar's speech to them at the end of the week sank in hard. "The doe is ephemeral, comes like a flash, first leaving you in doubt whether it's real. Don't dismiss that which you think is too feeble to deserve your attention. On the contrary, pay closer attention. That is how the inner compass works. It's neither vibrant nor loud, but a light feathered voice. It is not your intellect, nor is it your instinct. It's more subtle than that. It's your intuition. It exists. Follow it. You'll need it on Haack."

The meeting was set in advance. During the last full moons of the summer, in the middle of the night, nine bodies made their way towards Night and Day Inn, their meeting point. When the ladies arrived, the boys were already outside waiting. Borghis had the Exit Staff in hand, fully covered with a dark cloth in fear that the jewels on it would glimmer under the moonlight giving away their position. He was relieved that they hadn't crossed paths with anyone in the Black Forest on their way to the inn, especially no one from Falco's posse. At this point, that would have been the most catastrophic event in Borghis' life.

Helva, too, had her staff in hand, also covered with a cloth. Everyone had brought a little sack of some sort for essentials, but one large bag on the ground stood out from the rest. Since Nohlan was standing closest to it, Helva assumed it was his.

"What's in the bag, Nohlan?" she asked.

"Yes, Nohlan, tell her, what's in that bulky bag of yours?" Atlas asked, chuckling.

"Keep laughing! You just wait. You'll be begging me to share," Nohlan snapped back at him. Worried the journey might take longer than expected, Nohlan had packed a week's worth of food. The previous expedition to Master Sohan's domain taken with his friends had taught him precaution. He swore never to go hungry again.

"Nohlan, this is a drop and go mission. What part of Borghis' message did you not understand?" Atlas hectored again.

"Quiet!" Borghis interrupted. "Everyone listen: Nomi said this should be an in and out, no longer than a day. As for the Count's message, it's clear enough: once we enter Haack, we need to look for the Blue Navigator. Once we find him, he will bring Ezekiola to a bridge and will cross it with him. The rest of us do not cross this bridge. That will be our cue to exit. We don't hang around or chitchat. Understood?"

"So we're just going to leave Zek like that on some bridge?!" Nohlan asked.

"Stop asking the same question, Nohlan! I already went over that part. I don't want to see any of you waiting. Like I said, we need to exit as soon as Ezekiola is in good hands crossing that bridge. The Count knows what he's doing, and the Blue Navigator is aware of this journey, and will be waiting for him. Our task is to find him first," Borghis said, although his last utterance lacked the same note of confidence as the rest of his instructions.

"And who or what is the Blue Navigator?" Atlas asked for the first time.

"The Count didn't say," Borghis replied.

"Then how will you recognize it?" Atlas asked, concerned.

"It will be obvious when we see it. No more questions. We leave now. Follow me!"

Borghis was lying, of course. In fact, he had extensively discussed this point about who this Blue Navigator was with Ezekiola, but neither of them had come to a satisfactory conclusion. Ezekiola was lacking the same information. The Count had intentionally left them in the dark for their own safety. Should they be followed, the enigmatic figure of the Blue Navigator would not be easily discovered.

Atlas sighed under his breath, shaking his head. This was sounding like another one of those questionable trips he would come to regret later. Again, for the sake of his friend, he was tagging along while ruminating over who this Blue Navigator was. Borghis guided the group through the deeper, darker avenues of the Black Forest. The trees overhead obscured the moonlight. No one spoke. While walking behind Borghis in silence, Ezekiola's heart began pounding hard enough to reverberate in his ears. Something about this excursion sounded a different note for him. He could tell just by the way he had gathered his friends, as if he was ceremoniously preparing himself for a pivot point in his life. Where was he really headed? Who or what was the Blue Navigator and what is on the other side of the bridge? He had no clue but was confident that the Count was providing him with the best guidance. Somehow, hearing his friend's soft footsteps soothed him, a convoy of support, ready to accompany him as far as they could. As mundane as it seemed, it was significant enough to occupy a little sacred space in him. And for some reason, he was glad Atlas had come.

Borghis came to a stop, motioning Helva to come forward, pointing to a specific tree. They all stood aside, making way for her. Helva unveiled the impressive staff in her hands, supposedly hers. Upon seeing it, Borghis frowned. She smiled at him instead.

"Entry is as important as exit. Take it as a courtesy of the ladies, who never guard the Ladies Lodge as well as yours." Another stolen staff, Borghis thought. Helva had taken great pains to get this special staff that belonged to one of her teachers. Since it was summer, she reckoned its absence will go unnoticed for a few hours.

"Here, take it. This staff has entered many doorways. I guarantee you it's as efficient if not better than yours," she assured Borghis.

Borghis swallowed hard, then positioned everyone, coordinating who would enter first after his invocation. He had practiced this many times, envisioning it in his head beforehand. He reached for his pocket to be sure the Count's letter was safely tucked in there. With confidence, he spoke the sacred words.

Keenan was first to enter, followed by Gordi, then the ladies, with Ezekiola, and Borghis going last. Entry into Haack was a success. An exciting hum was buzzing through the group as they collectively congratulated themselves for having made it through step one.

"Shh," was the first sound uttered by Borghis, who like a frozen statue, was acclimatizing himself to the new environment. His eyes watered upon entry, and he blinked a few times. A carbon substance similar to charcoal powder permeated the air, thickening it, barely outlining the terrain in front of him. Everywhere he looked, it was a grim, ghoulish grey.

"It's dusty as hell here," Borghis muttered under his breath, unable to see the path ahead of him. It was almost a replica of the Herculean landscape Balthazar had programmed for him and Ezekiola to practice in. He secretly thanked his teacher for preparing them.

"And freezing!" Helva added. She took one step forward and gasped as a loud snapping sound was heard. "What was that?" she halted.

Borghis gave Keenan an interrogative look, motioning him to take something out of his bag. Keenan had brought a book, *The Death of Moons,* the only one he found which discussed Haack in tiny sections scattered throughout the book. He shuffled through the pages, then stopped when he found something.

"It says here '*due to the continual loss of heat, tectonic actions are abundant in some parts of Haack. The surface of the landscape continues to wrinkle, its interior shrinks, causing constant reverberations throughout the lunar mass.*' That's the sound we're hearing, like inner pockets crumbling," Keenan summed up what he had just read.

"So, this place is just disintegrating; horrible when you think about it," Helva remarked. Borghis walked around the perimeters and suddenly stopped, staring wide-eyed at something massive, an entrance of some sort. He dabbed the edges with his Exit Staff, which was now ready at hand to use at any given moment. He stood back, staring at something akin to the mouth of a cave.

"Helva, does your staff light up?" Keenan asked, squinting alongside Borghis at the impressive opening of the cave. Helva brought it forth, giving it to Keenan. The tip lit up cutting into the darkness.

"This is a good staff." Borghis gave her an appreciative smile.

"Do we go into the cave, or do we head the other way?" Keenan asked, looking around the scarce land. Dust combined with fog blocked much of their view, but in the cave, they might have some greater visibility using the contrast of the staff's light in the dark. Helva, Daria and Leanne came forward scanning the area. For some reason, the boys looked at them as if they held the final decision.

"What do you think?" Ezekiola asked after a moment. They nodded. "I think the staff brought us closest to our true entrance. We should enter the cave. The rest is just fog land, it won't lead us anywhere significant, that's my feeling," Helva finally said, her answer resonating with everyone.

Keenan was first to pass into the cave, followed by Borghis. Upon entering it, Borghis was struck with a flash of warning not to walk in the middle of the cave, but to stick to the sides. He remained quiet, however, not wanting to cause jitters in the group.

"It sure is dark, I hope there are no bats or anything like that lurking in here," Nohlan whispered from behind, following in the footsteps of his brother.

"You shouldn't worry about that Nohlan," Keenan spoke from the front of the line, guiding everyone with the lit staff. "Look around you. This place is not exactly thriving with life. There's not much here. It's the opposite. It's dying, so the chances of coming across animal life of any kind is quite slim. I'd be surprised even if we..." Keenan suddenly disappeared into a hole.

"Gordi!" he yelled while the book he was holding fell out of his hand. A fluttering of wings was heard simultaneously.

On reflex, Gordi caught Keenan's right arm to help, but instead, succumbed to Keenan's weight, while warding off things flying in his face. Gordi then got dragged on the ground, causing Borghis to mightily jump on Gordi's lower body to prevent him from being dragged further. Ezekiola, Nohlan and Atlas rushed forward, gripping whatever body part they were able to grab of Borghis, while Keenan's and Gordi's body dangled in the air. They were hanging off the edge of some hidden cliff, engulfed in darkness. Ahead of everyone, Keenan had walked right into a pocket of underground air, something that had once been dense land but was now crumbled away.

"Gordi, don't let go!" Keenan shrieked. Strange long white animals were flying around him.

"Hold on Gordi! Just hold on!" Borghis shouted for dear life. He glided slowly on the ground, getting a hold of Gordi's body first, while the girls moved in closer to help.

"No stay behind! All of you! There's a huge hole here, with flying animals," Borghis whispered fiercely, his veins popping out of his temples, fearful their weight might crack the rest of the fragile soil. That would be quite a swift end—tossed into some purgatory. With the help of Atlas, Ezekiola and his brother, Borghis was able to get Gordi out of the hole, who was then able to pull Keenan back up on the ground.

"Thank goodness we didn't lose this!" Keenan said half-jokingly once he got up, holding Helva's staff with shaky hands. He pointed the staff into the hole. It was a well of darkness. The fluttering of wings stopped in the pit. They couldn't see a thing. Neither did they hear the book *The Death of Moons* land at the bottom. That's when it hit Borghis. Upon entering the cave, he had a fleeting impression to be cautious, to stick to the sides of the cave and he hadn't paid attention to it. It was exactly what Balthazar was trying to teach him. There it was, the doe, representing his intuition. He should have caught on to that and acted. He had just put everyone's life in danger by not listening to his intuition.

"Everyone, move away from the center of the cave, and closer to the edges," Borghis finally stressed. "If this place is disintegrating, we need to hold on to each other, stay in line, touching the walls of the cave as we walk. Little steps."

"Is that hole bottomless? I didn't hear the book land!" Gordi asked, staring at the darkness below him.

"Well, we lost the book, so now we can't know for sure. Haack is spherical in form. It's almost surreal for it to just have hollow spaces in its core," Keenan looked down where he had almost disappeared, and his heart was still in his throat at how close he came to falling into an abyss.

"Well, good riddance to that long-expired book I say!" Atlas chimed in. "I can't believe you follow such outdated material in the first place. And for the record, there are living animals here.

It's almost better you don't have to carry that extra weight in your bag Keenan." Keenan chuckled although not sure whether losing the book was a good or bad thing.

"Alright, move along everyone, stick to the edges." Borghis was making sure everyone stayed in line. They walked for some time in silence, following Keenan and the staff's light that he carried. They often heard little sounds, which they assumed were nocturnal cave animals of some sort. Atlas, who had many things running in his head, still needed to get to the bottom of something far too nebulous to ignore.

"Where is the Blue Navigator? Shouldn't he be waiting for us here?" Atlas came back to his original query asked back in Circa. No one answered him. Everyone was watching their steps instead.

"Zek, talk to me here! Don't leave me blind in this cave! Do you at least know what he looks like?" Atlas asked.

"No, I don't know, the Count didn't say," Ezekiola answered with a deep sigh.

"Well did you ask him?"

"No, it didn't cross my mind to get details on that," Ezekiola said frankly.

"Wow, every time I go on a trip with you, it seems we wing just about everything, no map of any kind whatsoever here," Atlas exclaimed.

"Well Atlas, no one invited you to come along," Ezekiola said ruefully.

Atlas stopped and turned around, coming face to face with Ezekiola. "Really?" he said, his eyes narrowing like weapons. All the bodies lined up behind Ezekiola now had to stop and listen. "That depends on how you define inviting someone. Would it perhaps include putting someone in a tight position where they can't possibly say no because they'll get ostracized by their friend?" Ezekiola didn't answer, sidestepping him and his question with a faint smile, but he made sure to bump Atlas's shoulders.

"I take that as a yes!" Atlas yelled from behind.

"Well, would you look at that!" Leanne suddenly exclaimed. "There's some light over there, we can see the end of the cave," she declared, hoping that bit of good news would dissipate the tension in the air. It was amazing how darkness was conducive to conflict. A sigh of relief escaped from the group at the sight of additional light. They proceeded carefully for the rest of their walk. Exiting the cave seemed to take longer. The ground was uneven. Many times, they had to climb up on rocky steps, before swooping back down to ground level. They were just a few feet away from exiting the cave, when a loud gurgling sound was heard, halting everyone in their tracks. Whatever it was, it sounded very much alive.

"Nohlan, tell me that was your stomach making that noise," Atlas' voice was hoarse in the dark.

"You idiot! That sound came from outside the cave," Nohlan answered. "It sounds like an animal. Keenan, do you remember what kind of animals live here?"

Everyone looked at Keenan, who scratched his head. The Death of Moons book was gone. He had spent some time reading through most of the features of Haack before they left, but didn't recall reading much on animals. The only thing he remembered was that animals whose evolution had been arrested had wasted away in this land, slowly dying. Now he wished he could skim the book one last time.

"Just let me exit first," was the best Keenan could offer. "If there's something out there, I'll confront it."

"Hold on Keenan, let me go this time. You almost died before. Let's take turns brushing with death, give others a chance," Gordi offered, making his friends smile for the first time. But Keenan had already stepped forward before everyone else.

"Don't move," Keenan whispered upon exiting the cave. Something his size, on two legs, and a very long neck gawked at him. It was the sound they had heard in the cave right before.

"What is that?!" Gordi asked, coming next to him.

"Stay back, it looks like an ostrich," Leanne said as soon as she saw it.

"A what?" they simultaneously asked her.

"An ostrich, it's a bird we have on our planet, but they can't fly," she answered.

"You have birds that don't fly on your planet?" Nohlan asked in awe. Leanne nodded. Then to their surprise, especially Leanne's, a second bird came landing from above, next to the other, sounding a warble.

"Wow, they can fly! That's no ostrich but...I don't know what it is," Leanne said, shaking her head. As the warbling progressed, the two birds were joined by a third, and then a fourth. The sky suddenly filled with their kind. They landed one at a time, and for some reason, they headed towards Atlas, while his friends took the opportunity to back away safely.

"Whoa! What's happening here, Keenan?" Atlas asked in a panic. Keenan tried to search his brain, but he couldn't remember anything about birds on this moon. There was supposed to be very little life still on the moon.

"Oh wait, I think I read something about these birds." Gordi looked at Keenan, his eyes glowing with insight. "These birds were never admitted into Circa. I remember coming across their entry being declined on our planet. Something was off with their composition. Oh, what was it?" he mumbled, scratching his head.

"What's wrong with their composition, Gordi? They're big as hell!" Atlas' voice went up an octave.

"Now stay calm, don't display any aggression towards them," Gordi cautioned.

"Why are they heading only my way? Borghis, use your staff, Zek, pull your Emerald Belt out, do something!"

"My belt's not active," Ezekiola responded, while watching one bird try to snatch something off Atlas with its beak.

"I will not become their dinner! Shoo! Shoo away!" Atlas shoved the bird as far as he could. Another one tried to snatch something else off him, but again shooed him away too.

"Help me here!" Atlas yelled. Nohlan hesitantly took out some food from his packsack, throwing it in the direction of the birds. It didn't draw their attention one bit. They were still stuck on Atlas.

"What do they want?" a desperate Atlas panted.

"Oh, I remember! There was something about their vision. They're almost blind but not quite. Yes, that's it! They have no vision except for seeing one color only," Gordi said, and everyone looked at Atlas.

"You've got to be kidding me," Atlas looked down at his waist. He looked at the clothes his friends were wearing. Mostly dark tones. For some reason, he had not changed like his friends had and still wore his standard uniform. No one save for him carried that auspicious color on their waist, his red belt.

"Atlas, now slowly, remove your belt, and give it to them," Borghis directed, handling the situation coolly.

"This is *my* red belt, I graduated and earned it, it has one year seniority and has been through a lot with me. I will not give it up to a bunch of giant birds just because—" his voice drowned as the flock of excited bird squawked and started fighting amongst themselves. The birds violently struck one another, poking each other's heads and necks, making a crude spectacle. Atlas cringed at hearing several birds screech in pain.

"It's material Atlas, just give it to them! They'll kill for it!"

Borghis insisted. "Take it off, NOW!" Borghis shouted, the command in his voice scaring Atlas more than the screeching of the birds.

Atlas quickly untied his belt and threw it in the direction of the birds. On cue, a piercing cacophony was heard as the birds went wild over one piece of cloth, as if that's all that mattered in their world. One finally flew in the air, the belt in its beak. The other birds chased after it. Once they were gone, everyone rested their gaze on Atlas. He was staring far ahead with a mournful expression. Borghis motioned the crew to continue walking.

"Don't dwell on it, it's just material," Borghis repeated in a low voice as he passed by Atlas. "Now listen up everyone," Borghis gathered his crew's attention. "It looks like the mist is clearing up outside. I need your eyes here, so keep them wide open, look for the Blue Navigator. It could be anything, so start looking for something blue."

"Yes, good idea Borghis, and why don't we warm up with a little exercise here. Since the Count never told neither of you who nor what this Blue Navigator is, let's take some guesses. I'll go first. I think it's a Blue Robe," Atlas proposed.

"Navigator points to something that travels. Maybe a blue ship or something like that?" Daria suggested.

"A navigator is a guide. Birds are known to be great navigators, maybe a bird in the blue sky?" Leanne suggested. That rang true for Ezekiola and his friends. They exchanged a few looks. Indeed, they had been through that before, following a bird to guide them back home when they had ventured outside of Circa.

"I'll go with what Atlas suggested. I think it's a Blue Robe," Nohlan said.

"From what I gather, the Blue Navigator should be recognizable once we come across it. That's why Balthazar was keen on getting us tested, because he thinks we might doubt it at first," Borghis said.

"Could we be followed here?! Can we encounter any Sons of the Night Sky?" Atlas asked, his brow deeply furrowed.

"They don't use this ley line," Borghis answered.

"What's a ley line?"

"They are alignments between two places, connecting them. Like an invisible bridge," he answered. Atlas stared back at him, perplexed. His knowledge on worlds outside of his home planet was limited next to that of the Brown Robes.

After resuming their walk, the mist and greyness settled back in, and hours later, Borghis thought they were turning in circles. At some point, he asked everyone to trot along to pick up speed while keeping an eye out for the Blue Navigator. They walked for quite some time until the sound of rushing water drew their attention. Surprised, they stopped to find a small creek surrounded by rocks. It seemed this side of the moon held some life.

"Let's take a break, eat, recoup a little and figure out our direction," Borghis suggested, looking somewhat downcast.

"Oh wow! Look up! Quick!" Helva said. The mist had cleared momentarily. In a small opening in the sky, the dullness of Haack was suddenly compensated by something spectacular. A multitude of stars, colorful patterns, planets, and several moons hung over their heads, vivid and bright, as if meticulously brushed on a canvas by a flawless painter.

"This is the most terrific sight I've ever seen," Helva said. On Circa, they never came anywhere close to seeing such a display. More so for Leanne, who only could see her solo moon from her planet and only at times. Caught in a hypnotic trance, they continued to gaze at life above; it was the longest pause they took since arriving. Then the mist returned, blocking the heavens once more. Borghis continued to gaze upward, and as he did, a part of the Count's message came to him:

'Guide and deliver the ignited flame,
to its navigator, soundless and blue,'

Soundless and blue. Was the Blue Navigator a star or a constellation he needed to decipher and follow? Did the sky above hold the answer? Should he sit and wait for the mist to clear again? He couldn't figure it out. Suddenly, he was no longer sure of anything. He could sense despair creeping up in him. He knew it was only a matter of time before it settled on the group. With no sign of the Blue Navigator, he sat on a rock, and half listened to the conversation in the group.

"Repeat to me again what he told you," Atlas asked.

"He said: *Wait. Wait. Wait for it.*" Ezekiola repeated for the third time with a sigh. Every detail of the conversation Ezekiola had had in his mind with Count Meredus of Loggia was being broken down and fleshed out by everyone, from his intonation to the exact shade of his robe.

"What kind of an instruction is that?" Nohlan burst.

"I don't know. I cannot figure it out. I really can't this time," Ezekiola paced back and forth, wishing for some tangible answer.

"He repeated wait three times. That means it's longer than we would think. Well, how long is long enough?" Atlas speculated in his corner.

"Who knows how long this could be? A day, a week, a month, imagine a year!" Nohlan said with horror. "I haven't brought that much food," he added, petrified at this predicament.

"Stop. This conversation is going nowhere. We're just wasting time," Ezekiola said.

"Wasting time, you say? What time don't you have, Zek? You have all the time now. There's something Borghis and you have yet to figure out. Otherwise, we would be elsewhere, not pondering while sitting on rocks."

During the back and forth, Borghis was caught up in his own thoughts. Ruminating, he noticed something in the creek. For a moment, he thought it was a snake. It was slow, but not slithering. It seemed to rotate in the water, as if lost. Finally, it stepped out. It looked like a small animal. Across the mist, he saw a glimpse of its shiny shell reflecting the color of the sky above. It made its way into the mist and out of sight. Another small animal in this dying place. Borghis continued his thinking. Did he miss something? Was the Blue Navigator a cryptic message, and he just had to solve it? Did the sky hold the answer? Then for some reason, he looked up. He couldn't see the sky, only a dark fog. He thought of that shiny shell of the little animal he saw a moment ago. It was blue, reflecting the sky. He looked up again. The shell can't be reflecting the sky, not when the air is so thick with fog. The shell, the sky, the doe suddenly all merged into one in Borghis' head.

"THE BLUE NAVIGATOR!" Borghis yelled so loud, the surface of the water reverberated.

"What?" Ezekiola was first to react.

"Where is it? Where did it go?" Borghis said, frantic. He headed into the dense mist on all fours, searching for something with his hands, touching the ground, hoping not to squish it. Ezekiola immediately followed and found something.

"This thing?" Ezekiola asked, picking up the gentle animal in his hands.

"Put it back down! Don't change its direction," Borghis said, unable to contain his excitement.

"This turtle is the Blue Navigator?" Nohlan asked, pressing from behind to catch a better glimpse.

"Yes, look, its shell is blue," Borghis answered, with a sense of the mystery of the universe being solved at that moment.

They took turns holding the animal, amazed at its color, but more amazed at Borghis's fervent certainty.

"Are you sure?" they each asked in turn.

"Absolutely!" he answered. "Smart move, Count, choosing a turtle," Borghis spoke to himself. "Of course, they're great navigators, they can survive in almost any environment, on any planet even, with an exceptional inner compass, and that's why they live so long," Borghis said, his eyes vivid with light.

Against all rational explanation, Borghis ordered everyone to follow the turtle. The walk was long and slow, very slow. The gentle animal led them on mainly flat land, for what felt like several hours, and finally, they arrived at the edge of a cliff. That's when everyone came to a stop, but not the turtle. To their utter disbelief, the turtle continued to walk, as if on air. They watched as the Blue Navigator took its last step on land, and onto something invisible.

"The bridge!" Borghis was the first to see it. He was then overcome with dread when he realized what this meant for Ezekiola. He composed himself quickly; he had to stay strong, had to stick to his intuition. This was the right bridge.

"This is insane, there is no bridge!" Atlas remarked.

"Atlas, we're not in our world where we see dense land. This is a bridge. We just can't see it. Look closely. This is the ley line I spoke to you about before, that invisible alignment connecting two places. This is where the navigator crosses the bridge with Ezekiola, this is where we must leave him. I am certain of it," Borghis said.

Shockingly, the turtle continued moving forward as if stepping on something transparent. Ezekiola came close and touched it with his feet and realized it was sturdy. With one leg still on land, he held onto Keenan and extended his foot. Panic momentarily seized him. They made it this far, he can't just back out now. He didn't dare look down. While holding

Keenan's arms, he posed his second foot in what looked like midair. The turtle meanwhile was further away, having disappeared in the fog. Ezekiola had to follow quickly if he didn't want to lose track of the turtle. He finally let go of Keenan, and took one step, then another, and another. He turned around to look at them. "What are you waiting for? I'm okay. Go back!"

With their hearts on the edge of that cliff, they all moved back. They had come full circle. Borghis straightened the Exit Staff in hand, then uttered the words to exit. Leaving, they departed knowing their mission was accomplished.

Upon entering the other side, however, Borghis wished he could've taken some of the mist back from Haack to block his view. Several bodies stood waiting in a semi-circle formation at the exact spot where they re-entered Circa. At their center stood a man whose face glowed with victory. In the quiet of the forest, while the two parties stood facing one another in a tense atmosphere, it was Atlas who unashamedly broke the silence:

"Let me guess, this is the forest rat!"

Chapter 10

The Hunt

Dakor relished the sight of rows of children lined up in perfect order. Often, he spent quiet mornings watching them train while sharpening his collection of tools and weapons. Today, they had brought in their latest catch, future SONS in the making. As an Overlord, one of the highest rankings given to members of the Sons of the Night Sky, Dakor made selections early, based on their strengths and skills and appointed trainers for each. His authority was broad. Empowered to build the army needed to execute their Great Plan, Dakor meddled even in the smallest decisions. Start them young, mold them early. It was a principle he stood by. It's what enabled them to create a generation of life serving SONS. To many of his warriors, Dakor's achievements and extensive experience in combat made him a larger-than-life figure. But this morning, despite the scenic view of warriors in the making, such displays looked menial and no longer satisfied him.

Being one of the highly decorated Overlords among the SONS wasn't enough for Dakor. Within the hierarchy of the Sons of the Night Sky, there were still far greater than him.

Dakor was aiming for the pinnacle—to become a Nameless. As of then, only seven members of the SONS had achieved that great stature. They were called Nameless because they were unknowns, without features. Indeed, the seven who earned this title had performed such tremendous acts, irreversible deeds, that it caused them to experience extraordinary transformations. They understood how to use certain powers and manipulate matter to meet a desired outcome, and the more they used this power, the more their bodies and features blurred, rendering them faceless, the eyes being the last to fade away. Gradually, they became formless, and in that state, they wield great force. It enabled them to exercise terrific powers on certain planets, dominating them, but adversely it disabled them on others. Their formless bodies could no longer enter certain planets. This was the case with the twelve veiled planets, the original activators of the Fountain of Fire. The only way the Nameless could do this was through their agents. For that, Dakor was precious to them. He was on the cusp, yet in a position where he could access many worlds. And Dakor was about to execute the greatest act of all: accessing the Fountain of Fire. This would bestow them with access to all the universe, bending it to their will. It was the heart of their Great Plan—to establish their order. This would allow them not only to expand their dominion, but to reinvigorate their beloved home planet Brak that had seen its lifeforms and resources decline, its essence wither, notably since the Nameless grew in power and number. Harnessing the Fountain of Fire, now within reach, would allow them to thrive in limitless ways.

To become a Nameless, Dakor would have to perform a great feat which was now within his reach. He was in his tent, looking down at the organism that Rikka had grown, tenderly caressing its outer form, its inner poison holding the promise of his future. He often stroked his tools or his belt meditatively with his fingers, a gentle act before performing an act of violence. This time, however, the image was playing out in his mind. He was visualizing on how things would unfold. This wasn't just the execution of a plan; it was personal and held a special place in his heart. Best of all, this feat would single him out among his brethren. Who knows, he could even rise above the Nameless. Such was the greatness that lay ahead.

The sound at the entrance of his tent brought Dakor's attention back to the present. He had asked for the slave girl to be brought to him. He had promised something precious to her. Indeed, her six slave sisters had remained in Agiri, reserved for Dakor, as part of a future plan. Her acts would determine their fate. She waited in the corner, now a willing servant, to carry out Dakor's wish. He had several boomerangs brought in and requested that more be made in the exact shape and weight as the one Rikka created. Indeed, as soon as the SONS saw the shape of the venomous organism Rikka had grown and prepared for them harnessing the rays of Agiri's poisonous sun, different models of boomerang were built to practice with. Rikka had sold them a single product that could be used only once. Therefore, the SONS would get only one chance of hitting their target. For the victim to successfully succumb to the effects of the poison, there could be no miss. If the product burst hitting an obstacle such as a tree or it flew off in the wrong direction hitting the ground, the mission would be a complete failure. Dakor put carpenters, wielders, toolsmiths and other craftsmen frantically at work, giving them less time than needed to deliver, pressuring them to create faster.

"Come with me," he commanded the slave. A dozen warriors followed them from behind, wheeling the heavy load of boomerangs in a cart. Dakor's warlords hadn't wasted a moment. They carved out a plan to practice throwing correctly. And they certainly did not limit themselves to their planet Brak to practice. To achieve this mission, practice needed to be conducted on every variety of landscape, and on each, battle positions were enacted, faux fights staged, placing the slave in a position to throw a boomerang, and hit a target. They didn't only bring her to areas that were sparse with little vegetation conducive to throwing any weapon in the air to strike a target. They brought her to forests and jungles thick with trees, a taste of every possible landscape they might find themselves in, with very little space to throw an object in a straight line without getting it tangled in branches or bushes. Dakor spent valuable time with the slave, travelling with his inner circle, bringing her to far off vistas, planets, bright and dark ones, putting her to the test, preparing her. Often, depending on the material used to construct models of boomerangs, different sound waves were heard. Some echoed stronger, others reverberated differently. They remained discreet, choosing places closer to cliffs, oceans, or deep in the woods, far from life. The last place on their map was a series of dark caves, void of light, often those used for training the SONS. In the darkness, Dakor watched her, impressed at how her sight never failed. His slave saw better in the dark, he noted. Watching her perform and observing her attributes gave him an improved sense of direction on how best to execute their plan. There could be no failure. There were a few more days left for training when two of Dakor's top aides suddenly appeared, interrupting them.

"We've heard news from our huntsmen. Rumors are circulating in the Markets of Seve," one said, unable to contain his excitement.

"What of it?" Dakor asked, unimpressed, his eyes still fixed on the slave.

"A little girl dug out a book while playing in a forest, brought it to her illiterate parents, who then sold to a merchant.

This merchant knew its value just from the book's binding and sold it to a collector."

"And?" Dakor asked flatly.

"This merchant was apparently asking questions if anyone knew what a 'Fountain of Fire' was."

Upon hearing this, Dakor's attention shifted dramatically. He glanced at the messengers for the first time.

"I'm listening," he said.

"Their planet doesn't have this knowledge; they were not one of the twelve who were aware of this. We believe it's one of the volumes of the Kama we've been searching for many years. This book was planted there by that traitor, we're sure of it!"

"My Lord, if I may," the second aide interrupted, a perceptible delight in his voice. "Speaking of that traitor, early on in training the slave, we scavenged one of the planets we visited. One of our huntsmen came across a crazy beggar who was yelling the traitor's name and spewing profanities!"

Two sets of news Dakor did not expect came suddenly changing his mood. Could this be true? For so long, the SONS had been at work. Dakor had even sent out members of his own inner circle, his closest spies to collect precious information. Knowing his aides all too well, he knew there was content to this news. This was no fable. He sensed they had finally hit a mark. His spirits rose.

"Prepare the men and bring forward those huntsmen. I want to question them," he said. He then turned to his slave.

"You perform remarkably, especially in the dark. Serve me well, and you will be rewarded. You know what the consequences are for you and your sisters," he said before he left. His words echoed in her spirit like the soundwaves of a hundred airborne boomerangs. For her, there was hope.

Surrounded by his best tacticians, Dakor now found

himself with new variables to manage. There could be no room for failure. For that, he trod cautiously with his council.

"Show me where you think the traitor hides," he said.

"Here in this trivial dark planet run by giants, on the south side, closer to the sea, a planet called Voronar. In fact, we were there conducting our early trainings with the slave. She was throwing boomerangs right by a cliff," the huntsman answered, pointing on a celestial map that spanned across the wall.

"As usual, I sent out members to scavenge the area. One reported hearing a woman yelling his name. That name is not original to the planet. When I heard about this, I decided to follow through. I found the beggar and followed her. Her name was Yolsha, and she had no dwelling. I asked her questions about him, she just lashed out insanities. But right when I was about to dismiss her, she laughed and spoke of his one eye. That's when I knew it was him."

For the first time in a long time, Dakor had the sensation of being submerged in the exciting waters of hope, vengeance, and pleasure. *All this time living in the shadows, and you thought I couldn't find you,* Dakor mused. Several things flashed before his eyes. He realized that in fact, the very first training ground he brought the slave to practice had been the dark planet of Voronar. For so long, Dakor had been looking for him. That foul soul. To think, he brushed right past him, unknowingly, practicing throwing boomerangs so close to him. Indeed, this was remarkable news.

"And what about the book?" he asked. A warrior came forward, with a swift movement of his hand, shifted the image on the map. A new planet appeared.

"Over here, the markets of Seve, center opposite to Voronar. It's a brighter planet called Zoha, very sedimentary and crude. Most are illiterate, but apparently this merchant is not. We think he sold the book to a collector who knows about the Kama."

"My lord if I may," Dakor's right-hand aide interjected. "We can easily track that collector by getting ten of our spies in those markets, posing as foreign merchants willing to buy artifacts for a high price, especially books. This way, word will get around, and perhaps that collector will come to us," he said, looking at Dakor for approval.

"Not quite. A collector will not want to sell, especially that kind of book," Dakor said pensively. He had a habit of running scenarios in his mind to see which one stood out most. After a moment of silence, he spoke in a measured pace. "Find the merchant first who sold the book to that collector. See if he will lead you to the collector as well as the parents of the little girl who sold the book to him. Find the parents, ask them to take you there where their girl found the book. There may be more of them in that forest. Search the perimeters. In the meantime, I want a dozen of you in the outskirts of the market. Spend some time there, find out which collectors roam the market. Find and search their houses. Make sure to bribe the merchant so he'll identify the collector he sold the book to. They'll do anything for coinage in those lands. Follow the trace, and report back to me."

"Yes, my lord," the huntsmen responded, "and what do we do with the traitor?"

Dakor sat back in his chair. It was the kind of moment he knew would come only once in a lifetime. He stroked his chin, taking the extra time to think. He would only get one try at this. Many years had passed since the traitor escaped. Dakor had been unable to get his hands on him... until now.

"Gather our senior warriors. I want them as vanguard leaders of this assault. But I want to be there when you catch him. No one gets to put their hands on the traitor except for me," he said. "Bring our mappers in, I want everyone to be present to study every inch of that forsaken planet Voronar. We strike soon."

"Shall we bring the slave girl with us, just in case?"

Dakor was about to say yes but hesitated.

"No, she's here to serve one purpose only. I cannot risk any injury to her. She remains here under supervision," he decided swiftly, hoping it was something he would not come to regret later. He dismissed the council, and despite having much to look forward to, Dakor remained unsettled. A most important thing had not been dealt with. That's because he was still ruminating about it. His main warlord remained by his side, picking up on his thoughts.

"Have you given it some more thought? They're growing impatient," he asked.

Dakor nodded. They had another meeting ahead of them. He had to face the Nameless. With news of the Fountain of Fire being revived by a former member of the SONS, their very own Zeke, they were agitated, wanting immediate action, expecting results. Indeed, Zeke was Dakor's beloved pupil, and that's why Dakor had been appointed for this task by the Nameless. Like a child's pull towards its father, Dakor knew what it would take to draw Zeke back to him, but as anxious as they were to have Zeke back in their camp, something inside Dakor forewarned not to rush this, it would only botch the plan. He had to find the fine line, the right timing, and the right words for this mission to succeed, and eventually satisfy the Nameless. It was a balancing act. He walked into the dark tombs of the SONS' headquarters. There, standing in a half moon, were the seven great ones, distinguished by their dark, moving attire with no features, vertical black clouds in motion. He knew what their first question would be. As with everything, Dakor, endowed with the right words, always knew what to say. An eerie voice that can penetrate thickest walls and densest bones emerged from the shadows and echoed in his ears:

"Did you find the boy?"

Dakor smiled.

Chapter 11

Confirmation

Crossing an invisible bridge in midair wasn't as hard as Ezekiola imagined it to be. All he had to do was follow the turtle in front of him, watch his step, and not look anywhere but ahead. For that, the smog helped. So high up in the air, there was nothing here to see. His body could handle as much. It's what entered his mind that made the journey unbearable. So far away from home, in a lackluster setting and dreary isolation, Ezekiola entered an internal world of monologues. At first, the thoughts trickled down slowly, questioning his ulterior path every now and then: *Look at you, following a turtle. Have you lost your mind?*

After longer stretches of plodding behind the Blue Navigator, the thoughts multiplied, took on a new character, and escalated in tone – *Where the hell are you going, Zek? What's the purpose of all this? What if the turtle just falls off the bridge? What if YOU fall off the bridge, then what? This is insane!*

It did not help to be alone with his thoughts. Ezekiola didn't have anyone to use as a soundboard, to check his reasoning. He tried to share the Count's mind like he had in

Nomi's Garden. All he got was silence. He tried a few times, but to no avail. He finally lost hope of any contact with the Count. At a certain point, he thought he heard his friends Atlas and Nohlan laugh. He spun around searching for the source of their voices but was met only with fog. Then, Leanne's face inexplicably materialized in front of him. He stared at it, mesmerized. Her face then morphed into another woman's face. He continued staring at her; she was beautiful. Moments later, the woman also vanished. He heard other sounds, dreadful ones—fire crackling and whooshing in the air, clashes on a battlefield, high-pitched noises followed by the slashing of steel against steel. More than once, he heard the cry of a child. Ezekiola was sure he was going mad. After losing complete track of time, the prospect occurred to him that maybe he was walking aimlessly in the void. A sense of futility engulfed him, all his past and current endeavors weighed down on him. Nothing was making sense.

Just then, it was as if the protective dam in his head burst, thoughts that were never allowed to enter came merrily flooding through. With that barrage, the idea that he might forever be stuck on this forsaken bridge came on strong. Then another thought struck him. It was that in all practicality, he had been played the cruelest joke of all by his higher-ups. This included the headmaster, the Count, Igor Sanza, the leader of the Emeralds; Yossan, the one who was assigned to train him; and finally, all the Emeralds.

You're a fool! They're using you! How could you not have seen this coming?! After chewing on that some more, Borghis and his associates got pitched into this newly discovered traitor bucket. And who knows, perhaps Helva and Daria were in on this, too—and goodness, *Leanne!* Eventually, they all got dumped into the same miserable pail. Angry at himself for having so easily fallen into such a scheme, his thoughts raged uncontrollably, as if their very existence depended on occupying every corner in his mind. Ezekiola didn't know what was happening to him. He didn't have a name for this phenomenon, but it ate at him, holding him prisoner. Every time he tried to focus on the present moment, and this insufferably slow guiding turtle, that voice in his head doubled up in potency, and came wildly slashing forth on the ultimate subject: *'Fountain of Fire? You think you're special? There's no such thing. It's a myth, it's all in your head. You can't be an Emerald, you can't even fight. Let it go. Turn around. Go back home!'*

But home was far. He couldn't just turn back, he had to continue. Regardless, going back by himself without the navigator seemed like a worse alternative. A dim thought resurfaced in his mind, and it was the only thing that kept him moving forward, keeping him somewhat sane. It was the initial certainty he sensed when Borghis saw the bridge. *'This is where the navigator crosses the bridge with Ezekiola, this is where we must leave him. I am certain of it,'* Borghis had said. At the time, Ezekiola was certain, too. But once on the bridge, the certainty of it had vanished into thin air. It demanded a Herculean effort to pull that image out from the remotest corner of his mind and keep his attention on it amidst the inner turmoil. To stick to that very first decision, believing that it was undoubtedly the right one. It was very little to hold on to, but if he did not hold on, the journey would destroy him.

Suddenly, Ezekiola had the sensation of lacking air. Had they changed altitude? Was the turtle going up or down? He glided his hands along his chest, resting one on his heart, and found it was beating normally. So why did his chest feel compressed? He inhaled deeply a few times, slowly letting out a long exhale each time. Somehow, this little exercise made his head spin. The thought of fainting crossed his mind. He forced himself to stay alert. This was the last place he should faint. It would be a sure death. Tormented with such a possibility, the surprising sound of water momentarily pulled Ezekiola out of his unease. He was hearing a flapping sound. Was he hallucinating again? His breath shortened further, while the volume of the splashing increased. He thought that was it, he was going to collapse. And then, finally, a dreamlike vision appeared before him—a shoreline. At that instant, the turtle did something unbelievable. It dove into the water. Ezekiola halted abruptly. Panic seized him. *Where is the Blue Navigator going? Is it coming back?* He followed the turtle's blue shell with his eyes as it swam deeper into the water, until he could be seen no more.

Ezekiola shut his eyes and opened them again. He looked down to see where he was standing. He was on a rock in the middle of a sea. The wind was blowing, lifting the fog at odd intervals, giving him a clear sight of what lay ahead. A shore indeed! A sense of euphoric relief overcame him, and for a moment, his eyes welled up as he laughed with delight. He stopped laughing when he came back to his senses, realizing what he had to do. He had to swim. He gaged that the shore was not too far. He scanned the sea; it was calm enough to swim in. He could do this. He took off his clothes and shoes, packed them in his sac, and dove right in. The water was fresh, and salty, so salty in fact, that he was almost floating in it, making it an effortless swim. He arrived at the shore, and noticed barrels placed close to the seashore. Some barrels were filled halfway with what looked like salt, others were empty. He dabbed his fingers in one and tasted it. It tasted good, and different than the salt back home. Someone lived here. He scanned the perimeters to see if anyone was around. He barely had time to look up the cliff when a deafening roar hit his ears, and something vicious with a white body and black mane came descending in fantastic leaps. Instinctively, Ezekiola dropped his bag and dove right back into the sea, swimming as far as he could. The animal didn't follow him into the water, but paced back and forth, roaring some more, standing guard at the shore.

"Andiya!" A loud voice came from the top of the cliff, followed by a whistle. Ezekiola took his eyes off the beast for the first time. A man, somewhat plump, was calling the animal. He wore a patch over one eye.

"My cat," the man yelled from on top, clapped a few times and whistled his cat back to him.

Cat?! Ezekiola was stunned. This cannot be a cat. This must be something else. He had never seen such a thing before. Suddenly he realized it was a Solev, the very cat Leanne talked about during their stroll in the forest, dubbing it a huge lion. Obeying its master, the cat backed away from the shore, and climbed up the cliff with amazing agility. The man stood still as a statue, observing Ezekiola. After a long pause, he motioned for him to come up. Then he said something that made Ezekiola wonder if he had heard right.

"Load the empty barrels with salt, hoist them up, then wait for me." He disappeared right after.

Perplexed, Ezekiola slowly swam back to the shore. He put his clothes back on and checked out the vicinity. Who was this one-eyed man? Why is he asking for him to bring up barrels? He thought of climbing up first to ask questions. What if that cat comes back down again, making him fall off the cliff midway? He hesitated. Since nothing in this journey made sense, Ezekiola grabbed a shovel. He checked a few times to see if that beast would descend again. Thankfully it didn't. After a few trials, Ezekiola figured out the lift system, and eventually managed to lift his first barrel after filling it with salt. He climbed up the cliff, and the first thing he spotted was a little cabin stationed not too far from the edge. He looked back down from the cliff and noted the splendid view. The sun was high. It must be midday, he thought. He was taking in the view when the next command came in:

"Place the barrel here, go back down for the rest." Ezekiola turned around to speak to him, but the man was gone, disappearing into his dwelling.

"Wait, who are you?" he asked.

"Who I am doesn't matter," he heard from afar.

Ezekiola sighed. He tried dragging the barrel forward, but it was too heavy. He struggled just sliding it an inch forward. He stopped and walked towards the hut. He needed a minimum of answers.

"Can you tell me where I am? Are you the one I'm supposed to meet?"

As he walked towards the hut, Ezekiola spotted a green belt next to a floor mat inside the cabin. He froze. It was a sight he did not expect to see.

"I told you to place the barrel and go back down for the rest!" The man snapped at him.

Ezekiola backed away, his eyes still fixed on the belt, or rather on an *Emerald Belt?* Yet the braids on it were different, as if it was some other version of what he had. The man stormed out of his hut, closing the flimsy door behind him with a clunk. He obviously didn't use that door much. It could barely close shut.

"These are the rules here: I talk, you listen. I lead, you follow. I order, you obey," he said, coming face to face with Ezekiola. "Understand?"

Something about this man's countenance suddenly made Ezekiola think of Igor Sanza, the leader of the Emeralds. The man even looked like Igor, too, similar in expression and features. Ezekiola was about to protest, but the image of the belt he had just seen flashed in his mind. Whoever this man was, he was the one he was supposed to meet. That was his first unfortunate realization. The second was that he was sure this man could bring him back to Circa. Ezekiola had a choice. He could dismiss the orders or obey. He so badly wanted to go back home but had no clue how to get there. So, he wisely shut up and nodded instead.

"Good. Now watch how you move barrels. I use these special ropes to glide them. I'll show you only once."

Watching him demonstrate, Ezekiola thought of Igor Stanza again. The two had similar physical traits and even a similar vibe: small in words, harsh in expression, short on temper. He hoped this wouldn't be a repeat of that experience. Was he really the one the Count intended for him to meet? He hoped he hadn't crossed that bridge of hell for nothing.

After showing him once, Ezekiola was left alone. To his credit, he managed well. After lifting the third barrel, the night sky set in. He looked up surprised. It would normally take a lot longer for the sun to set from that high position. This sun descended like a falling ball. Curious about it, he had questions, but on orders remained quiet instead. Every time he came close to the man, he attempted to read his mind. Unfortunately, nothing was going on. The man didn't think. Wasn't he at least curious about Ezekiola showing up by the shore of the sea? The only logical explanation that came to Ezekiola was that the man had been expecting him. He knew.

With the work completed, Ezekiola was given a cloth, to sleep on the ground. Mental and physical laboring had taken a toll on him. As soon as his head went down, he passed out. Barely having recuperated, the sound of something walking on gravel woke him up.

"Wake up, there's salt to harvest below," he heard him say. It was still dark outside. Ezekiola was sure it was the middle of the night. Reluctantly, he got up and obeyed. Unbelievably, the sun rose quickly thereafter. What kind of place was this?

Things seemed short and fast. The days were quiet; the work plenty. He spent many days this way, wondering what his purpose was with this man, and after a while, he stopped posing questions in his head. He woke up early, toiled, spoke little, and funny enough, got used to it. He also got used to Andiya, the massive cat. So much so that Andiya started following Ezekiola instead of her master, dashing up and down the cliff, accompanying him every time he drew the barrels. She even allowed Ezekiola to pet her. And not long after, Andiya nestled next to Ezekiola's cot instead of her master's to prepare for sleep. The man noticed Andiya's change of behavior, and since then, something changed in him, too. Ezekiola could tell.

When market day came, Ezekiola was briefed little, and instructed to help. He had never seen giants. His first sighting made his heart palpitate. Andiya's presence was reassuring, however. If need be, the large beast would be able to handle giants. The market was a confusing jumble of sound, images, and atmosphere. Every moment, someone yelled something in a language he did not understand. Half the time, Ezekiola couldn't tell if they were just talking or arguing. When asked to purchase a loaf of bread for their lunch, it took him three times longer to get his loaf than newcomers asking for the same thing, all because he didn't know how to hustle his way through the crowd. When the boisterous giants came in waves to purchase their favorite salts, he tensed further. Just their size was astounding and made him shrivel. He wore his Emerald Belt underneath his clothes, in the unlikely chance that it would activate itself and be of use.

With their produce sold at the end of the day, and his guide gone to get the wagon and horse, Ezekiola was left alone to pack. While moving one of the empty barrels, he heard a contemptuous laugh behind him.

"Oh my! What do we have here? A handsome boy!"

Ezekiola spun around to see a raggedy woman standing behind him. Her clothes had so many gaps, the edges barely held together. The moment she saw him, she gasped.

"Fire! Fire!" she yelled, eyes shut. Ezekiola looked around to see what she was alluding to. Nothing around him was on fire.

"Oh, the fire!" she said again, squinting heavily. She couldn't quite open her eyes to look at him. She wailed, in pain or delight, Ezekiola couldn't tell. Her wailing got so loud, curiosity got the better of the merchants, and in no time, a large crowd gathered.

"Where? What fire?" someone asked in the crowd, as more people came.

"The fire! I can see the great fire!" she announced to everyone around, seizing the momentum. "The fire is among us! This boy, this boy, look at him! This boy is fire!" She pointed at Ezekiola.

Upon hearing '*This boy is fire,*' Ezekiola's breath caught in his chest. Her words contained a strange convergence of truth and fiction. What was she really saying? Ezekiola wondered how she knew about the sacred Fountain of Fire that he had reignited with Leanne. Was she talking crazy or had word gotten out this fast, even outside Circa? He glanced at the merchants around him who were looking at him with genuine curiosity. The wailing woman kept her eyes shut, and every time she looked up at him, she shut her eyes again, as if blinded. Ezekiola couldn't tell if she was putting on an act. What went on in her mind as he read it was as confusing as her behavior.

"Gespar! You vicious snake!" She suddenly yelled, looking behind Ezekiola, spitting on the floor. Ezekiola turned to see his guide emerge from behind the cart. So that was his name, *Gespar.*

"Get out of here, Yolsha!" he yelled at her, visibly shocked at seeing her and the attention she had garnered during his short absence.

"You are pure evil you, Gespar! May the fire in the boy kill you! That's if they don't get you first!" she yelled louder this time, laughing. "Stay away from him!" she told Ezekiola, "he will end up in the abyss!" she hissed her last words.

Ezekiola noticed Gespar loading the barrels in a hurry. He also kept checking faces in the crowd. This was the first time Ezekiola had seen him distressed. Even as they exited the market, he kept checking behind to see if they were being followed. It got so bad that Ezekiola broke his silence.

"Are you in trouble, *Gespar* is it?" he asked, emphasizing his name. He caught his eye.

"Don't ever say my name in public," was the response he got.

"The woman at the market said your name. Do you know her?" he asked.

"Yes, she's a Kozi, small like us. She went crazy many years ago," Gespar answered, suddenly talkative. Ezekiola seized the opportunity.

"Why did she say those things about you?"

"She says many things, you have to ignore her," he answered briskly.

"Why did she say about me '*this boy is fire?*'" he asked, looking intently at Gespar, who in turn gave Ezekiola a thoughtful glance but said nothing. Ezekiola kept looking with greater intensity, capturing something that Gespar had been concealing up until then. *Oh, he knows,* Ezekiola suddenly realized after reading his mind. *He knows about me and the Fountain of Fire!* Just like that, he got his first insight. Gespar did a double take at Ezekiola, looking cross this time. It seemed something had just hit him in the face.

"Are you a mind reader?" he asked Ezekiola, a crazed look

appeared in his eye. Surprised at being asked such a question, Ezekiola stared right ahead and didn't dare to look back at him.

"Did you just read my mind?" Gespar asked him again. Ezekiola didn't dare answer that question either. Gespar abruptly steered the wagon on the side of the road, bringing it to a sudden halt. He looked at Ezekiola with intensity.

"Don't you ever read my mind! You have no right to enter that space and extract information. I forbid you to go there. Understand?" Gespar said, the tone of his voice frightening Ezekiola for the first time.

"Understand?" Gespar repeated a little louder this time, forcing Ezekiola to answer loudly, "YES."

"Say it! Look me in the eye and say I will never read your mind, Gespar!"

"I will never read your mind Gespar," Ezekiola proclaimed, disgruntled. Both remained quiet after that. During their silent moment together, it occurred to Ezekiola that the woman Yolsha at the market may not be as crazy as they thought. If she spoke of the great fire, she can't be too far off from reality. And yet, she also spoke of Gespar being pure evil. This was something that got Ezekiola seriously worried.

That night, whether it was the incident at the market, or talks of the great fire, Gespar did something different. Accompanied with Andiya, he brought Ezekiola to a hidden zone in an adjacent cliff, higher in altitude than where they were stationed.

"Put your belt on," Gespar said, mentioning the word 'belt' for the first time. Ezekiola was astonished but did as he was told.

"Now give me your word," he told Ezekiola.

"What word?" Ezekiola asked.

Gespar looked at him, somewhat puzzled. "Your word, give me your word!" he said again, irritated.

"Alright, alright, here: I GIVE YOU MY WORD," Ezekiola said loudly, whatever that meant. Since he couldn't read his mind, he really had no clue as to what Gespar wanted. Gespar shook his head.

"They taught you nothing did they, those Emeralds?" he said. The dumbfounded look in Ezekiola's eyes confirmed everything Gespar needed to know. It made Ezekiola wonder just how much Gespar knew. He had underestimated this man.

"It's a pledge you give as warriors before training, to respect the warrior code. I'm guessing you have no idea how to fight either, do you?" he assumed more than asked. Ezekiola shook his head.

Gespar walked behind the semi-circle to a clandestine spot to retrieve something. It looked like he had a secret stash hidden in the back somewhere. He came back with a thin black cloth and started wrapping it around Ezekiola's eyes. Ezekiola backed away instantly.

"What are you doing?" he asked, alarmed.

"Training you," Gespar said.

"Why do you need to cover my eyes?" he asked.

"Will you trust me?" Gespar asked instead. This prompted a pause on Ezekiola's end. What was his other alternative? He had no immediate answer to that.

"Fine," he sighed. He recalled the strange ways the Emeralds experimented on him. It felt like another one of those episodes. With his eyes sealed from the outside world, he heard Gespar whistle Andiya back to him. Why was the cat coming into this?

"First, we work on instinct. Learn to sense your enemy's approach before seeing them," Gespar stated, and whistled a new variation of sound to his cat.

"What am I supposed to do exactly?" Ezekiola asked, blinded, spinning in a circle. He heard a whooshing sound as if

Andiya climbed up the wall, followed by a strange silence in the air. Then, the weight of the cat struck him down. He fell to the ground on his right side, groaning in pain.

"Get up, fast, she's coming at you again," Gespar said sharply.

"Are you crazy?" Ezekiola shouted as he got up. "You're asking your cat to attack me?!"

"Move around, don't rest in one place, don't get comfortable," Gespar directed.

Ezekiola heard Andiya go up again, and when it went silent again, he quickly moved to change direction, but only managed to avoid a full body collision. Andiya rotated herself in midair and extended her paws, striking parts of his body. Ezekiola was about to remove his binding and stop this outlandish training. And yet, a distant voice in his mind told him to continue instead. After a while, he didn't pay attention to his bruises, nor parts of his body that stung, mostly caused by Andiya's claws as she inadvertently sliced his skin here and there. Every time the whistle came, Ezekiola learned the pattern, and where the attack would come from. Suddenly, he communed with Andiya's mind, and the direction she was about to take. Ezekiola moved at the right time, in the right place, made the right move, avoiding all contact, looking like he was dancing instead. He never calculated his time, but the sun had risen when Gespar stopped him.

Exhausted, Ezekiola had his best sleep ever that night. They went back to that cliff several days in a row, training different techniques, no longer needing Andiya. On the fifth day, Gespar took out that green belt Ezekiola had spotted at his hut. His face bore a faraway expression. As much as he wanted to, Ezekiola restrained himself from going anywhere close to reading Gespar's mind.

"Take off your belt, and give it to me," he told Ezekiola. His voice held a new note, Ezekiola noticed. He took the belt, and there was something strikingly disciplined in the way Gespar handled it, an adroitness he had never witnessed. He held Ezekiola's wrist, ran the belt around it, crossed two strands underneath once, and ran it again over the wrist, with a final knot beneath the palm of his hand. He then took his own belt and did the same thing on his wrist. He paused, holding the tips of both their belts before tying the final merging knot.

"Now being a mind reader, I want you to focus on the warrior in me. Focus on my skills and focus on what I learned as techniques. You do not go anywhere else in your intent," he instructed Ezekiola.

"Are we about to engage in the forbidden Caspol Dance?" Ezekiola asked. Gespar smiled for the first time, and despite having one eye, it spoke volumes in that one moment.

The instant the belts connected, Ezekiola felt a surge of something, a new element invading his body, expanding him, stretching him from the inside out. He recalled experiencing this with his twin Zeke once, and now again as he merged with Gespar. He had an initial glimpse of Gespar's abilities, then rapidly became submerged with his essence. He was aware of every one of his skills, as if he was Gespar himself. Instantly, the knowledge on how to manipulate weaponry, command an army, prepare for battle, and face imminent death fused into his mind. A robustness and a bravery he had never acquired in life suddenly flowed into him. He blended with Gespar. The two became one. He was tempted for a moment to probe further into Gespar's past, for he sensed much lay there, but held himself back to honor his word.

When Gespar disconnected the belts, his one eye was glazed. He looked into Ezekiola's ocean blue eyes with a sorrowful expression, as if he had just been pierced in the heart. He saw something, Ezekiola could tell. What intent did

Gespar have before they started the Caspol Dance? They never talked about that part. What did Gespar see in him? Without saying a word, Gespar resumed the session. But something heavy hung in the air. That night, neither of them slept.

The day after, Gespar was not the same man. Miraculously, his conversation tripled, and he chattered as if overnight a bird's vocal cord had been switched with his.

"Yesterday we merged, today we fight. I want you to tap into the warrior, use the skills you need, and apply them," Gespar guided. The blindfold came back on again. Ezekiola knew exactly what to do and how to strike Gespar. Gespar used all sorts of tools he dug out of his secret stash. Arrows, spears, flying axes, all were thrown in Ezekiola's way. Gespar kept testing him repeatedly, waiting for something.

"Next, you learn the wielding of your belt. You must turn it into fire. Remember that fire is created. It does not exist by itself like a rock does. There are many grades to fire. It is not of only one type that lights up wood. The principles governing the element are the same. It needs to be activated. To make it come alive it needs friction. The belt has a similar fire as the one you see burning in the woods, but this fire is connected to you. It will do as you ask of it, bending itself to your will. Learn to create that friction in your mind, follow it with your movements, and gradually transfer it to your belt."

Ezekiola started with whipping his belt around in the air. Having seen Gespar demonstrate, he knew this was possible. The gradual whipping turned into sparks, and after several trials, Ezekiola's excitement ascended to a new level. Even blindfolded, he could sense his belt was on fire. He also knew the direction Gespar was aiming his belt and met it with impact. Fire crackled in the air, creating miniature lightning bolts which could be seen from afar. It was during one of those moments when Ezekiola slashed his belt in the air that something detonated, and a tremor was felt beneath him. Just the sound of it shook his insides. He could smell dust, a lot of dust suddenly. A moment later, he could barely breathe.

"Gespar," he called. There was no answer. "Gespar!" he shouted this time. After a moment of waiting, Ezekiola took off his blindfold, holding it underneath his nose instead. He couldn't see a thing, nor breathe right. Dust was everywhere.

"Gespar!" He couldn't hear anything, nor did he see Andiya. Did they just disappear? Ezekiola exited their training ground and started searching the perimeters just behind the rocky areas.

Gespar was thankful to have the arms he did, thankful for the heavy barrels he had to lift that were full of salt, that made his forearms and shoulders the strongest parts of his body over the years. He could hang onto anything. And right now, he couldn't believe he was hanging by the edge of the cliff where he had brought Ezekiola to train. It was a strange position to be in to receive something special: a confirmation. This was the boy, alright. The Count was not lying. He had his first taste of truth—the Fountain of Fire has been reignited. The boy just needed to learn how to wield it. Suddenly, it wasn't his weight that Gespar felt, but the one for guiding him correctly.

"Over here!" Gespar yelled from afar.

Ezekiola ran close to the edge of the cliff to find Gespar struggling awkwardly with legs dangling just to get back on top.

"What happened?" Ezekiola asked, shocked.

"Go get Andiya first, she's over there," Gespar instructed. Andiya too, had been propelled in the air somehow, struggling with her legs on the edge.

"How did you end up here?" Then the unimaginable occurred to him. "Did I ...? No, I couldn't've," he said in a daze.

"Aye. Who's the special one you linked with?" Gespar

asked at this inconvenient moment, propelling a smile on Ezekiola's lips.

"Leanne, she's...umm...from Planet Blue. But she's with us on Circa now," he said as he helped Gespar get back up.

Training after that was of a different grade. They changed location, staying away from cliffs. Ezekiola took turns testing with intensity, applying it in crescendos. Controlling was hard, but Gespar was patient. Uncharacteristically patient. On the third night, Ezekiola couldn't sleep. Tasting that fire, familiarizing himself with it, energized him, even at night. He stood wide awake. He rose and went to the edge of the cliff, then came back. Gespar was sleeping soundlessly. His patch that night however had come off. Ezekiola had never seen an injured eye before, and curiosity got the best of him. He approached Gespar's face to observe. At the sight of it, blood drained from his face. It wasn't the contorted skin that made him tremble, but that it had been branded with something, a symbol of some sort. He couldn't make it out in the dark, so he came closer. His eyes adjusted; the symbol looked familiar. He stretched his mind to find where he had seen it. The drawings in the astronomy room of the Ye Ole' Brown Lodge flashed into his mind. The dark corner, the imperfect triangles, the faded shady symbol of the Sons of the Night Sky. It was the one branded on his eye. Gespar mumbled something in his sleep, shifting. In one move, Ezekiola leaped back into his cot. He stayed immobile for the rest of the night. Sleep never came easily after that.

On their way back from training the day after, Andiya was not there to meet them halfway to walk the rest of the trail. It was unlike her to miss greeting them. Ezekiola was several steps ahead of Gespar when his body fired up. It wasn't just his waist. His hands, all the way to the tips of his fingers had the sensation of fire flowing in them. It was far too disturbing to continue to act normally. In the quiet of the forest, he stopped and stood immobile. He felt eyes on him.

"What is it?" Gespar asked from afar.

Ezekiola looked around and spotted something massive hanging from a tree. His first instinct told him to run. But that thing hanging was a familiar sight. His eyes could not believe what his mind was telling him. His heart plunged into his stomach. He turned around to stop Gespar, but it was too late. Gespar's world crumbled.

"No!" Gespar screamed. Andiya's lifeless body was hanging upside down. Gespar tried to move forward, but his body wobbled instead. When Gespar took Andiya in his hands, turning her over, he was horrified further. An arrow had pierced her left eye. His knees locked, and he fell to the ground. In the quiet of the forest, Gespar's grieving was interrupted by a wicked laughter coming from behind a tree.

"Your story ends here Gespar," a malicious voice said. Suddenly, a tall body emerged. His face was veiled save for his eyes. He was looking at Gespar, pleased with his sight. But then he saw Ezekiola, and froze, his dark eyes growing wide at the sight before him.

"Zeke," a faint whisper came to his lips. Five more men appeared from the surrounding trees. All of them seemed caught in the grip of shock.

"RUN!" Gespar uttered a deadly shout, seizing the momentary inertia of their adversaries. He grabbed Ezekiola by the arm and headed in the opposite direction. A cacophony of chaotic shouts was heard from behind, and as the commotion grew, it was followed by fire crackling. The men were fast, and Ezekiola knew they would catch up to Gespar. In that frantic moment though, he knew what to do. His body still fired up, he stopped, took his belt off and powerfully struck the ground, sending a wave of energy into it. It traveled deep into the soil, and a moment later, he got his results. The surface of the ground shook violently, cracking in half in the direction of their assailants, knocking them off balance, sending trees falling and rocks tumbling on them, thrusting them into turmoil.

Gespar had no choice but to lead Ezekiola into an underground maze that existed on Voronar. It's how he had discovered the planet in the first place when he escaped, using a sporadic door. Today, he would break his vow to never enter Circa. And as he did, he knew he was entering something far worse, a new cycle of chaos unlike one he had ever lived. It was at this moment that he realized what had transpired. Without knowing, Ezekiola had uprooted him. That boy had dug out the far ends of even the deepest roots of what had comprised him up until then. He was brought to a new fork in his life, one which he never imagined reaching. What will he become after this? Gespar headed straight for the Emerald lodge, risking more than his life. It was dark outside, with one small torch perceptible from afar. They saw a body standing. As they moved towards it, Ezekiola recognized the familiar face of Yossan, the very warrior who had supervised his training during his time spent at the Emerald camp. Yossan was standing guard, as if waiting. His body stiffened at seeing Gespar, as if he was half expecting, yet still was shocked. Gespar said something to him in an unfamiliar language, but Ezekiola saw Yossan's face lit up. It was a facial expression Ezekiola had never seen before, not even after spending a whole month training with him.

"Come this way," Yossan told them. In the dark of the night, three bodies crept into the Black Mountains of Circa. At dawn, only two emerged. Of those two, one finally made his way back to Cypress School.

Chapter 12

New Nemesis

Helva realized quickly that any request done on behalf or for the sake of Leanne to accommodate her in Cypress School would be approved graciously. Her sole purpose was to relocate Leanne into a dorm with her and Daria. Thus, with the little time left before school started, Daria took it upon herself to do an almost impossible task—a massive restructuring of the ladies' dormitories. She spent days swapping girls back and forth in other rooms, pleading with some, begging others, all in return for favors. Some students were not easy to convince; they had impractical conditions, and others wouldn't budge if they didn't have their best friends transfer along with them. Lady Marmel, the school clerk, seemed to be physically pained each time Helva stepped into her office that summer to report dormitory related changes. Yet, she conceded every time. And for those students unfortunate enough to be away off season, a not so small surprise awaited them when school started. They came back only to learn they were uprooted and sharing new dorms with girls they barely knew. Just a few days short of starting school, the names of Helva, Leanne, and Daria had been circulating unfavorably on pursed lips.

One sunny afternoon, Leanne, Helva, and Daria were sitting in their new dorm, freshly decorated with sojas that Helva recently plucked, merrily shuffling papers back and forth, and organizing their schedules. Classes here were far more interesting than what Leanne was familiar with on her home planet. Considering the special circumstances she found herself in: no belt had been assigned to her, nor any specific classes. Instead, at Cypress School, a floating curriculum was recommended for her. This year, Leanne could choose and engineer her own schedule, all according to her interests, although the whole was subject to the final approval from the School Council. She could take any introductory class she wished, from any belt category she desired. If halfway through the year, Leanne lost interest in a class or two, she could simply switch out for another. The hope was that by the end of the year, this formula would help narrow her interest to a specific field.

As she browsed through the school folder, she noted it was divided into different colors, representing all the categories of belts. At first, she landed on the Red Belts, and glossed over some of the courses—*Arithmetic*, *Logic*, *Mind and Matter*, *Rule and Order*, whereas others like the Emerald Belts had quite the captivating classes such as *Cosmic Evil*, *Mastering Rivalry*, *War of the Surrans*. But when she flipped the pages and found herself in the silver and white divisions, the classes listed had her in awe.

"Oh, this sounds interesting! '*Explore a myriad of suns in the galaxy of Arithea and their influence on orbiting planets,*'" she read out loud. "This class is called *The Suns of Arithea*. Did any of you ever take it?" she asked her friends. Daria and Helva simultaneously shook their heads.

"How about *Charts of Circa?* It says here '*this class explores the astrological symbols governing Circa and how to interpret its evolution using geometrical charts.*'" The girls shook their heads again. Next, Leanne skimmed over a class called *Planetary Grades*, which compared different planets coming from one and the same galaxy. She was overawed just reading some of the titles.

"You're in the advanced sections of the white and silver categories, dear, you'll be lost in those classes. Move over to the introductory brown division a little, so we can have a class or two together," Helva counselled, shuffling the massive school folder until it landed in the brown category. She then slapped additional history classes into Leanne's schedule.

"No, wait, she can't take this one," Daria intervened; "This teacher's just awful. You'll barely make it through the first half of her class, she'll put you to sleep."

"What about this one?" Leanne asked, pointing to another teacher.

"Oh, no, you don't want him. Just the clothes on him will be an eyesore," Daria cautioned. "Remember what happened last year, Helva?"

"Oh yes. He wore them so tight, then sat on his desk right in front of us, we could barely concentrate. And every time his legs shifted on that desk; all we would do is stare at them, waiting for those pants of his to rip. We even wagered when they would finally shred, and I hit the right date! Ha!" Helva said proudly, provoking laughter from her friends.

"This one's great! She's our favorite, always sidetracks and tells stories, you won't get bored in her class," Daria offered.

"What's this?" Leanne asked, looking at a special paper placed inside her welcome folder. The quality of the paper was different, akin to a delicate parchment. It was addressed to her specifically. Helva was standing up and was the first to read the letter diagonally. From her bird's-eye view, her eyes quickly landed on the signature at the bottom. The name Falco Rasspan was elegantly calligraphed at the end. Her brows shot up.

"Is he kidding me?" Helva pulled the paper out before Leanne or Daria got to the signature line.

"Hey, we didn't finish reading the letter!" Daria protested.

"No need," Helva confidently told them, ripping the page into pieces. "Leanne, we will pretend this was never in your folder. Just act dumb and innocent if anyone asks you anything. There are some things I need to take care of myself."

"What was it though?" Leanne asked.

"It's a request from the forest rat, which we hope never to see again," Helva stated, then dumped the paper in the trash. She didn't want to add that creepy request to Leanne's load, especially not at the start of school.

"Oh wait! He mentioned something to me when he saw me with Ezekiola in the forest. Does the letter have to do with me having to visit their sanctity house, or whatever that place is called?" Leanne asked uneasily.

"They call it Sanctuary, and it's anything but!" Helva quipped. "Let's keep that rat Falco in the dark. We need a plan to counter what he did!" Helva's eyes swelled up suddenly, remembering what had happened to Borghis after they had exited Haack. They had no idea that on Circa they had been missing for three days. Unbelievably, it had felt like hours on Haack. When Borghis finally brought them back to Circa, Falco Rasspan, and his crew, were eagerly awaiting him. Indeed, Falco had arranged to have every portal closed in the Black Forest save for one, and like a conniving fox, waited for his target to come out of its hole.

True to his words, Falco had Borghis officially suspended for transgression until further notice. He had cleverly planned his stratagem. Beforehand, Falco had modified several rules governing Brown Robes which, on their face looked unexceptional. He submitted them to the headmaster just on time. What he did was to give additional grounds for Brown Robes' suspension and expulsion. One of them, trivial as it sounded, pertained to the use of *other* staffs when personal ones were confiscated. Thus, it was easy for Falco, in front of so many witnesses, to prove the theft and use of the Exit Staff by Borghis when the latter's personal staff had been confiscated by Falco himself.

Borghis' refusal to submit to a formal inquiry, in addition to his refusal to disclose where Ezekiola was located, further aided Falco's case. Instead, Borghis confessed to a master plan for the whole escapade. He admitted to stealing the Exit Staff, lying to all his friends on where they were going, and ultimately, shielded all involved but himself. Borghis's now fantastic story also included having stolen a staff from the Ladies' division to enter a portal. That fabrication was to keep Helva out of trouble. And the more incredible the story, the more Falco gloated. To him, it was ecstasy to hear such words flow out of Borghis' mouth. It gave Falco unending pleasure. To the Forest Council members, Ezekiola had gone missing, and by default, they blamed Borghis for it. Now, his fate at Cypress School dangled from Falco's fingers. Indeed, Falco wanted to make an example of Borghis, show his authority and command respect from the students. He thought the headmaster at Cypress School was too lax, unable to discipline and disorganized. But deep down, Falco harbored a secret desire to become headmaster one day. He wanted to have power over all the students at Cypress School, not just one division. Nothing was out of reach for him, and it was only a matter of time before he would add the title of headmaster under his belt.

"That rodent will pay a price for what he's trying to do, I

just haven't decided what price yet," Helva stated with sangfroid, her determination sending an icy chill down Leanne's back.

Leanne was glad to have Helva around. She admired her stamina, how she went about doing things, often with no forethought to the consequences. Yet she managed all the same. Helva always stated that when you do something for others, life will find a way to place things back in order. You just won't be privy to the details of how and when.

This made Leanne ponder on what happened to Ezekiola. The last she saw of him, he was crossing that invisible bridge. He was still not back from his trip, wherever he ended up going. They were discreetly told by Nomi that he had made it, was alive and well. No more. With no set date on when he would be back again, Leanne did her best to pass the time, despite being downhearted at his absence.

A few days into school, Leanne could not have been more enthralled by one of her classes. As plain as it sounded —*History of Circa*—was more fantastic than she ever imagined. The planet was so old, its age was unimaginable. So much turbulence had happened here, Leanne was surprised how it could even continue to exist. It was a story of one battle after another, not only with neighboring planets, but hollowed asteroids inhabiting different clans of race, all seeking one and the same thing—dominion. A tipping point in the history of Circa was when the Surrans fought one of the greatest battles to aid Circaens. The Surrans were seventeen-foot beings with ferocious bodies and wings. Wings! Leanne's eyes almost popped out when her teacher exposed a three-dimensional holographic image of one such impressive Surran in the middle of the classroom, almost standing next to her. Their wings were not feathered like birds, but skin like, forming part of their body. Leanne couldn't help but make parallels to what was found back in her own little world of Planet Blue. She thought maybe that's where the folktale of large human bats came from on her planet. It seemed as if the history of one planet imprinted onto the next, but was registered with nuances, never in its original format. The stuff of myths.

Later, although Circaens had been one of the few hosts to accept Surrans on their planet, their kind was decimated when a large group of Emeralds, the very group who became the Sons of the Night Sky betrayed them in a monumental coup, annihilating almost their entire species. The surviving Surrans scattered to neighboring worlds. By the end of her class, Leanne was a little crestfallen learning about the Surrans. She wondered what happened to the ones who survived. It seemed surreal that in the vastness of the universe, there could still be a homeless species unable to find a proper dwelling where they can coexist with others. She was also surprised to learn that the Surrans had many prophecies related to the Fountain of Fire. That part truly sparked her curiosity about their species. She would have to take another class just on the Surrans to learn more about them.

She enjoyed the rest of her classes that day but was surprised that no one really came to greet her. In fact, Leanne found that most ladies here were courteous, but not very expressive. Not like Helva and Daria, at least. They smiled curtly at her, but no more. She found it curious that none of them talked to her, considering she was new, and literally from another planet.

At the end of the day, on her way to the dorm, she got hold of the first quarterly publication of the school journal that was being distributed, *The Eclipse*. It was the welcome back issue, the largest of the year, encompassing several articles from students in every single category of belt, topped at the end with a sensational collection of poems, words of advice, and abounding rumors. Casting a look at the first page of *The Eclipse*, Leanne's good humor was suddenly slapped down. She stopped walking and dropped her bags on the ground. After shuffling her way through every single page, she quickly stormed into her dorm.

"What is this?" Leanne asked, holding the bulletin in her hand, only to find Daria alone, shuffling through the very same newsletter. Daria immediately straightened up and bundled the paper in her hands.

"You have to ignore it, it's nothing," is all she managed to say. Leanne noticed Daria also had a letter in her hand.

"I can't just ignore this! Did you read what's in this thing?" Leanne asked.

"It says nothing significant, just pointless chatter from ladies who have nothing better to do with their time," Daria said.

Leanne shook her head and turned the pages once more.

"I can't just leave this be; it's so wrong! Why would they even say this?" she blurted out, her eyes moistening for the first time.

"Daria, you won't believe what I just—" Helva walked in, stopping abruptly as soon as she saw Leanne. Helva's eyes were also welled with tears.

"What's going on?" Helva asked, noticing *The Eclipse* in their hands. Helva hadn't picked up a copy yet.

"It's what's written in this," Leanne said, flustered. Helva took her copy and her eyes fell upon the cover page, conveniently entitled '*THE GLAMORS OF FIRE,*' written in grossly large print, with a background image of a blazing red fire.

"We shouldn't pay any attention to this paper!" Daria interjected before Helva even turned the page.

"Give me a moment here Daria," Helva said, her voice shaky, as some additional weight had just been added to her chest. She didn't even get a chance to tell Daria what had just happened, that there was something else she was dealing with. She turned the page and started her first reading, jumping through some, and reading bits and pieces of others:

Welcome note: Beware Ladies. The word fire, lately, has been tarnished, overused. It has become a word spoken far too many times, painfully so by newcomers from doubtful provenance. Ladies, those with unprincipled audacity such as these novices will only contribute to further distorting its true meaning we Circaens need to shield...
Words of wisdom: to the ladies of Circa, the true Circaens, protect yourselves from ethereal distractions. A time to prove our solidarity is upon us, let us not decline in the face of these glamors, 'fiery' as they seem, and remember that glamor also works under the guise of evil. The call is being sent, we need to sanitize our environment, will you hear the calling and join in protecting our lands?

Helva looked at Daria, then at Leanne, her eyes no longer tearful as when she walked in. Something else had taken its place. She forced herself to continue turning the pages while pacing back and forth hypnotically in their dorm. The words of wisdom section were followed by the poetic one. A short story was selected for the first edition of *The Eclipse*. It was titled 'The Rogue and the Charlatan.' She quickly read that one. In short, it narrated the story of a disguised gentleman and a lady who begin their lives on a ship named Spring of Fire, only to end up revealing their true selves as a rogue and a charlatan. Their ship also happens to get wrecked by a powerful fire, turning the couple's life altogether into tragedy. Helva almost tripped over Daria's cat while reading it. She strained her eyes to carry herself onto the last page, the rumor segment:

One noble ladies' encounter at the Lake of Maji during the last full moons of Circa foreshadowed a warning. A great evil is upon us, for a black sorceress will come in our midst, disguised as a white enchantress, only to deceive us. Will it be one infiltrating our inner circle who will betray us? Isn't it always so? Rumor or truth? Only time will tell.
Your Rumor Lady

Helva's jaws dropped. She quickly closed her mouth and composed herself. She looked up at her friends. A moment of silence ensued. Their thoughts though, were anything but still.

"They're talking about me, aren't they?" Leanne said.

"But it doesn't mention your name anywhere. I checked," Daria said, meekly.

"Daria, you know very well that Leanne is on EVERY one of those pages. There's no need to mention her name. Ezekiola, too, is in there. They are laughing at them and the Fountain of Fire! Let's not kid ourselves,' Helva stated it plain. 'This is Poisy, Chace, and Laurel's work. I know it. These three vicious ladies are behind this, and we will figure a plan to deal with them. We need to, umm, we need to first—" Helva stopped short when her gaze fell on the empty vase next to her bedside.

"Where are my flowers?" she asked abruptly, looking at Daria. Daria took out the envelope she was holding in her hand.

"I found this next to your vase when I got here. I didn't want to upset you with it, I was going to go look for another soja to replace it with."

Helva looked at her friend confused and grabbed the envelope. She quickly saw its provenance with a glance of the initials 'F.R.' on the seal. It stood for 'Falco Rasspan.' Just that image got her heart pounding. She tore it open and read the letter. The Forest Council was requesting a meeting with her.

Several articles were conveniently transcribed naming the new sections created covering 'The flowers in the Black Forest,' and all acts warranting decrees, which included the plucking of a soja.

"Who came into our dorm?" Helva demanded, her voice fierce. An invisible line had been crossed.

"I don't know. It's what I found. I was the first one here," Daria answered.

Helva looked at Leanne, then at Daria. 'Daria, I need you to do me the biggest favor. I'm being watched wherever I go. And Leanne here is under prey's watch too. You seem to be the less targeted among us. I need you to get Atlas. I never thought I'd say this, but we need his help.' Daria nodded enthusiastically, hopeful at the news.

"Oh, what was it you wanted to tell me when you walked in?" Daria asked, suddenly remembering.

With all that had just transpired, Helva found herself in another chaotic space. Things had piled up at an unprecedented speed. Her breath shortened suddenly, forcing her to sit down. She made the effort to compose herself before speaking again. Through teary but determined eyes, she said:

"Borghis has just been expelled. Brace yourselves ladies, we are at war."

Chapter 13

The Sacred Books

Sitting on a rock by the edge of an unknown sea, Gespar found himself in a strange moment of time. It was the kind he rarely visited in life, maybe once or twice before. And yet, here he was at a new juncture in his journey where decision was knocking at his door. A small voice told him what to do, while every ounce of him resisted. He wasn't in for an easy ride. That much he knew. He was like a little tugboat struggling through rough waters to pull the larger ship to safety.

This voice didn't just call for his attention, it sought to forge a new path. He couldn't ignore the fact that the Count had been right. He did not just place blind faith in him. He had leaped and had entrusted Gespar with Ezekiola. Unbelievably. As much as Gespar was in the habit of self-deprecation, reducing himself to a meaningless life, he had achieved that one task of training Ezekiola the best he could. It upset him that he had just started working fruitfully with Ezekiola when his time was being cut short. He still had something to give. He stood up, moving closer to the seashore, to once again hover his hand over the sand and water. Where was that spot that land, water, and air met, where it was neither wet nor dry? Although he couldn't figure it out, he somehow sensed that the decision he would take would bring him closer to unraveling this mystery. He also knew that the decision he would make now would bring him closer than ever before to death. His only solace was that it would be an honorable one. Any other way would be dishonorable. Difficult as it was, at least in this manner, he could choose.

First on Gespar's list was digging those books out of their holes. He was the perpetrator who had hidden all five volumes of the Kama. One by one, he would retrieve them and bring them to their rightful proprietor. The easiest one accessible was on the planet Zoha, the closest located to Voronar. He recalled hiding the first volume on the lower lands in a forest close to a village. He had never dared to enter any of the planets where he hid the books, never knowing who was following him at the time. When Gespar exited Circa, he had asked Yossan to lead him exactly here. Advanced Emerald warriors like Yossan knew most portals on their planet, and with the use of their belts, they could easily travel in and out of Circa.

Gespar noticed Zoha hadn't changed at all from the last time he had been there. Planets like these take ages to evolve, if not aided by neighboring worlds. It was like Voronar, except no one wanted to live on Voronar because of those hostile giants. Gespar had originally memorized the configuration of the trees just as he had star constellations where he had hidden the first volume of the Kama. In fact, it was the geometrical placement of the trees that made him choose the spot. There was a formation of eight older trees amidst young ones, making it an octagon like structure. He walked for some time coming closer to his destination. He suddenly stopped when he heard shouts of children playing not too far. He paused to listen for a moment, carefully scanning his environment. No child was in view. From afar though, he could see something dark lining the ground. He couldn't tell what it was exactly. He walked over to take a closer look, and as he did, his chest tightened. There, in front of him, extended a long stretch of tilled soil. He followed it, and with every step, it became harder for him to breathe. When he reached the spot where he had buried the book, it looked like the ground had erupted from beneath. Fresh earth was piled on the sides in little mounts. There was no question that the ground here had been thoroughly dug up.

As he stood staring into a large, deep hole in front of him, Gespar's mind came to a standstill. He had not foreseen this. His mind plunged into a dark space as he continued staring into the blackish void with nothing visible but earth. He couldn't have come here for nothing. He must find it. The voice of children nearby snapped him out of his stupor. He looked up to see little faces smudged with dirt staring at him wide-eyed. None of them dared to speak.

"What happened here?" Gespar asked the children, breaking the silence.

"My sister found a book," a little boy emerged out of the lot, answering proudly. "Why do you have a patch over one eye?" he then asked, curious.

"Where is the book?" Gespar asked, his heart pounding in his chest.

"My parents sold it," the boy answered. "What happened to your eye?" he asked again.

"Who did your parents sell the book to?" Gespar panicked. Life seemed to have other plans for this book.

"To a merchant. What's so special about this book that so many strangers are after it?" The boy's question sucked the air out of Gespar's chest. He hoped this was not true.

"Why? Who came here before me?" he asked.

"Strange people came to dig to find some more," the boy answered.

"Yes, they were strange, weren't they?" a little girl in the group interjected.

"Why do you say that?" Gespar asked, looking at her.

"They were dressed dark, with coverings on their faces. But we could still see their eyes. One of them had a marking on his temple, see right here," she motioned the side of his face where she had seen it. Gespar's gut wrenched at hearing this. They had gotten to it before he did. The Count had been right again. *"They will find the books eventually if you don't retrieve them. It will end up in their hands,"* he had warned. While Gespar was sleeping away in his solemn life, there they were, treasure hunting. The Sons of the Night Sky.

"Did those strange ones find the book?" Gespar asked.

"Hmm, not sure. I think the merchant had already sold it long time ago to someone else," the boy added. Gespar's heart stopped. The book had gotten too far. Now he worried about the rest. How was he going to disentangle this mess?

"Do you know who the merchant is?"

Some of the children shook their heads simultaneously. This world Gespar had just entered began to collapse on him. His hands were shaking. He turned his back to the children to control himself a moment, looking back into the deep hole, not knowing what to make of the situation. Where is the book now?

"But I saw him at the fair yesterday acting funny," the youngest in the group suddenly said. "It's still going on for another day. He had a big purple hat on with purple plumes. He let me touch it!"

Gespar's ears pricked up, and hope was kindled at hearing this odd detail. Many things flashed in his mind, notably that pigmentation of such colors was hard to find in this desolate barren planet, let alone the knowledge on fabricating hats or how to dye plumes. It's one of the reasons why he buried such a book here. They were far behind on their evolution and would not grasp its content. He never calculated that a little girl could find it and her parents sell it. He hoped there was still time. He had to find this merchant.

"Thank you. Can you tell me how I can get to the fair?" he asked.

"Yes, but can we see your eye first?" the boy persisted, putting Gespar on the spot. Gespar sighed deeply. Slowly, he walked up the little mound where the boy was standing. As he approached, he could see the children were unnerved by his proximity. He bent down to place his face right in front of the little boy's and stared deep into his eyes with his one eye. The boy's countenance suddenly changed.

"Something vile and terrible pesters in there, and if you look at it, even for a moment, it can suck you into a deep hole like this one here," Gespar said, pointing to the ground beneath them. The children stared at the hole for a moment, then back at him. "Are you sure you want to look at my left eye? You might disappear after and never be found," Gespar said. The boy's eyes widened at the thought of it and instinctively shook his head.

"That's what I thought," Gespar said, smiling at the children for the first time. "Where is the fair?" he asked.

"Walk north five thousand steps, then head west at the fork in the road with a grey market flag, for another thousand. You'll hear the crowd before you see them," the eldest girl in the group said. Gespar nodded, realizing again how rustic the society was, measuring distances in steps. He bid farewell and headed north.

In the first half of his walk, Gespar scolded himself for

having carried on with his life without any afterthought to what he had done. How could he have been this reckless, not having thought of the possible consequences and outcomes? Under great pressure, he had made hasty decisions. He had been in a rush to hide the books. At the time, his life had been at stake.

The children had been right. He heard the crowd before getting to the fair. He had crossed paths with a few passersby on his way, all who stared at him quizzically. They could tell he was a newcomer. Before getting to the fair, Gespar put his cloak and hood on, so as not to draw further attention. He appreciated the fact that this world was more docile than where he used to live. There was no yelling or shouting, though judging from the type of tents and tools they used to mount them, they were much further behind in knowhow.

He glanced around and initially saw no one with a plumed hat. In Voronar, Gespar had learnt several dialects and instantly spotted one spoken by a salesboy.

"Have you seen the character who was here yesterday, the one with a purple plumed hat?" he asked him in his language.

"Yes, over there," he pointed. Gespar turned around and in the crowd, he could see a man with high plumes atop his head.

When Gespar found him, he was laughing deliriously, spiraling on a podium, as if drunk. To Gespar, his senses seemed clearly altered, but surprisingly, he didn't reek of anything. Gespar had spent enough time in lowly taverns with giants to know what the effects of spirits had on a body. This was something else. As the man spun around in a disorderly fashion, staring into the air, almost dancing with his arms spread out, the inside of his coat flapped open a few times. Something in there caught Gespar's eye. There were several vials with something purple in them.

"Trade runner, can I get me some of what you got?" Gespar asked capriciously, motioning inside his coat.

The merchant touched his breast pocket, a scary smile stretched across his long face. "These are precious. Depends on what you give," he replied.

"On second thought, I'm not so sure of their provenance, they could be fake," Gespar said.

"Oh, this is no fake. It enhances life. It will make you feel alive, so alive!" he exclaimed all jittery, extending his arms skyward again.

"Impossible. Such things are not found here, just look at the color. It's a fake, I say!" Gespar said loudly, making sure the crowd heard, intending to provoke him further.

"No! It's not! This is real! I procured them from my tradeswoman."

Tradeswoman? Something about hearing that name troubled Gespar. He had dealt with one such woman who went by that name in his distant, wretched past. Not having lived that life for a while, he could only assume many went by such names. He comforted himself knowing the tradeswoman he once knew would have nothing to do with this madman.

"It's a lie," Gespar ventured. "You just want to steal goods from honest buyers while selling sham mood swings in vials. There's no such tradeswoman."

"YES, THERE IS!" the man blurted out, almost tipping over the podium. He took out all his vials and held them high up in the air. "She exists! I tell you! Her eyes are cloudy, and hands are purple. And she said these precious vials come from great sacred, immortal caves. They're called Fountain of Fire. It awakens the fire of life, you'll always feel alive, and never die!"

Upon hearing *purple hands* and the jumble of warped words on the Fountain of Fire, a cold wave submerged Gespar under new waters of terror. He shuddered at his next thought. *It can't be, it can't possibly be,* he repeated to himself. He had known too well of such caves found on a wretched planet,

Agiri, and especially of a tradeswoman operating there. It couldn't get much worse than this. In fact, he had visited the Caves of Agiri many times before, yet a part of him still didn't want to believe, so he pressed further.

"I wonder what you traded for her to generously give such life altering goods. They are not easy to find," Gespar mused. He noticed the man's expression shift suddenly, stiffening. Gespar was coming close to his target, he could see. He came up on the podium where the man stood, closing the gap between them. The man looked momentarily scared, as if he had lived this moment before. Something about Gespar and his eye unsettled him too. But Gespar had to know.

"What did you give this tradeswoman that she could have possibly wanted from this drab planet of yours?" he asked, his lone eye a shade darker.

The man gasped, shaking suddenly. "We don't want your kind here! I already told you I sold *the book* a long time ago! Your party already came scavenging our lands! You wreaked havoc, turning many of our houses upside down!" he boldly asserted.

Gespar got his dreadful answer. His heart sank. "I am not part of that clan. You should've thought twice before giving away something you don't understand," he said grimly. He turned around and left, thinking in turn that he should have himself thought better than to plant things in places of no value.

Alone with his own thoughts, Gespar wondered how far did the Sons of the Night Sky get? Did they find the book? They obviously ransacked the area and didn't find anything else on this planet, though they tried. Gespar had only buried one volume of the Kama here. He entertained a slew of more troublesome thoughts. He couldn't stop worrying about that particular shade of violet on that merchant's hat and the Agiri tradeswoman he sold the book to. Most of all, he worried about the SONS' involvement in all this, possibly with the tradeswoman from Agiri whom they knew well, and what all this could well mean.

Chapter 14

Gathering

The cafeteria food on that sunny day wasn't sitting well with Atlas. His stomach tossed around, making a few awkward noises, loud enough for his classmates to notice. The food that day was fish, and it had smelled funny. The side dish was potatoes with a mix of greens. And those, too, Atlas thought smelled funny. But because everybody was eating it, he ate it all too. By early afternoon, Atlas felt a few shivers go up and down his spine, making him want to take a hot bath in the middle of the day. But he carried on. Sometimes, he crouched in his seat during class, and found this hunched position to be somewhat helpful, as he tolerated the sweat pouring down his forehead. He wanted to but couldn't start skipping classes just yet, it was too early in the semester to do that. And although he couldn't wait to go back to his dorm and curl up in a ball, his day was far from over. Daria had sent him a frantic message that same morning, claiming some emergency his sister and the ladies had. What could possibly be so urgent? He could never understand her demanding ways. Of course, he had said yes to meeting them at Night and Day Inn in late afternoon. He just didn't think he'd be feeling this way after lunch. He banked on the hope his digestion would get better by the end of the day.

Upon arriving at the designated inn, he first spotted Helva facing the door, and waved at her, then noticed Daria and Leanne sitting across from her.

"Thank goodness you're here!" Helva stood up to greet her brother. The place was loud and busy. Very busy. In fact, every table was occupied.

Upon sitting down, the first thing Atlas spotted were his sister's eyes. They were red, and her face looked like she'd lived a whole month in a day. He greeted Daria next, and she looked like a distressed cat. He couldn't help but notice how untidy and loose her hair was. He then looked over at Leanne who bore a glacial expression. He was still looking at Leanne trying to figure out what was wrong with her when she suddenly jerked in her seat. A serving faun approached the table to take their order, but Leanne had never seen a faun.

"I'll have three pints," Helva ordered first. Atlas looked at her in surprise. Never had he heard his sister order in such quantity.

"Three pints?" Atlas asked her, shocked. His question caused Helva to throw him a stern look in his direction.

"What's wrong with that?" Helva asked her brother. He remained quiet, closing his eyes instead, looking as if he was trying to breathe normally. Noticing him acting strange, she commented further. "Your face lacks color. What's wrong with you?"

"I don't know. I'm not having a good day," Atlas said, pushing himself to raise his voice above the noise. A powerful whiff of ale and other spirits penetrated his nostrils when he spoke, stirring his insides even more. Perhaps it was best to talk less.

"Do you know what's happened?" Helva asked. Atlas shook his head.

"You don't know what happened to Borghis?" Helva questioned. Atlas shook his head again, then forced himself to formulate a somewhat concerned look: "I haven't seen him since we came back from Haack," he answered plainly.

"He got expelled, Atlas!" she blurted out, slamming the table so loudly it caused neighboring tables to look in their direction.

"What?! When?" Atlas asked, surprised. Nohlan hadn't told him anything about that. Then again, he hadn't seen Nohlan all day. Helva's throat tightened, her eyes welled with tears. She looked away for a moment, unable to answer.

"He got expelled yesterday," Daria answered in her place. "And we can't find him now. We think he already left the school premises."

"I didn't even get to see him to say goodbye," Helva's voice shook. Momentarily, she recomposed herself. "Atlas, I need you to find him for me," she said with sudden determination. "I need you to help me figure out a way to speak to Nomi about this, and speak to our School Council, and the Brown Robes, and the Forest Stewardship Council, and the Emeralds, there must be someone who can possibly be—"

"Whoa, Helva!" Atlas defensively raised his hands in front of his face. "You're all over the place. You can't just get the whole school involved in something like this, it's specifically the Forest Council who decided—"

"No, it's not the Forest Council! Wake up, Atlas! We know who's behind it! This rat has got everyone agreeing to his demands! And those Emeralds... how can they go along with such a false accusation that Borghis caused Ezekiola to disappear? It's as if they don't even care what happened to Ezekiola, nor Borghis, for that matter! And I can't believe Headmaster Nomi would approve of such a thing!"

"Shouldn't it be the headmaster who has final say on expelling a student from his school?" Leanne asked, looking intently at Atlas.

"Yes, shouldn't it be that way?" Daria repeated the question.

"I, umm—I think—" Atlas sighed, rubbing sweat off his forehead. The place was getting louder, and he couldn't quite bring himself to talk without weakening his body further. Considering his state, this conversation was demanding too much effort to think. Regardless, he didn't have solid answers, only suppositions. Truth was, he had never investigated school rules in the past. Never had to. In his recollection, no one had been expelled before. The Brown Robes, however, were governed by their order, and now he wondered how much the school rules overlapped with their order's rules, and vice versa. How did that work?

"Nomi needs to give final approval, doesn't he?" Helva pressed Atlas again.

"I'm not sure. Did you talk to Keenan and Gordi?" he asked his sister.

"I tried to look for them, but I can't even find them. They are no longer in their lodge. Can you at least go find them, please?" Helva pleaded.

"Helva, I don't know if I can really do something here," Atlas said, his feeble body speaking more than his mind. It amazed him at how quickly physical unease disabled his willpower.

"I helped you in the past, didn't I?" she said, desperation in her eyes.

"Yes, and look at the happy direction that took us!" Atlas retorted with a frown.

"Well, you got what you wanted for your friend," she said.

"And I had to pay a dear price for that!"

"Atlas, it's only a matter of time before this forest rat will be all over us. He's already sent me a request because I plucked those protected flowers of his. This floral extinction phenomenon is a fabrication of his, I'm certain of it! There's no proof that such a species is disappearing from our lands. He acts like the Black Forest belongs to him and he decides whatever he wants! And soon, watch. He'll be at it, sending new rules to govern our school, and not just Brown belts or Brown Robe students. It will include everyone. Wait and see. He's scheming big. Don't think you're untouchable, just because you're a red belt. He'll find a way to bypass that, just as he got Borghis expelled. The longer we wait, the harder it will become to pluck the roots of this sick growth out of our grounds."

A concerned look crossed Atlas's face. He lowered his eyes to the table thoughtfully. While thinking, the caption 'FIRE' written large captured his attention.

"What's this?" he asked.

"Oh, please go ahead, we brought you a copy to read," Leanne said, crossing her arms over her chest. With a tilt of her head, she motioned for Atlas to grab a copy of The Eclipse, waiting to read his expression. Atlas regretted having said anything, suddenly noticing that Leanne's demeanor hinted at another dilemma.

Atlas read the first page quickly, moving over to the next, reading diagonally, and then just a few words here and there. His eyes widened when he got to the short story.

"The Rogue and the Charlatan! This is about Zek and you?" he asked, stunned. Leanne's gaze made Atlas's blood run cold. He flipped to the end, reading the rumor section last.

"Who's writing this?" he asked, incredulous.

"Three brutes. But we can handle this part," Helva

answered. "This is your copy by the way. We wanted you to be aware and let Zek know what's being said when he gets back. We will figure out our battle here, but I need you to help me find Gordi and Keenan first. I'm sure they know where Borghis is. We can meet again to figure out a plan to get him back. I'm not letting this go, even if I get kicked out of here, Atlas. I swear it on all the moons of Circa!" Helva said. Atlas nodded, worried at how far his sister was willing to take this.

"Alright, I'll go look for them now. We'll get to the bottom of this. Find out who prints these in your division, and make sure you run a counter print or something against this idiocy!" With these last words, Atlas exited with his copy of the newsletter, and made his way to the Ye' Ole Brown Lodge as promised. He could have searched for Nohlan instead, but that would have extended his path. The lodge was closer.

His initial search was unfruitful. As Helva foretold, Keenan and Gordi were not at their main lodge. He searched around the perimeters, into the gardens, the surrounding Black Forest, even their dorms. They were not there either. Where could they be? His stomach was somewhat comforted after leaving the noisy inn, walking in nature eased it a little, but now worry settled in. The sun was setting low, and he really wanted to get back to his dorm. But Helva's pleading voice reverberated in his head. And not finding Gordi and Keenan was now arousing his suspicion. Walking weakly but steadily, he persisted in his search, asking other Brown Robes about Keenan and Gordi, but no one knew where they were. In fact, he was struck by their nonchalance. Brown Robes didn't seem to know each other's whereabouts, nor care at all. After doing enough rounds, he stopped for a moment and thought hard. Gordi and Keenan didn't get expelled, that much he knew. They should be here, but evidently, were not. His thoughts brought him back to that day when they exited the dead moon,

Haack, and saw the entourage of Falco standing in front of him. As he revisited the chronology of events, an image suddenly came to his mind. Atlas realized he forgot to look in an obvious location. How could he have missed it? It was the one place he never bothered to check. The *Sanctuary*.

He had to be careful. Those Forest Council members were adamant about keeping non-members off their grounds. He came close, noticing the absence of bodies around the stark structure of their dwelling. It looked morbidly stark. More like depressing, thought Atlas. He also noticed the place was in shambles. The outside structure looked like it was decaying, and even the greenery looked like it was dying. He had never seen it in such bad shape. Was he going to just enter the Sanctuary like that? In the quiet of the forest, while ruminating on how to best enter, which pretext to use, a few faint voices reached his ears. They were coming from behind a smaller structure, a part of the Sanctuary located not too far from it. He thought he recognized one of the voices belonging to his friend Nohlan. This was reassuring. He ignored his physical discomfort briefly, and headed towards the sound, hugging his stomach tight. As he came closer, a vile stench hit his nostrils. It stirred his guts, stopping him dead in his tracks. A gutter smell mixed with some other revolting stink circulated the structure. He heard that voice again and was now sure that it was Nohlan who was speaking. Ignoring the smell as best he could, he forced himself feebly to take the additional steps to come closer. He came up from behind, only to find Keenan, Gordi and Nohlan, all three of them on their knees, deep in mud, digging around a structure, while something awful bubbled on the surface from a broken pipe. Different sized pipes, some broken, along with shovels and tools were all laid on the ground. The realization hit Atlas like a brick in the face, and his stomach, too. They were in the latrine zone.

"What are you all doing?!" he asked in shock, looking at the three of them. Nohlan especially looked embarrassed. Keenan however, seemed to have a different attitude.

"Well, Atlas, take a wild guess?" he said, taking a break from shoveling something in the ground.

"This is the most disgusting thing I've ever seen!" Atlas exclaimed.

"Well, hello to you too, Atlas!" Gordi then greeted him. "Believe it or not, this is the reductional work ascribed to us by Falco, the forest rat, as part of our punishment for acting as accomplices to Borghis."

"You have to clean the latrines?"

"Not just that, he wants us to fix a burst pipe linked to their latrines underground plumbing," Keenan answered.

"What?! You need a plumber for this," he said, barely able to pronounce words. Upon speaking, Atlas had to inhale, and a tapestry of new sound, smells and colors invaded his senses, striking past the zone of tolerance.

"Yes, I think so too, but Falco thinks we can handle this ourselves," Gordi interjected disdainfully.

"And why are you in here? Aren't you supposed to have class?" Atlas asked Nohlan.

"I'm a brown belt, so..." Nohlan answered, his head hanging low. It pained Atlas to see his friend this way. Atlas still couldn't come around to accepting such a sight when Keenan spoke again.

"Atlas, it's not as bad as it seems. There's good and bad news here. The good news is that Falco's bowels are acting up on him, several times a day and now we know why," Keenan said, with a smirk on this face. To Atlas's shock, it seemed to liven up Nohlan's face when he spoke next.

"Yes! He has stomach worms, and they're all over in here. The worm's head though hasn't come out, which means it's still in his stomach! Ha!" Nohlan said jovially. Atlas shuddered at hearing this. Keenan then dumped whatever he picked up in the ditch into the wheelbarrow placed next to him.

"The bad news is Falco wants us to use this as fertilizer for his garden, raising vegetables, and as the Forest Council has been long doing, giving extra to our cooks in our cafeteria," Keenan said, Atlas stared at Keenan in astonishment, looking wide-eyed at what Keenan was shoveling out of the ditch. He then turned his gaze towards the substance gurgling out of the ground right in front of Keenan, then to the brownish-black substance dumped inside the wheelbarrow.

"Is that... is that... is that his shhh—" Atlas lost his voice as the sound of bubbling grew, and more percolating feces surfaced from the ground, emitting a horrendous stench. The whiff, the worms, the compost, the cafeteria meal all merged and mashed as one in his guts, causing bile to rise to his throat. Suddenly, it was as if the fish bites that Atlas ate at lunch that day reconnected in his stomach coming alive, and with a mighty thrust, wriggled its way out of his mouth, taking along its side companions of greens and potatoes with it. The force of it took him by surprise, propelling him forward. Too weak to hold upright, Atlas lost his balance and landed in the ditch next to his friends and all the feces. Everything came out.

Atlas would never forget that day—it was the day he became one with the plight of his friends. After pouring his insides out, a zealous willpower overcame him, replacing what had just exited his body. He sat down on the ground next to his friends. It was in the ditch that the most important gathering took place between four bodies—Nohlan, Atlas, Gordi and Keenan carved out what would become their greatest mission yet. And this is how Atlas gained his first taste of the power of union. The four of them threw all sorts of ideas back and forth during their planning:

"It won't be easy, Falco is squeaky clean and abides by the rules," Gordi whispered.

"Oh, I'm not so sure about that. I've spoken to a few Gemins and they're really not happy with him. He has been ignoring them and sending out new rules for them to follow. I'm not even sure he's allowed to be doing that. He claims dominion over the Black Forest. Plus, the Sanctuary is falling apart, and the surrounding area has never been in worse shape. Something is not right. Give me some time, and I'm going to find a way to trap that rat. He's fond of rules, but I think he's breaking some without knowing it," Atlas responded.

"What about Borghis? How will we get him back?" Nohlan asked.

"We'll find a way Nohlan, don't worry, we'll get him back," Keenan said.

"Where is he now?" Atlas asked. He wanted to give some news to his sister.

"Nomi has a brother in Cypress City who is a carpenter. He sent Borghis to live with him so he can work alongside him, at least for now. I'm not sure what his plans are, but they don't know about our plan. We'll get him back for sure," Keenan said hopefully.

Atlas went to visit Nomi sometime after with a list of requests. Nomi wasn't just surprised, but relieved. Atlas could see the hope that glimmered in his eyes. It was as if he had taken a weight off his headmaster's shoulders. And when Atlas left Nomi's quarters, he made sure to bring along a trolley on which he stacked the piles of documents cluttering his headmaster's room, the very ones that were handed to the Headmaster by the Forest Stewardship Council on rules and regulations. Only one thought permeated Atlas's mind: search and you will find.

Chapter 15

Dancing Darkness

Accompanied by his right-hand man, Dakor chose his crew carefully. This was his most important task yet. The chosen were composed of new graduates who had been under his tutelage for many years. They were zealous, eager, and with every fresh opportunity presented to them, hungry to work their way up. But most of all, they all knew Zeke when he was among them. They had trained with him, then bitterly watched him rise in rank quickly. Zeke was endowed with something more; they couldn't dispute the obvious. His mind reading skill was a gift few possessed. And what could be more fulfilling than hunting down and crushing the very person who had surpassed them in the past.

As pressure mounted and preparations continued for the conclusion of the Great Plan, Dakor was both anxious and furious. It haunted him that he had missed the greatest opportunity of all—catching Zeke. There he was, standing in front of him in Voronar. Painfully, he replayed that moment many times in his head. Had he brought the skilled slave alongside him, things could have ended up much differently. He scolded himself for lacking the foresight to handle the possibility of what was such a serendipitous event. What upset him most though was his initial reaction when he saw Zeke. He froze. How could he? The only explanation he found was that his emotions betrayed him. He was unable to come to grips with the sight of Zeke, standing next to the traitor. And what happened next had him completely unprepared: Zeke used a power that caused an extraordinary tremor beneath his feet. Dakor could barely make a move on his own. Like dry leaves trapped in a whirlpool, Dakor and his crew were tossed about helplessly, swayed by the cataclysmic forces of nature that shook them. The ground quaked, cracked open, threatening to swallow them whole. He lost two men that way, crushed by the boulders that fell on them in the ditches. Without thinking, Dakor had grabbed onto a tree, holding onto it for dear life, hoping the tree wouldn't succumb to the violent forces. Everything happened so fast, only after did he realize how terribly he had handled the situation. This was unprecedented. He had never seen such a show of power. Now he had a taste of it. And he knew what it was—the Fountain of Fire. Dakor had his first glimpse of what he was up against. What he was planning next had to be done skillfully, carefully, and most importantly, with patience. There could be no room for any mistakes. Not one.

When they exited Voronar, Dakor was able to relieve only part of his fury. Indeed, after a long pursuit, his huntsmen finally discovered the abode of the purchaser of the sacred book. They traced the very tradeswoman to whom the merchant of Seve sold the book. It brought them straight to the caves of Agiri. It was a place Dakor had suspected this world was holding a secret from the start. With evidence on his side, he didn't hold back his rage one bit.

"You witch! You lied to me!" Dakor thrashed the table Rikka was working on.

"What are you talking about?" Rikka replied innocently, scrambling into one corner of her workroom as furniture and glass were smashed and shattered all around her by the SONS.

"Don't insult me with stupid questions! How long did you think you could carry on before we found out? I can cut you to pieces for this! Where is it?" Dakor grabbed the chair Rikka was sitting on, throwing her off, and smashed it against a wall.

"I don't know what you want!" Rikka shouted back.

"That's how you've been thriving here, in the business of reviving the dead. You used the teachings, didn't you? And now, I hear you're busy making copies to trade!"

"That's not true!" Rikka said.

"Where is the book?" Dakor asked, infuriated by the answers she was giving.

"It's not with me! It's with scribes in another world, translating. I swear it on the life of all my Agiri Mystics, they took the book away!" Rikka confessed. Then, to redress herself in this powerplay, she added defiantly: "If you kill me, I will not allow my Mystics to give you that book."

What she said made Dakor pause a moment, a dangerous glee shone in his dark eyes. He tilted his head to catch a glimpse of his men around the room to watch their reaction, then started to laugh. Almost immediately, his crew released themselves and laughed in unison along with him.

"You think *you* are going to hold us prisoners?" Dakor asked, a malevolent smile cutting across his face. His tall body finally reached the corner where Rikka huddled, he bent down and grabbed her by one arm, raising her off the ground. With one hand on her throat, he tightened his grip, holding her against the wall, her feet dangling in midair. She struggled to grab his arm with her hands, but they were like feathers on steel.

'Listen to me carefully. I will only say this once. I want the original book in my hands,' he said calmly, then tightened his grip further, choking her. He stared into her eyes, watching her face change color. She attempted to speak, but a gurgling sound came out instead. Dakor continued to speak as if he was in the calmest of setting: "And I want every single copy made by those scribes of yours in my hands too, not one shall be left in Agiri or elsewhere. Your world is our prisoner now, and I will burn it down if I need to, and I will make sure the smoke will suffocate every one of your kind in these forsaken caves. This is the doom that awaits you and your world if you do not give me what I want." Rikka's eyes rolled in the back of her head. Dakor finally let go of her, and she fell to the ground with a hard thump.

"Wake her up," he ordered his men. "As soon as she awakes, destroy the whole marketplace. Gather her Mystics. Throw three of them in the pit. Make her watch. All of it. She needs to know we mean what we say."

The SONS carried out their orders. Before they destroyed their main marketplace, Dakor stationed an army in Agiri, to search every corner and retrieve whatever copy of the book they could find. He assigned a special crew of his men to escort Rikka to her hidden Mystics where the original book was said to be kept. All the Mystics including Rikka were held prisoners, their release only to come when the original book would be in Dakor's hands, and all the copies made afterwards by the scribes. Anyone trying to escape would end up in the pit.

In the meantime, Dakor and his men took away whatever they could find valuable, including all the hordes of slaves kept prisoner on the planet. Indeed, unbeknownst to his slave girl, her clan of sisters was taken possession of and brought onto Brak, the SONS dominion. As part of her release package, he ordered Rikka to harvest more of the poisonous organisms that look like a boomerang. He wanted rows of them planted. With too much at stake, Rikka had no choice but to follow such orders.

Next in the execution of the Great Plan of the SONS was a visit in another sort of cave. This one however, was located on Brak, their home world. With torches in hand, several members of the Sons of the Night Sky escorted Dakor through a long dark passageway, a centuries old maze composed of a system of underground tunnels. Here, the prisoners' dwellings were built. For those forsaken to live several feet below ground, light would become a distant memory. Cries were heard from different cells, some in anguish and pain, others of lunacy. In such hellish digs, there was never an in-between; it was either pain or madness. The sound of footsteps echoed in the dark as the group approached the end of the passageway. They could hear keys tinkling as they closed the gap. A lock was being opened by a guard.

"In here," the guard motioned to Dakor. He entered a larger cell where several men stood facing the wall. They were covered with filthy rags, once upon a time their clothing. They looked barely alive. A particular stench emanated from this group. Despite his tolerance for such things, Dakor stood far from them. Often, this smell was indicative of imminent death. Those too weak to withstand the pestilence that would often hit them usually wasted away in their cells. Many had died this way. Observing the ones lined before him on shaky legs, Dakor could tell it was an effort for them to stand up. Then he spotted the weak one, crouched on the ground on his knees, head resting against the wall.

"Get up!" he ordered. The man attempted, using both hands and knees. Too frail to stand up on his two feet, he fell to the ground in an awkward balled up position.

"Bring him to me," Dakor commanded.

Two guards held the man upright, one on each side. The

prisoner groaned in pain. Hollow cheeks and a thin layer of skin outlined the frail bones of his body. He looked like he hadn't been fed for years.

"How would you like to taste freedom?" Dakor asked.

The man did not answer. He gazed at Dakor with weary eyes, as if his world had been crushed ages past.

"What if I were to release not just you, but everyone else here, all your comrades?"

The prisoner's countenance shifted; a faint glimmer of curiosity inhabited the expression on his face. It was the first time such a thing was being said within these walls. With the little light left in his mind to think and reflect, he could tell something was up, else such a thing could never come out of the SONS.

"Speak!" Dakor commanded to him.

"Ahhh... ahhh... ahhh—" the man mumbled away, unable to pronounce a word.

"He was in the silent cell, my lord. He hasn't spoken for years, he's lost his speech," the guard explained. Prisoners held in the silent cells were those on whom additional sentences were imposed. To remain forever silent. Speaking would only get them killed. Dakor looked at the prisoner and pondered for a moment. This prisoner was dangling on his last thread of life. Not much was left of him. So frail, so weak, he would probably not make it past a few days of freedom in the outside world. Just the shock of it would kill him. He liked that outcome; it would serve them well.

"I'll take him. Keep him in his cell until we're ready. Give him water only, just enough to keep him alive. He'll be a sight to behold," he said, and left the vile dwellings of their underground prison.

When the last of the news came to Dakor's ears at nightfall, he was elated. After a long search of a specially assigned crew, his huntsmen had found the traitor. It would be a matter of time until he would fall under his grip, too. After getting one precious item at a time, one valuable piece of news after another, Dakor was now ready to face his next and final assembly—the one to receive his blessing. He made his way into the great halls of the Nameless. In the center of a circular room, Dakor stood tall, addressing the shadowy silhouettes, his superiors.

"We found the boy," he said, relishing in his own statement.

Agitated upon hearing such news, the Nameless circulated around him creating a black vortex, ethereal and chilling, a dancing darkness. Dakor was pleased. He could sense the effect his words had on them. It fortified him, elevating his spirit to a new level.

"Where is he?" the collective voices of the Nameless hissed simultaneously, echoing in the room.

"He's been dwelling in Voronar, training with the traitor," Dakor answered. Thinking back, he could not believe the sight of them side by side. But in hindsight, once he thought through it strategically, he understood how that came to be. It was ingenious. And incredibly daring. The more he contemplated the reason behind the coupling of the traitor and Zeke, the more he realized it was truly a work of art.

"Isolate the boy. Separate him. You know how," they commanded him. Dakor knew exactly what they meant by such words. They weren't merely alluding to separating him physically from those around him. It went much deeper than that.

"Does the boy know who the traitor is?" a Nameless asked.

Dakor paused for a moment, his expression deepened. A dark smile curved his lips as he mused on that last question. "No," he said, reveling in his answer. He knew this knowledge would serve him as a great weapon.

"Good. You may go forward. Consummate the Great Plan in our name. Our might is yours." With that, Dakor received his blessing and exited.

Now Dakor's greatest strength was to be put to the test. His patience.

Chapter 16

The Surran's Massacre

The humdrum of everyday life was back in orbit at Cypress School. With all well underway, classes continued, and routine resumed. After training with Gespar, Ezekiola was glad to be back on the familiar ground of his school. It gave him a sense of normalcy to begin his theory classes as an Emerald Belt student. It's what Igor Sanza, the leader of the Emeralds, had planned for him after all those flopped training sessions. Igor had been disappointed in Ezekiola. His attempt to revive the warrior or draw out of him the powers of the Fountain of Fire had completely failed. In the end, it wasn't Igor who was able to ignite the powers of the fountain in him, but Gespar. Indeed, after reflecting on his recent encounters, Ezekiola noticed that a strange nostalgia overtook him after parting from Gespar. Despite the short time they had spent together, it was as if he had lost a sibling. Even after day-to-day life resumed at Cypress School, thoughts of Gespar often surfaced. Like a leaf suddenly blown into a stream, Ezekiola wondered which way the current had taken Gespar. Although he had fond thoughts of him, every now and then crazy Yolsha's words about Gespar being *pure evil* would creep up on him. And there was also that branded eye of his, stamped with the very symbol of the Sons of the Night Sky. How did that happen? Gespar's expression after the Caspol Dance when they first merged with their belts also mystified him. He could tell Gespar was struck by something. What did he see? The puzzling portrait of Gespar had several missing pieces to it. This often nagged at Ezekiola but refusing to dig further in pursuit of completing this puzzle, he pushed it into the back of his mind.

Back at school, the group of friends finally had the long-awaited opportunity to reconnect. From the lot, it was Leanne who was most thrilled. Any advice ever given to her in the past about keeping a safe distance from Ezekiola spectacularly flew out the door. It seemed what she enjoyed most was time alone with him. She rearranged her schedule, bringing numerous changes to her curriculum, scheduling her classes in tandem with his to spend whatever afternoons they could together. Despite the many times her friends offered her to watch the sunrise, she had kept that moment to share with Ezekiola. They were finally able to see the sunrise standing atop the White Mountains by the amphitheater. They walked every path in the forest several times, even took a painting class together, one of the classes open to both male and female divisions. They were just one step away from being called a couple.

Atlas, on the other hand, spent an extraordinary amount of time in the library, which even for him, was unusual. He was onto something and had undertaken conducting tedious research. He got several of the librarians in a fit of frenzy with special requests, going as far as making them order books from the Cypress City Archives. Part of the reason was that Atlas didn't dare take anything out of the Brown Robes archives. He was being extra careful not to arouse suspicion. The Cypress

City Archives held a copy of every original book ever written on Circa. Some were ages old. Those age-old books, however, were like artifacts, too ancient and fragile to leave the premises of the city archives. When Atlas landed on one such book that he needed to access, delight twinkled in his eyes.

Luckily for him, after months of school, the first holiday was coming up—*The Surran's Massacre.* Thus, he found the perfect excuse to plan their first school related outing—a day's visit to the Cypress City Archives.

The Surran's Massacre was a dark holiday to say the least, and the story behind it—one of tragedy. In a long ago past, the Surrans, a tall and powerful, distinct species with wings, were known to be great destroyers but also great healers, with the ability to extinguish or revive life at will. They had the power of invocation far beyond the normal, allowing them to exercise control over many kingdoms including the animal and vegetable ones. Circa was one of the few planets who had given the Surrans their Word—to safely share living space with Circaeans. But they were deceived. The Surrans were hence annihilated at the hands of a large group of Emeralds, the very band who would later split to form the Sons of the Night Sky. With most of the Surrans decimated on Circa, a small number of survivors escaped and scattered into other worlds. For the Surrans, Circa failed to honor their Word. To Circaens, it was a shame they had to bear, something in their past that had never been resolved.

Helva had been begging to go to the city, too. Atlas had been patient with her. He had to speak to his sister several times to hold her back from just escaping to see Borghis. Since he had been expelled, Helva and Borghis had communicated through letters only. Helva was a Brown Belt and although she was in the female division, she was under the ultimate authority of none other than Falco Rasspan. That's what Atlas had uncovered when rummaging through their regulations. If Helva was caught leaving the premises during the school year, that would play in Falco's favor. When Atlas saw what he did to Keenan, Gordi and Nohlan, he knew how far Falco could go with his sister, savoring his power over the entire Brown Belt and Brown Robe order. And Master Falco had his eyes on Helva, waiting for the moment she transgressed. She had borne his scorn for plucking sojas, something she considered ridiculously minor. Falco, on the other hand, made it sound like she had desecrated the entire forest. *His* forest. To send a strong message, Falco held a formal court, making her stand in front of the entire Forest Stewardship Council. He reveled in how she had remained quiet and obedient all along. But Helva wasn't being obedient to Falco, but rather to her brother. In fact, Atlas pleaded with his sister to admit her wrongdoing and remain quiet, which she did so reluctantly.

"You're caught in a chess game now Helva, and you need to play right. If you want to capture the king, you strategize and swallow your pride. Your pride is like a pawn. Be ready to lose some while you plot something bigger," Atlas had cautioned her. Luckily, it made an impression on her.

Atlas grew closer to his sister during this time, supporting whatever emotional outbreak she experienced every so often. He was onto something bigger, he told Helva, and she should be patient. He was on the verge of possibly unseating Falco from his throne. He, on the other hand, appreciated his sister's foresight. Helva had been right. Falco's tentacles went far and wide, inspecting every single student, no matter their order, including their progression, classes they attended, their whereabouts, and even which books they borrowed from the Brown Robe's lodge, in both male and female divisions. The logbooks tripled, and he kept track of everything, even strolls in the Black Forest. Countless new rules sprung up like grass in springtime, some on exercise, others on communal work. There were even new rules enforced for Gemins, though they were not well received. Gemins were now being told what to do, which paths to walk on, where to garden and on which days. Under Falco's governance, every activity and leisure ended up in a logbook. Brown Robe and Brown belt students' whereabouts were monitored, transcribed, and before long, several students were put on suspension, and others were assigned communal work. They were on a very tight leash, held by the terrible hand of one supreme leader.

"We leave at dawn," Atlas said the day before the holiday.

"Why so early?" Nohlan asked.

"We have a big day in front of us, Nohlan! I have to maximize my time in the morning to sift through the archives so we can meet Borghis afterwards. I already sent word to Borghis that we'll be in the city and where to meet us for lunch. My sister hasn't seen him for a long time. I want to make sure she gets the extra time with him. In the afternoon, we'll leisurely visit the city and catch the parade. Oh, and I need to stop at Old Hermie's antiquarian bookshop at some point."

"Whoa, Atlas! That's a lot of stuff packed into one day. It takes about an hour to get to the city, an hour to get back, and now you've added a city visit in there, a parade to watch, and do you really need to go to this bookshop? What if we want to do something else?"

"Nohlan, this is a highly coordinated schedule. We can't change it now. Everything I planned fits in a day, and all you must do is follow along. It will work seamlessly. And don't worry, you'll have enough time to do what you want in the morning while I'm at the archives. And yes, I really need to stop by the bookshop. I'm out of books."

"But you've been at the library forever, Atlas! We've barely seen your face! How could you be out of books?" Nohlan appeared dumbstruck.

"*My kind of books*, Nohlan! The ones *I* read. The stuff I'm borrowing from the library has nothing to do with my interests. Besides, our library here needs some serious revamping. I plan on calling a meeting with those Silver Robed librarians. I find they're operating on a very low caliber lately, almost half asleep."

Nohlan sighed. He didn't dare question Atlas any further. He sounded highly prepped for whatever was going on in his mind.

The next morning, the same crew of friends who had once journeyed to the moon Haack, minus Borghis, made their long trek to the city. Someone new, however, came along. Yossan. The Emerald warrior who originally supervised Ezekiola's training at the Emerald camp all summer, was now back in Ezekiola's life, this time to act as a bodyguard. His presence was mandatory. This was the new rule Yossan had explained to Ezekiola after he got back from Voronar and learned that he came face to face with the SONS. Leanne and Ezekiola couldn't leave Cypress School unless accompanied by him. Ezekiola wasn't sure if this new rule came from the Emerald leader Igor Sanza or just Yossan himself. He wagered on the latter. Igor wasn't a fan of Ezekiola, and it wasn't like Igor to send away one of his best warriors as a bodyguard. It seemed the leader of the Emeralds was kept in the dark about the time he spent on Voronar. Ezekiola sometimes wondered why Igor wasn't privy to this. And each time he thought of Igor, Gespar's face would also come to his mind. There was a strong parallel between those two characters that left Ezekiola intrigued. He went as far as thinking that they could be brothers.

As Yossan tagged along with them to Cypress City, he garnered curious glances here and there from the friends, especially from the ladies. His imposing presence was anything but subtle. The elegant Emerald Robe he wore made the crew look like they were his escorts instead. Characteristic of him, Yossan remained quiet. As usual, Ezekiola could not read a thing from that stoic warrior's mind.

The morning schedule went as planned. Atlas beamed with joy exiting the archives, as if he'd just won a reading prize. Meeting Borghis was next on their timetable. In alignment with the holiday spirit, the chosen meeting venue was a tavern called none other than *The Surran's Massacre*.

"Who picked this place?" Ezekiola was first to ask as soon as they walked in.

From the outside, the sprawling two-story tavern was nothing short of inviting. The outer frame was surrounded by elegant canopies, flowing linen canvases and golden glass lanterns, providing a warm feel to the place. Inside, however, was another story, symbolically portraying what happened to the Surrans. Circa, the welcoming planet, had ensnared them with its inviting beauty only to terminate them upon entry. Once inside, no one could come out unaffected by the haunting decor. It was dark, and the first thing noticeable was the fires flickering from torches mounted on the wall. The first floor was long and rectangular, and the second floor could be seen from the ground. A few steps in, an imposing circular staircase spiraled up to the second floor, every stair decked with goblets of fire on each edge. Magnificent chandeliers made from axes hung across the ceilings, with a multitude of candles adorning each. Rows of cutlasses and mirrors embellished the unusually high walls of the tavern which were so magisterial, they were the reason most came here. They depicted bestial scenes of Surrans and every battle they fought throughout the ages on Circa, with the years calligraphed at the bottom along with the name of the artists who painted them.

The images were gruesome, and cleverly placed mirrors reflected those images from every angle. Some Surrans were speared, others decapitated, their heads poked onto a spike, while others had their wings cut off, held in the air by the mighty hands of spiteful Emerald warriors. One scene in the middle of the tavern depicted a great feast with body parts of conquered Surrans on the table. Leanne almost tripped over a chair when she saw the ghastly feast, especially after all she had learned about the Surrans in one of her classes. The slashed wings especially were most repudiating to her, for it was believed that the healing powers of the Surrans resided in them.

'*You betrayed your Word*' was written beneath almost every image, immortalized on the walls.

"It doesn't matter who chose this place! Stop staring at the walls. Oh, there's Borghis!" Atlas jumped over to the table adjacent to the masterful painting of the horrific feast. Borghis was sitting at what appeared to be a communal table, next to others who were having their meals together. Ezekiola didn't like being seated in the center of the room, nor being seated next to strangers. He looked up, and a large scythe, adorned with a massive chandelier held by chains was hanging right on top of their table. He looked around to see if there were other tables available. The tavern was busy so everywhere he looked, not a single table was free. Whether it was the gory image in front of him, the dangling scythe overhead, or the fact that they were so centrally located almost on display, all unnerved him. It was like being in the middle of a battle scene in the most vulnerable spot. He reluctantly sat at the very edge of the table, next to Leanne and Yossan, while constantly shifting in his seat, his eyes skimming the surroundings now and then.

Upon seeing Borghis, Helva wrapped her arms around him. 'I missed you!' she whispered. They held each other tight for a while. Borghis was dressed in simple brown trousers and a brown shirt, the trademark of Cypress carpenters.

"You don't get enough of the color brown, I see." Atlas's remark had both Borghis and Helva chuckling.

"I heard the same about you, Atlas! That lately, you like to get dirty in brown things, no matter the texture." Borghis' comment had everyone laughing, even Ezekiola, although he seemed very tense.

"So, how's carpenter life in the city?" Keenan asked, sitting across from his friend.

"Actually, I enjoy it far more than I thought," Borghis answered. "Nomi's brother is quite skilled. You should see some of the things he's built. In fact, our school—umm, I mean Cypress School—is requesting new bookcases for their library," he said briskly. Everyone spotted that minor correction Borghis made in his sentence, and the ever so slight sorrow in his voice when saying his school's name. Keenan and Gordi came closer to him, hunching forward on the table.

"Borghis, we're onto something, and very soon, you will be a very happy brown whatever you wish to call yourself," Gordi said, smiling.

"No, no, no," Atlas clicked his tongue, grabbing everyone's attention. "We agreed not to talk about this in public, remember?" he told Gordi, with quick side glances at Keenan and Nohlan. They looked away and held their tongues. This got Borghis curious.

"What are you talking about Atlas?" he asked.

"Something that will have you greatly indebted to me. I would even say a lifelong debt," Atlas answered with a smirk.

"Ha! You wish! No seriously, what's going on?" Borghis asked, looking at the rest of his friends. Gordi didn't answer, neither did Keenan.

"Nohlan? Want to tell me anything?" he asked his brother.

In answer, Nohlan shrugged his shoulders. Borghis looked at the girls, then Ezekiola, getting nothing out of them either.

"Alright. Fine. I see what's going on here. Can you at least tell me if this has to do with my expulsion?"

"Yes and no," Keenan said. "It's a story about a falcon, a forest, and a very special rodent who claimed dominion over the forest, only to eventually get caught in the falcon's claws." Borghis chuckled at hearing this, deciding to leave to his imagination what his friends were up to.

The conversation was lively after that, the words *forest rat* and *rodent* being repeated numerous times between the friends. Once their meals were served, a better mood permeated the room despite the somber decor. The group even got a few laughs from Yossan, who uttered some words after being prompted by Leanne, Daria and Helva sitting closest to him. It seemed the ladies had the best luck getting him to speak. The boisterous tavern was in full swing when Ezekiola broke his gaze from his table and looked up to the second floor. Immediately, his eyes fell on a woman already staring at him. The moment he locked eyes with her, his body fired up. For some reason, he could not bring himself to break away from her gaze, nor pay attention as to why his body felt that fire. Everything was the same around him—the crowd was boisterous, laughter was heard, and servants moved to and fro among the tables. Nothing had changed. And yet, her eyes were hypnotizing, filled with an almost palpable intensity. He continued to stare at her, mesmerized, observing how distinct her eyes were—they were larger, with white lashes. Never had he seen such outstanding eyes before. A movement on her table suddenly diverted his attention. A man comfortably seated with his back turned was circling the edge of his cup with one finger. It had a large onyx ring on it. The finger continued to swirl round and round the cup. That movement... that strange caress. It hypnotized Ezekiola more than the woman's eyes. Time seemed to stop. Watching that movement, a haunting familiarity crept up on him.

"What is it?" Yossan asked suddenly, breaking his trance. Ezekiola looked at Yossan, somewhat dazed.

"Nothing, just—" Ezekiola paused for a moment, his mind still on that finger caressing the cup. "It's just, something that umm... felt familiar."

Upon hearing those words, Yossan pushed his chair to stand up and draw out his belt, but it was too late. Almost instantly, something blasted in the tavern, and the scythe located right on top of their table came crashing down, along with the chandelier hanging off it. Borghis, Keenan, Gordi and Nohlan, among others, were ejected from their seats, landing several feet away. Yossan just had enough reflex to shield the girls with his body, shoving them beneath a side table. Ezekiola, in turn, was also ejected, landing dead center of the tavern, his ears deafened from the sound that reverberated in his head. What just happened? Did the scythe accidentally fall? He thought he lost his hearing, but it was the astonishing loud voice of Yossan that clearly confirmed otherwise.

"GET OUT! EVERYBODY OUT!" Yossan finally pulled out his belt.

Suddenly, a meteoric shower of lightning and dust filled the air. Fire crackled close to the ceiling, and shouts were heard. Men out of nowhere appeared standing atop the banister of the second floor, brandishing what looked like whips, in reality, their belts. Bolts of fire spiraled out of their belts, all shooting in the direction of Yossan. He wasn't the only warrior in the room. He was surrounded by a considerable number of his greatest enemies. Like water seeping into cracks, Sons of the Night Sky sprung out of every corner of the tavern. Inundated with shots, Yossan struggled to ward them off on his own. As mirrors broke and chandeliers shattered all around him, Ezekiola laid sprawled on the ground, hardly able to pick himself up. Blood trickled from the side of his head, his hands were cut, pieces of glass stuck out of his skin, and his ears were buzzing. What just happened started to sink in. The scythe falling was no accident. Nor was the tremor, nor the fire. He gathered his strength and crawled towards Yossan, attempting to stand.

"Stay down!" Yossan yelled and pushed him to the floor. Consumed in action, Yossan couldn't determine which angle the SONS were coming from, nor was he able to keep a count of how many there were. His attention split in several directions, and then quickly got disoriented as flames lit up in several spots in the tavern. Tables, chairs, drapes, paintings were all catching fire one by one.

Ezekiola remained low on the ground. He looked to his side and could see barrels bunched in a corner that had also caught on fire. Although he could feel the warmth of that element, the heat emanating from them was nothing like the fire that kept swelling inside of his body. He had the sensation of being amplified, as if not a space more could be filled by that strange blazing element inside of him. He looked up to the second floor where he had seen that woman with the white lashes. She was gone, and so was the man sitting across from her. He saw a glimpse of two tall bodies leaving the tavern. With no tangible proof, he just knew they were the heart of the danger. He looked at Leanne further away, hunched in a corner next to Daria and Helva. They had their eyes shut, frightened out of their minds, screaming every time glass shattered on the ground and fire sputtered next to them. Ezekiola gathered his strength and stood up again.

"Take the girls and get out of here," he told Yossan, motioning an exit door.

"Stay down I said!" Yossan glared at him, distraught. This was not the time to disobey orders.

"Just do as I say and don't follow me!" Ezekiola continued as if Yossan never spoke.

"STAY DOWN!" Yossan yelled, tossing Ezekiola to the side. Fire spiraled in their direction, just brushing Ezekiola's neck.

"Take the girls and leave, Yossan!" Ezekiola repeated, louder this time.

"What?!" Yossan was stupefied.

"Don't follow me! Just get them out of here!" he said fiercely. He then looked intently at Leanne and back to Yossan again, then shouted something that left them even more confused:

"Don't follow ANY of me."

Amid the chaotic scene, Ezekiola started clapping. It wasn't just random claps, but a sequence. From her corner, Leanne could see what Ezekiola was doing. She stared at him, stunned, wondering if he wasn't losing his mind. Just then, something familiar dawned on her. She remembered when that malevolent Zeke had once clapped in her presence; a clap that had set Madame Camille's shop where she used to work on fire. But as Ezekiola clapped away, it seemed he was trying something else, and wasn't quite getting the right sound. Suddenly, he came down on his knees, and slammed the ground with his right hand, as if it needed correction, then clapped a new sequence. What happened next astounded everyone, especially Yossan. While Ezekiola remained crouched with one knee on the floor, another Ezekiola sprung out of him and stood up. Yossan's eyes widened as he stared at what looked like a double of Ezekiola. Like a shadow flying in the air, Ezekiola's double jumped sideways onto the closest wall, pushing himself upwards, and onto the second floor, aiming straight towards a SONS. Another sequence of claps was heard from the still kneeling Ezekiola, and two more came out of his body. And there sounded another sequence of clapping, and out sprung more bodies. Ezekiola multiplied himself in front of everyone's eyes, leaving anyone who witnessed such a scene, including frightened victims in the tavern, agape. Every one of Ezekiola's doubles dispersed in different directions, like flying tornadoes, attacking the assailants from every corner, creating a confounding diversion. Anyone glancing inside the tavern would have thought the Surrans on the walls had come alive.

Terrifying sounds emanated from Ezekiola's belt as it clashed against others. The flashing lights became too blinding to see. Those caught in that crossfire had no choice but to keep their eyes shut.

"Get out now!" Ezekiola yelled at Yossan, who was standing in shock. For so long, they tried to resuscitate the warrior in Ezekiola and draw the powers of the Fountain of Fire out of him. And there they were, Yossan's first exposure to them, bearing witness. At that strange moment, Yossan was glad not to have given up on Ezekiola.

"Take them to the Watchtower, call for the Emeralds!" Ezekiola ordered. Their roles seemed to have reversed. Yossan grabbed Leanne and the girls, and by then, Borghis and the boys had stepped out from the back door, getting lost in the disoriented parade crowd, which was already moving away from the burning tavern.

"He's a fake!" One of the SONS suddenly yelled. He realized that the multiplied versions of Ezekiola were only shadows of his real self, casting the illusion that he was attacking, coming down hard on them. The men stopped fighting suddenly.

"Look, look here! He's a fake!" he said again, next to another double of Ezekiola. His arm went right through Ezekiola, and the shadow of him disappeared.

"It's ALL fake!" he yelled this time and went to pass his arm through another double of Ezekiola. This version however was the real one. Ezekiola struck him in an instant, his belt flawlessly wrapped itself around the man's waist, sending him flying, soaring upwards, crashing him on the infamous feast wall of the tavern.

"Get him! Over there! He's the real one!" came shouts from the men. But Ezekiola multiplied himself again, and out sprung ten of him from the same body, creating additional confusion. The Sons of the Night Sky didn't know which way to look, which one to attack. Every time an Ezekiola approached them, they would still have to fight and expend their energies for they didn't know which one of him was real. One by one, Ezekiola struck the SONS, and by the time they were all down, he searched for the man and white-lashed woman he had seen leaving not long ago. Where did they go? He stepped out of the tavern and ran for his life.

When Ezekiola reached the Watchtower, the scene that unraveled before him looked like a mirage. At first, a hazy image of unrecognizable bodies appeared, and then, when he could finally make out bodies and faces—he was in disbelief. What lay before him made his run-in at the tavern look like a warmup. There in front of him stood a far greater batch of SONS than the ones he had just encountered. On the right side of the Watchtower could be seen Yossan, Leanne, Helva and Daria, who were already in the grips of the SONS, held as prizes. In the center was an unrecognizable, frail man sitting on his knees. And Gespar, who he hadn't seen since he got back to Circa after training with him in Voronar, was now dangling off the Watchtower's cliff, just on the left side. Above Gespar stood a tall man, ready to do something. As Ezekiola drew closer, he caught a glimpse of the ring he had seen on the man's finger in the tavern. For some reason, the white lashed woman was not there.

Ezekiola's body quivered as he went up the hill. He was walking as there was no need to run. He sensed the foreshadowing of something abysmal, as if a new version of the Surran's Massacre was about to take place. Fear struck at the core of his heart. Despite feeling the strength of the fire in him at the tavern, it now seemed to recede with every step he took towards the Watchtower. One thing however he knew for certain: they were all waiting for him. While Ezekiola gathered whatever courage he had to face whatever lay ahead of him, unbeknownst to him, Leanne was, for the first time, engulfed by a strange fire, the very same one that had filled his entirety just a moment earlier.

Chapter 17

The Violet Haze

"**O**ur precious host has arrived."

Dakor's voice was smooth, measured, his countenance impeccably serene. This tranquil state was starkly juxtaposed with the agitated waters of the sea below. Spray from the waves—violently crashing on the rocks that bordered the Watchtower's hill—filled the air. Under the rays of the setting sun, Dakor's eyes glowed like black diamonds, magnetically drawing any onlooker onto him. Even from afar, Ezekiola was pulled into those spellbinding eyes. Those eyes... now that he had time to look at them, they were stern, resolute, and hauntingly familiar. The markings on the side of his face, were vaguely familiar, too.

With a pounding heartbeat, Ezekiola scanned his immediate setting, registering the numbers, the positions. At a glance, he saw Yossan shirtless on the ground; Gespar dangling off a cliff; Leanne, Daria and Helva in a corner, each held by the hands of a SONS. The lone man who looked like a prisoner, his hands bound trembling, was in front of the Watchtower. As if the matter in his mind dispersed into his surroundings, Ezekiola could feel everything and everyone, be they the assailants, the prey, the Watchtower, even the boulders. Ezekiola looked in Yossan's direction again but could not make eye contact with him. Yossan's body and face were crushed against the ground under the weight of two men pressing him down. In that moment, he knew he had to tread cautiously. Any quick move on his part, and one of them would surely pay the price for it. This wasn't going to be a simple battle. The set-up was too sophisticated for that possibility.

As he slowed his steps, Ezekiola observed the matching dark attire of the SONS. Some of them had their faces veiled, while others were exposed, but with thick black marks cutting across their faces. Ezekiola's outfit was as dark as theirs, darkened from the fumes they absorbed in the tavern. His skin also had a dark film on it, with a line of charcoal spread across his face, covering dried blood marks caused by chandelier glass that had cut into his skin. To Ezekiola's dismay, he fit their side of the decor, as if he himself was one of the SONS. Ezekiola's gaze once again came to rest on the man with the dark eyes. The man stood on the highest pinnacle, right at the edge of the hill next to the Watchtower, where his feet brushed against Gespar's hands. Upon seeing it up close, terror spiraled through Ezekiola, making his stomach clench. He saw how in a moment's time one foot could easily push Gespar over the edge.

Ezekiola came to a standstill at an invisible line. Crossing that line further would cause a move on the other side. The two glared at each other for what seemed like a long moment.

"Don't you dare," Ezekiola spoke.

Dakor raised his eyebrows and smiled. As if in acquiescence, he momentarily moved away from Gespar's struggling hands.

"My dear Zeke, how I love that you can read my mind! I

always let you do that to me; did you know that?" Dakor said, gazing towards the sea, letting his eyes relax on the setting sun.

"I am not your dear Zeke," Ezekiola said sternly.

Dakor laughed softly.

"You may not remember me, but I remember you," he said. It was a tender laugh, one that burned Ezekiola from the inside. "I can see why you think so," Dakor continued pensively, "but you haven't seen everything. Much has been kept hidden from you." He swiftly lifted an arm and motioned his men to raise Yossan from the ground. Yossan grumbled as he was dragged forward by the arms on the stony ground, then dropped in the center, next to the frail man.

Ezekiola immediately gripped his belt tighter and came forward, but a scream coming from Helva stopped him dead in his tracks. A cold sharp dagger had just pressed itself against her throat.

"Tsk. Tsk. Tsk," Dakor clicked his tongue, drawing Ezekiola's attention back to him. 'There will be no using those powers here,' he said, keeping his gaze on Ezekiola. Paralyzed by horror, Ezekiola glanced at Helva, who had her eyes shut, her face contorted fearing the threatening movement of the blade. He looked towards Leanne and Daria. Their faces were stricken and pale, being held back, possibly next in line, then back at Dakor as if he were the puppeteer of the show, pulling his desired strings.

"Good," Dakor said, continuing his speech. He shifted his attention to Yossan and, pointing to the prisoner, asked: "Yossan, do you recognize this man?" Yossan didn't answer, but stared hard at Dakor instead. He was quickly met by a blow on the side of his body by one of Dakor's men.

"Give an answer if you don't want the prisoner dead," Dakor demanded.

"No," Yossan muttered under his breath.

"Do you recognize him?" Dakor asked the prisoner in turn.

The man lifted his bound hands motioning to Yossan and mumbled a few words.

"Ayee, ayee noo," he mumbled. "Ayee, ayee, noo hmm!"

"Yes, yes, of course you do. You know him," Dakor said smoothly.

"Yoosssann," the prisoner pronounced as best he could. Yossan's eyes widened. At first glance, Yossan was sure he did not know that man. But now looking closely, recognition dawned on him, despite the features having undergone an incredible transformation.

"Sayat?" Yossan whispered in disbelief.

"That's right. The man has a name: Sayat!" he said, as if learning it for the first time. "See, you do know each other. Now Sayat would testify here that many of his kind are still alive, held prisoner. Isn't that true, Sayat?" Dakor asked. Sayat nodded in every direction, looking at everyone, in hopes that his persistent nod would convince everyone of that truth.

"Thouw, thouw, thouwzz..." he uttered.

"Thousands, yes, thousands. That is correct," Dakor clarified the answer, then addressed his audience. "Thousands of Emeralds, still alive! And not just alive, but waiting for their freedom, freedom that I'm ready to grant. Freedom, as you all know, comes with a price," he said with a measured pause, and met Ezekiola's eyes. "I have an offer to make you, and my proposition is a simple one: come to me, and you'll have an army liberated, including your friends here, along with this prisoner," he said, pointing to Sayat.

"HE LIES! Don't accept it!" Gespar yelled suddenly, his voice thick with conviction.

"In every man's life, comes a moment of truth," Dakor made his next statement, ignoring Gespar's outburst. "An opportunity to embrace his true self, who he really is, not what others make you believe." With a motion of his arm, Dakor opened an image in mid-air right in front of Ezekiola.

"Don't look Ezekiola! He creates illusions!" Yossan was next to shout but was quickly struck to the side again.

"Why don't you decide for yourself, Zeke? They've hidden too much from you," Dakor said, with knowing eyes.

Ezekiola's attention narrowed on Dakor as he weighed those words carefully. His options were limited. He could see Dakor had made up his mind already and was not going to leave without him, whatever it took. In truth, Dakor was merely giving him the opportunity to save the few lives of his friends. That's it, no more. Not another prisoner was to be released. This was all for show. And although Ezekiola did not seem to know Dakor at that moment in time, he could sense the relentlessness in him, that he would never stop. Ezekiola could have closed his eyes and not looked, but if he did, he knew this beast would come again to try him. So instead, he tacitly accepted the invitation by looking in the direction of the vortex that opened before him. Almost instantly, a myriad of images scrolled. At first, Ezekiola was the observer, witnessing a panorama of events as they came and went. Then, as the actions increased, he was immersed in them, as if he were living them right there. Soon after, he was no longer the outsider, but found himself merged in the scenes. He was center stage now, seized body and mind, living a plethora of emotions one after the next. The further the scenes progressed, the harder it became to live them. He saw much, then suddenly, there was too much. No longer was he observing acts, but was perpetrating them instead, carrying out deeds, terrible ones. How could he have possibly done such...

"It's not real! You're fabricating this!" Revolted, Ezekiola tore himself away from the swirl of images. But Dakor's expression remained unaffected, he looked down upon Ezekiola, as a father would look upon a child uttering useless sayings.

"This is no fabrication Zeke. Don't you know who you really are?" he asked. Those words. Undesirable as they were, pierced something in him. More dangerously, it opened his appetite to know.

"Don't listen to him Ezekiola! He only shows what he wants you to see!" Yossan interjected.

"Who do you think you are, Yossan?" Dakor shot back, shifting his attention to him. "You're but a cruel man, so cruel that you're ready to drop your imprisoned comrades easily for this one boy who doesn't mean anything to you. You didn't even train him, did you? It took the mind of a greater one to risk something you poor Emeralds would never dare to try. You deemed unworthy the one thing that was worth expending on. And you failed, Yossan. Your whole lot failed! You're not worth anything to them, Zeke. They NEVER believed in you!" Dakor hammered out his last words and Ezekiola could see he was speaking from a deeper place now. Those words could not all be falsehood. He knew that much after going through his personal ordeal with the Emeralds at their training camp. Indeed, he felt they had given up on him.

"Don't believe his empty words, he's manipulating you!" Gespar shouted suddenly.

"Gespar, poor Gespar," Dakor said, turning towards him.

"Zeke, I would like to tell you something Gespar never dared to share," Dakor said.

"No matter what he says, don't let him decide for you! Don't ever give him that authority," Gespar said in a tone as if they were his last words.

"Would you like to tell him Gespar, or shall I?" Dakor asked, walking back to his advantageous position closer to the edge of the cliff. Gespar was still struggling to hang on. All the while Dakor had been presenting his offer, he had been dangling with just one arm, to give the other a break, alternating with each. In that moment, only one arm was supporting his weight as Dakor's feet gradually stopped next to it.

"Don't you dare touch that hand," Ezekiola said, leaping forward. On cue, several SONS rushed towards him, but Dakor halted them with a motion of his arm. On the contrary, he wanted Ezekiola to come closer to him. Their eyes met as they stood face to face, closer than they had ever been.

"I won't push him. No, I think you might have the honor to do that," Dakor responded, surprising Ezekiola with his answer. "I think it's only fair you know the truth. Go ahead, Zeke, read my mind, it's all yours," he offered, his eyes emitting a fiery intensity, enticing him to plunge into them. Ezekiola could not help but do just that. He had to know. And then he saw it... the beginning. His beginning. His mother, his father, his twin brother, his separation from them. And there he was, the familiar face of Gespar, in their midst, inside his home. Realization struck him, and it struck him hard. Harder than he could handle.

"He's the one who stripped you away from your mother, Zeke! He separated you from your brother!" Dakor said with false compassion. "He carried out the recruitments of the children for the SONS. But don't be sorry for him because his story was vile from the start. Have you wondered why he's not an Emerald and not allowed on your planet? He was once one like Yossan. That's right, an Emerald warrior! He wanted to rise in the ranks of the Emeralds, become their leader, and gain more power. But he didn't get what he wanted, so he thought better to join our ranks and flourish there. He became one of us, and after so many years of leading the SONS, he decided to strip himself from us too. We call those a traitor by nature. Traitors, as you know, have a stench and Gespar is reeking of it. We caught him, but he escaped. Ask any Emerald here, they have a price on his head too, isn't that right Gespar? Banished from both worlds. The executor is now the executed. Gespar deserves his end. He's but pure evil," Dakor said, staring down at the dangling man.

Ezekiola shook his head. The story sounded like a suspicious tale. It could not be true. But those words 'pure evil' echoed in his mind. It made him think of crazy Yolsha, the old beggar in Voronar who uttered follics, while pronouncing some truths. She had said the same thing about Gespar being 'pure evil.' He was caught in the grips of confounding stories. Which one was true? Then the vision came to him, of Gespar's reaction right after they merged with their belts. He appeared heart-stricken. Ezekiola came on his knees and crouched down to look over the edge at Gespar.

"Is it true?" he asked, his voice cracking.

Up close, Ezekiola could see Gespar's face and arms were bruised, and blood trickled from the back of his head. Down below, blue waters crashed onto formidable boulders. From this vantage point, he could see why the Watchtower was built on this spot, for the rocks were condensed in this area, giving a better foundation to support the construct. And a sure death if one was to fall.

Gespar's one eye was glassy, filling with that translucent liquid that speaks first before any other faculties of the body.

"You knew all this time," Ezekiola whispered, then shut his eyes. It was as if someone had taken an invisible knife and cut ten inches into his soul.

"This is why I give you the honor to render justice where it is deserved," Dakor spoke, leaning closer to Ezekiola.

"Don't listen to him, Ezekiola!" Yossan interjected suddenly. "Dakor was Zeke's mentor. Before you start pointing fingers at who a traitor is, say it. Say what YOU did!

He's the one who viciously killed Zeke's woman and child! Yes, he had one. He had them thrown off a cliff!" The unexpected statement snapped Ezekiola out of his moment with Gespar.

Ezekiola looked at Yossan, unsettled by the meaning of such a declaration.

"What did you say?" he asked, stunned.

"That's right, Zeke had a woman and child. They were innocent and Dakor killed them! I was there, I saw it with my own eyes when he—," Yossan's voice was cut short as he was met with additional blows by the SONS holding him down. They continued pounding on him to shut him up.

Upon hearing this, a strong impression gripped Ezekiola. How could Yossan make such a thing up? He always found Yossan to be a different warrior from the other Emeralds he had interacted with. He was quiet, distant, yet strangely protective. That warrior had known something all along. There it was, he had seen something and kept it hidden. All this time, they were trying to conceal Zeke's past from him.

Ezekiola looked at Dakor intently and the familiarity of him crawled up in him just as a dream might be recalled in early morning, where fragments resurface from the back of the mind. He continued to look hard at Dakor to see if he would expose his mind to him just as he did earlier. To his surprise, Dakor was waiting for him to do just that. That's when he saw her face, the same woman he had seen when crossing that invisible bridge behind the Blue Navigator and heard the cry of a child. The woman he kept seeing in his dreams, as if all this time, parts of Zeke trickled itself into him, finding any small outlet to bring that other self alive. A strange sensation overcame Ezekiola, an awakening of sorts, as if he had been asleep all this time. He could feel his body trembling. This could not all be fabricated.

"Did you do it?" Ezekiola's voice shook with passion as he confronted Dakor.

"I never killed them," Dakor stated matter-of-factly. Ezekiola probed further into his mind to see. And there it was, the woman had no choice but to jump off the cliff as the alternative was to be killed by the SONS. She chose death by falling with their child in her arms, with Dakor standing not too far from them, then looking down that cliff to make sure it happened.

"No, but you sent the order, didn't you?" he said, with greater authority, and edged dangerously close to him, while Dakor slowly took a step backward. Ezekiola could see there was not an ounce of shame in Dakor for having perpetrated the act.

"I had no choice," Dakor responded with unexpected sincerity.

"Alhena," Ezekiola suddenly remembered her name, as if he merged with Zeke, becoming one and the same person. Just at that moment, rage overwhelmed him. Submerged in the image he saw when reading Dakor's mind, he forgot everyone around him, including Gespar, Yossan, Leanne or the ladies. He forgot his purpose, forgot about the Fountain of Fire in him, or what brought him to the Watchtower in the first place.

"LIAR!" Ezekiola shouted, crimson with fury. As he lunged forward, he saw a quick movement up in the Watchtower. By the time he looked up, it was too late. The spiraling sound was heard first, then something he did not see coming hit him in the back of the neck, bursting upon touch. The physics of it didn't make sense. How could something he saw coming from the front hit him in the back? Whatever it was, it wasn't hard enough to knock him to the ground, but rather make his body wobble at most. Instantly, Ezekiola looked up where the object came from and locked eyes with her. There she was, the woman with the white lashes and large eyes he had seen in the tavern. She had been standing by a windowsill up in the Watchtower all this time. Ezekiola thought he had regained his balance but caught himself struggling instead. Whatever it was that burst on his neck, it suddenly produced a cloud of purple and blue around him. He instinctively touched the back of his neck and could feel fluid where he had been hit. He looked at his hands and saw blood mixed with a film of blue and dark purple. Confused, he looked at his arms and feet. They were bluish purple. His clothes, the same, he looked all around him, and saw he was in a cloud of some sort. From afar, everyone could see. Ezekiola was covered in a violet haze. It surrounded him, engulfing him. Then he smelled it, and the essence viciously overtook his senses as if someone had soaked him in a barrel of perfume. A tremor went through his body, and he shuddered violently. He struggled to keep control of his body, but he could no longer stand. His heart pounded wildly as that strange element flooded him. He met Dakor's eyes, and he could see a triumphant smile wash over his face.

With his calm demeanor, Dakor had been quietly moving back, keeping himself away from the violet haze. The choice for his slave was the best decision he ever made. His slave hit on target, on time. Everything else was to be made history from here on. He just knew. Dakor watched as Ezekiola fell to his hands and knees, his body convulsing close to the edge of the cliff. Leaving him to suffer in that state, he turned his attention to Gespar, moving with a patient efficiency, and pulled a dagger out from his side.

"I never finished my job the last time. Symmetry is always preferred, don't you think?" he said, looking into Gespar's only eye, stepping on his hands. Gespar groaned in pain. In a surprise move, Dakor stepped off of the hands for a moment and bent down to come closer to Gespar's face.

"You can always choose to let go and die in the petty dignity you have left. I have a preference for watching people fall off cliffs," he said with a wicked smile, sure that Gespar would choose such an alternative. But Dakor had never known what had become of Gespar all those years he spent on Voronar. He only knew Gespar when he was among the SONS. He never knew Gespar through years of hauling barrels of salt up a cliff. Nor did he know about his overdeveloped shoulders and arms. Hanging off a cliff was what Gespar liked to do most when he spent time with Andiya, his beloved cat. He would often test her to see how long or how far she would go to try to save his life. They played long hours like that, and it was the most fun he would have with his cat who had died at the hands of his enemy.

Gespar didn't waste his chance and seized the opportunity. In that unsuspected moment, he hollered a name at the top of his lungs, taking everyone, especially Dakor, by surprise.

"LEANNE!" he shouted, remembering her name. That special name was given to him the last time he was dangling off a cliff right after Ezekiola had tapped into the Fountain of Fire, propelling him into the air. Upon hearing her name, Dakor started laughing. He turned his back to Gespar and looked over the opposite end to see which one of the girls was Leanne.

"IT'S NOW OR NEVER!" Gespar screamed his last words. In an unprecedented move, Gespar swung himself and snatched Ezekiola's arm that was within reach. In an instant, both were in a freefall.

On cue, a cacophony of sounds ensued—seeing Ezekiola fall off that cliff, deadly shouts flowed out of an enraged Dakor, cries emanated from the SONS, Yossan yelled for his life, but all those sounds were muffled by another powerful one. Leanne, unable to withstand the tension in her body, the rising fire that was inhabiting every inch of her since they arrived at the Watchtower, let that strange element erupt out of her in the form of her voice. She tore away from her assailant, sprang forward, falling on the ground. She screamed, and as she did, something more engulfed her scream, amplifying it. She couldn't tell whether the ear-piercing sound that reverberated all around came from her or not. It was deafeningly loud, and, in that instant, she shut her eyes and clamped her ears. When the piercing sound finally stopped, and she reopened her eyes, things were not quite as they had been. Leanne couldn't see. She could barely breathe. In fact, no one around could either. Dust was everywhere.

Chapter 18

The Lady of the Mountains

With shaky hands, Leanne grabbed her shirt and pulled it up to her nose. It was futile. Dust particles penetrated her nostrils in even larger quantities, causing her an intense coughing fit. She quickly shook her shirt, removing as much dust as she could, and brought it back to her nose. It helped, somewhat. But the dust wasn't settling. Her eyes burned, and tears streamed down her cheeks. Her body had barely adjusted to the changes when something else baffled her. She stilled her senses for a moment and listened. It was silence. The kind of silence that reigns in the aftermath of a calamity. A moment ago, everyone was yelling. And now, there was not a peep. Where is everyone?

She peered into the dust, but still could not see a thing, as if she was watching the world through a dirty lens, a sandstorm suspended in time. She patted the ground; it was the same texture as she had felt a moment ago when her palms had touched it. The disturbed dust that was once on the ground would just not clear away, nor settle down to its original position. Something was amiss. She could only see what was in proximity to her. She observed closely and noticed something strange. It wasn't just dust in front of her, but other particles. She crept towards a concentrated batch but did not understand what she was seeing. Bits of rocks mingled with the dust moving in odd patterns in the air, as if mimicking the motion they would if under water. It was simply unnatural. Suddenly, a shadow approached her from behind. She gasped and quickly moved away. To her relief, it was slow-moving and not much of a threat. In fact, the large mass she saw was so incredibly slow, she could easily follow its trajectory with her eyes. She looked wide-eyed, realizing what it was: the massive boulder she had been standing next to a moment ago was now literally floating in front of her. What's happening? That's when she heard the laugh. It was muffled, coming from afar, but Leanne could tell which direction it was coming from. It was a deep, hearty laugh, coming from a restrained belly that hadn't contracted in ages, which had finally been given a blessing to release an all-out guffaw.

It was Gespar, feverishly, boisterously, laughing whole-heartedly.

Trembling, Leanne forced herself up. Picking her way carefully, she made her way slowly through a miasma of dust. Why was Gespar laughing? Where were those men who had surrounded her moments ago? She took advantage of the dust to navigate a few steps closer to where her friends were standing.

"Helva? Daria?" she asked, her voice shaky.

"Over here!" Their voices came. Visibility, it seemed, was their main obstacle. She followed the sound, waving her arms in front of her on reflex, attempting to clear the dust. As she approached, she could hear the muffled coughs of her friends, then suddenly started hearing others coughing as well. Drawing closer to her friends, the octaves of the voices she heard were deeper. She reckoned the SONS were still close by. She saw shadows of her friends gathered in a small corner and touched them.

"What happened?" Leanne asked, troubled.

"I don't know, but something happened when you fell on the ground and screamed. Those men just let us go. I don't know where they are now, but they seem to be at a distance. We just can't see them," Helva said, grabbing a hold of her and Daria. They heard Gespar's laughter from afar.

"Let's go this way," Leanne said, leading her small crew. She felt confident the dust would camouflage them enough to help them escape.

"Gespar?" Leanne called as she walked carefully, relying solely on her memory of where the cliff was located, and where she had seen Ezekiola last fall in front of her eyes. She still hadn't processed what Gespar had done in that last moment. She knew Gespar only through Ezekiola's accounts of him and his adventures on Voronar. She was only now beginning to grasp his wild nature.

"Ah, you did it, Leanne, you did it!" she heard him say, elated, laughing again.

"Did what?" she asked, squinting. She still could not locate him.

"You removed order," he laughed again, unable to believe the extent of her power.

As the three ladies came to the edge of the cliff, they were finally able to catch a first glimpse of something: Gespar's shadow next to Ezekiola. Leanne did a double take. She looked wide-eyed at the image in front of her, as did Helva and Daria. Ezekiola and Gespar were both airborne. Floating. She looked up further, and could see shadows of other bodies, they were floating too.

"What do you mean 'removed order?'" Leanne asked Gespar, incredulous.

"You removed order and reintroduced us into chaos. That's right, you removed a force governed by the invisible world of your nature. Gravity. Our kind cannot operate when you do this," he said, chuckling.

Removed gravity? Leanne was dumbstruck.

"You will pay for this, Gespar!" Dakor's voice suddenly reverberated from somewhere in the air. Though they were several feet away, his shadow seemed to lurk closest to Gespar. His body was awkwardly moving in circles it seemed.

"Ha! Dakor, you should've known better than to capture women and expect nothing to result from it," Gespar said. His laughter ricocheted in the air.

"You're dead, Gespar! You hear me? DEAD!" Dakor spat out furiously from his airy position.

"Whoa, Leanne!" Helva whispered as Dakor continued to lash out. "This means, umm, that...umm..."

"Means what?" Leanne asked.

"That you tapped into the Fountain of Fire," Helva finished her sentence.

"What?! How?" Leanne replied, confused.

"How is it we're not floating?" Daria interjected, adding to the confusion. The three ladies exchanged looks and Helva quickly caught on, her face bearing an expression of wonder.

"Because it's a force of *our* nature. Leanne used the fountain's power to incapacitate the polar opposite—the male." Helva answered, grasping what she was witnessing. "But of course," she continued, as if speaking to herself, "it's the force that holds everything together in place, even the planets in our galaxy, yet you never see it. It works invisibly. Remove that force and chaos ensues. Brilliant," she said, slightly rapturous.

Leanne shook her head. "I don't know how this happened. I

just fell to the ground and I—" she trailed off, remembering the overbearing heat she felt on the inside. Her mind could just not explain the phenomenon. "Is that Ezekiola next to you?" she asked Gespar to be sure.

"Yes," he answered. Leanne sighed with relief.

"Leanne!" Yossan's voice was heard from behind. It was coming from the same direction where he had last been seen. "Over here, get me down!" he beckoned them. Subdued shouts were heard closer to him. Several shadows of the SONS moved closer to each other, grabbing one another, while one singular one stood out.

Realizing the land was theirs to move freely on, the three friends ran into the Watchtower. Inside, visibility was better. The dust there hadn't stirred as much. Suddenly, the shadowy figure of a female moved swiftly, and a thump was heard, followed by footsteps.

"Someone's leaving!" Leanne exclaimed nervously. They dashed up the stone stairs two at a time and stared out of the window. There, they saw a faint shadow move away.

"Someone's running away!" Daria exclaimed.

"Never mind her, grab that rope," Yossan said. The ladies looked up from the window, and there in front of them, they could see Yossan's body awkwardly hovering at their level. Yossan had seen a woman climb down from the rope that was hanging from the windowsill. Leanne quickly pulled the rope up that was tied to the windowsill, while Helva sat at the edge of the window, positioning herself. They swung it several times in Yossan's direction, but in vain.

"Can you try coming closer?" Helva asked Yossan.

"I'm trying," Yossan moved himself forward, waving his arms as if he were swimming. He wasn't sure if it was having any effect.

"Hold on, let me try," Daria said, switching places with

Helva. After several attempts at throwing the rope towards him, the situation looked worst, as if Yossan was floating away.

Leanne then took her turn. She dropped the rope at one point and extended her body as far as she could from the window. Her hand was finally able to connect with Yossan's, and as soon as he grasped her hand tight, the extraordinary force of gravity pressed Yossan down. Instantly, his weight dragged Leanne down too, and she screamed.

"THE ROPE! GRAB THE ROPE!" Helva yelled, while Daria and she both held onto Leanne. A once floating Yossan was now dangling off the edge of the Watchtower, his life in the hands of Leanne, and by extension, Helva and Daria. Anxious giggles at such an inappropriate time broke out from the ladies as they took miniature breaks to adjust and reposition themselves. Their efforts were inconceivably mixed with the reality that they could just all die if they fall off the Watchtower. A determined Yossan was finally able to grab the rope while holding Leanne tight onto him and successfully pulled both their bodies back up.

Meanwhile, the SONS were yelling madly in their language, and Dakor's commanding voice reverberated in the air like a thunderstorm gathering clouds. As if in conglomeration, they concentrated themselves in one zone.

"Don't touch any of them," Yossan said catching his breath, pointing to the shadows that looked like miniature dark clouds in the air. First, he found his old friend, Sayat. As if that invisible force bestowed by Leanne followed his touch, Yossan brought him down with the help of the rope, and in a blissful moment, hugged him deeply.

"You fools! This is not over! I will see you meet your doom!" Dakor's words fired out in a fit of rage. Suddenly, his shadow vanished. One by one, shadows once discernable disappeared. Only two could be seen from afar—Gespar and Ezekiola. Yossan motioned for everyone to follow him.

"Gespar, I'm here right at the edge where you were last. Can you try coming closer with Ezekiola?" Yossan asked. He tied the rope to a post located near the Watchtower and then to his waist, preparing himself.

"Yes," Gespar said and started doing strokes in the air. He maneuvered Ezekiola's motionless body, placing it in front of him so it could extend towards the cliff. He spun around aimlessly a few times, then finally got to a better spot where Yossan was able to see a leg.

"Stay still and hold on tight to him. You'll both fall when I touch him," Yossan instructed. As soon as Yossan grabbed Ezekiola's ankles, both succumbed to gravity. Aided with the knot at his waist, Yossan held himself in a position to support their weight. The ladies held onto the rope as well, pulling from behind.

It was only when they made it onto the ground that the severity of the damage hit them. Ezekiola lay unconscious, his face colorless, with blood oozing from behind his neck. Gespar immediately took his shirt off and pressed it against the back of his head to stop the bleeding. Gespar checked his eyes. They were bloodshot. If it wasn't for the small perceptible pulse felt at the wrist, Ezekiola's body looked lifeless.

"Don't touch him, he's been poisoned," Gespar said, scanning the rest of his body.

"What kind of poison?" asked Yossan.

"It comes from the Agiri sun. They prepared this for him," Gespar said knowingly. Gespar had gone searching for the sacred books in Agiri, only to come out with the terrifying knowledge of something else. The SONS had been tracking him long before he made his way to Circa, and caught Gespar right before he was able to warn Yossan.

"What is the Agiri sun?" Leanne asked, panic-stricken. Just seeing Ezekiola's motionless body sprawled on the ground caused her enormous turmoil. Now there was talk of poison.

"Agiri is a planet where the rays of its sun can be harvested to poison and kill. They infused a product with its essence to cause this. It wasn't a blade they used, but something else. This means they wanted him alive, but—" Gespar said, unable to finish his sentence, realizing the plot behind their risky plan.

"Will he live?" Leanne asked. No one answered.

"We need to find an antidote," Helva blurted. "I can find Gemins who can help."

"We've got no time for that. They'll be back for him. The SONS know they have a small window to act, and they'll use it," Gespar said, frowning. "You went too far this time, Dakor, too far," he said after a pause, speaking to himself.

"I have to alert the Emeralds," Yossan stated, meetings Gespar's eye. It was something Gespar wasn't ready to hear, nor confront. *I have no choice*, Yossan's eyes spoke.

"You can muster a legion of your warriors, but that won't save him now. He won't last. The Agiri poison is complex, and the antidote cannot be found here on Circa. We don't know half of what it's done," Gespar said, looking troubled. Yossan could hear the fear in his voice. Gespar looked downcast, his thoughts spiraling into darkness, a weight unlike any he had ever felt pressed down upon him. It was a life and death call. He's seen poison act out before, but poison from the Agiri sun was of another order. Very few survived the lethal effects of that wretched planet's sun. As he brooded over the matter, a thought suddenly flashed in his mind. He looked at Yossan, a flicker of hope gleamed in his eyes.

"There's one who can help. If the ladies take him to her now, he might survive," Gespar said, sounding hopeful.

"Who?" Yossan asked, perplexed.

"The Lady. Do you remember which portal brings them there?"

Yossan's eyes widened. "You want to send him to HER? Ezekiola can't walk on their land!" he protested.

"Exactly. This works to our advantage. Dakor won't ever take that path and send his warriors searching there," Gespar said.

"But he could die there!" Yossan argued against it.

"The Lady is the only one who can help! I am sure of it!" Gespar insisted.

"Which lady? What land? Where?" Helva, Leanne and Daria talked over each other, unable to follow the back and forth between Yossan and Gespar.

"The Lady of the Mountains," Gespar responded.

This time Helva spoke. "You want us three to bring him to the Lady of the Mountains, the land where no man can enter?" she said almost breathless. Being a Brown Belt student, she had learnt much about other worlds and dwellings. One that had always intrigued her was this famed Lady of the Mountains said to have great healing powers.

"Yes," he answered.

"But how can we bring Ezekiola?" Helva questioned the obvious. "The female chase, ensnare, trap, hunt and kill every man that walks on their land. We three ladies can enter, yes, but if Ezekiola touches their ground, they'll never let him out alive."

"He won't walk. A mare will carry him," Gespar answered, providing his jaw dropping solution. "You don't go against the law of their land this way," Gespar continued, then looked at Yossan. "Can you help me find a mare in the forest right here?" Pressed for time, overstressed, and with no other alternative to present him with, Yossan, who initially hesitated, conceded.

"Alright, follow me," Yossan said. He went to grab Ezekiola, but Gespar prevented him, taking the risk of carrying him on his back instead. The small group made their way to the nearest forest adjacent to the Watchtower. Yossan quickly went looking for a mare, while Gespar turned to Helva and Daria.

"Can you find something to slow down poison?" he asked. They both nodded. "And do you know how to make drowse essence from plants?"

"I do," Helva answered.

"Good. Bring me a handful," he said. A blend made from certain leaves was used to knock someone unconscious. Without questioning further, Helva moved swiftly to search for it. With everyone dispatched to do a chore, Gespar turned to Leanne.

"I need you to stand guard next to him. Don't touch him, the poison could still be acting. We'll be back with a mare," he instructed. He got up, and to her surprise, she saw Gespar take out a knife and rope, the very ones used by Yossan a moment ago. Stunned, she watched Gespar turn Ezekiola's body over and tie his hands behind his back.

"Precaution," he said, and left.

Leanne found the tying of the hands was taking it too far. The more she observed Gespar, the less she warmed to him. The man was outlandish and unpredictable. She brushed off his manners and focused on Ezekiola. This was the first time that day she was left alone with him. She closed her eyes, taking a moment to absorb the silence and whatever tranquility it could offer in the aftermath of what had transpired. How did all this just happen? She opened her eyes and looked at Ezeki-ola. She couldn't hear him breathe. Worried, she came closer, bringing her ears next to his mouth. This close at odd intervals, she could feel the soft warm breath of his inhale and exhale. Instinctively, she gently touched the scars on his cheekbones, completely forgetting Gespar's instruction to her a moment ago. The blood had dried on his face. She traced her fingers over the rest of his features. Suddenly, the phantasmagoric thought of waking him up with a kiss came to her. She had seen this happen so many times in fantasy stories told back in her world... how a prince can awaken a damsel from her slumber with a kiss. Foolish as it sounded, maybe *she* could wake a boy up this way using the fountain's power that was apparently in her. After all, Helva said it—Leanne had somehow tapped into the fountain's power. She stared at Ezckiola's lips. They were soft, slightly curved at the edges, nicely rounded, and in that moment, inviting. She looked around, no one was in her immediate surrounding. There was nothing to lose if she tried. Immersed in such rosy thoughts, she failed to see the flickering of his lashes as she closed her eyes and gently pressed her lips against his. When she pulled back, his eyes were wide open, giving her a penetrating stare.

"It's just like the first time we kissed," he said. She gasped and moved back.

"Don't be afraid," he said. Leanne stood motionless, her face stricken and pale. How did Ezekiola just awaken like that? Did the kiss work? He shifted his body sideways, and despite his hands being tied in the back, with effort, he managed to come up resting on his knees.

"Stay where you are," Leanne said shakily, slowly moving back, unsure of what was happening. She looked at his face. He was far from looking fresh. His eyes were blood red. He looked like he had just crawled out of a grave.

"I need your help. Please, Leanne," he pleaded, motioning his hands. As Leanne cautiously edged further away on her behind, Ezekiola slowly walked forward on his knees. For some reason, she was not reassured by his awakening at all. She saw him scan their environs, his eyes making a sudden stop where Gespar had left his knife, right next to a small bush. He suddenly shifted his gaze back to Leanne and in that instant, she spotted the devil in his eyes. Instinctively, she turned around and lunged forward to reach for the blade. With incredible agility, Ezekiola moved with his free legs, stunning her. He gained speed and right when Leanne caught the blade, he jumped on her, his body crashing over hers onto the ground. They tumbled around, whirling left and right in a wild match of who would gain control of the blade. With Ezekiola's hands attached, Leanne pushed him away, hitting wherever she could, not knowing where her blows landed. Groans were heard, but it didn't stop his resilience. She kicked him at one point, and he groaned in greater pain. Every time Leanne tried to break free from his grip, he caught her with his legs and tried to subdue her. After several attempts, he mounted her from behind, locking her body at hip level, crushing her beneath his weight while she was facing the ground. Luckily, both of her hands were still holding the blade tightly, compressed right under her chest.

"Get off of me!" she yelled.

"Give it to me!" he spoke roughly in her ear.

"I can't breathe," she said, panting.

"If you want to live, Leanne, you will give me that knife," he said, his breath heaving in unison with hers. Leanne tried to move, but the more she did, the more her lungs were crushed under his weight. Any effort spent to break free drained her energy further. At that awkward moment, she understood Gespar's warning and why he tied those hands. She just could not believe that the boy she was supposed to save was turning against her. She stayed immobile and passive for a small moment, making him think he had won this bout. Then, using one of her greatest faculties, she screamed at the top of her lungs.

"HELP!"

Almost instantly, a heavy load came off her. Gespar's strong hands gripped Ezekiola, shoving him aside on the ground.

"WHAT HAPPENED?" Gespar's voice thundered in the forest. Leanne turned over, catching her breath. Gespar saw the blade in her hands, then saw her face. Bruised on one cheek, blood seeping from the other, her hair wild, her body trembling. He looked at Ezekiola, and turned him roughly on his stomach, putting a knee on his back.

"Are you alright? What happened?" Daria and Helva rushed over.

"Go ahead Leanne, tell them what you did! Tell them about you kissing me," Ezekiola suddenly said underneath Gespar's hold, shocking the witnesses who heard him. His voice sounded terribly different. Everyone looked at Leanne, with puzzled looks on their faces. Leanne could not believe what she was hearing.

"Did you kiss him?" Gespar asked, incredulous. Leanne was speechless. She couldn't bring herself to answer such a plain question.

"Oh, she kissed me alright, she wanted it, you should have seen her when—" Gespar pressed his knee higher to his upper back, causing him to shut up and growl in pain.

"Hush! Did you find what I asked for?" Gespar asked Helva, distraught. She nodded and handed Gespar a poultice covered in part of her shirt she'd ripped off, in order to carry it.

"Be careful, it's potent," she said. Gespar compressed it on Ezekiola's nose, testing it, instantly knocking him out. He turned over to look at Leanne.

"I asked you to stand guard and not touch his face. He is not who you think he is right now! We don't know what this poison did to him, nor what it can do to others who touch him," he stated. Gespar had suspected the poison would do this. The reality of it however hit Leanne like a ton of bricks. Gespar was ready to bear the effects of that poison on him by manipulating him, all the while trying to keep everyone else at bay. At that moment, she was appalled by her imprudence.

Yossan arrived with a mare. His eyes registered shock when he saw Gespar pressing down on Ezekiola's back. He looked at everyone else after and unravelled the story fast.

"He woke up?" he was quick to ask Gespar, who nodded in turn.

"He's out again, the poultice worked—but he's definitely not himself," Gespar said, staring hard into Leanne's eyes to pass the message again. They both placed Ezekiola on the mare, carefully tying him onto it. They spent a while going back and forth with alternatives on how to best keep him in place and unconscious until he was with the Lady of the Mountains. They placed the drowse mix close to his neck, where he could smell it easily.

"Follow me," Yossan said after they were done. The Emeralds knew most of the portals on Circa. He turned his attention over to Helva, explaining on how to get to their destination.

"There's no need of staffs. The Lady will bring you back," he said at the end, making his voice deep and reassuring. Helva nodded. Right before entering the portal, Gespar held the ladies back for a short moment, too, and added one last piece of advice:

"Remember, the Lady heals. Don't be afraid," he said.

The ladies crossed the portal anxiously, not looking back. The mare was calm, steady, a reassuring presence. Ezekiola's body was bound tight onto it. They could only hope for a smooth course. The land of the Lady of the Mountains bore its name well. Mountains spiked the landscape wherever they walked. Valleys comprised the areas in between, and steep cliffs made it a haven for fowls, with an all-encompassing view enticing any flying animal to make its home there. They walked quietly at first, with Helva leading the mare, Daria in the middle, and Leanne walking last. Since the incident in the forest, Helva's brows remained furrowed.

"What happened back there, Leanne? Did you really kiss him?" she asked, her back to her friends. Leanne flushed. Not again. It was bad enough when Gespar scolded her, acting as if he was her father.

"Yes, and I shouldn't've," she responded briskly.

"That's all right. Who knows if I would've done the same if it was Borghis," Helva said pensively.

"He just attacked you like that?" Daria asked this time.

"He saw the knife Gespar left behind and we both went for it," Leanne answered. Although she was trailing behind, Leanne could sense the array of thoughts circulating in their heads like active molecules.

"It's the poison. It must have ignited Zeke and raised him or something. Ezekiola would never dare do that," Daria reasoned. They went quiet for a moment. The subject seemed to have died off.

"Make him pay for it," Helva said, suddenly.

"What?" Leanne asked.

"Make him pay for what he did," she repeated.

"Make Ezekiola pay for what he did? But he wasn't himself. He was acting like his twin—"

"Doesn't matter which one he was. Zeke, Ezekiola, Zek, whichever one he thinks he is, make him pay for it! Every action has a consequence! Maybe he'll have better control of his other self, you never know," she blurted. A groan was heard from Ezekiola, as if he had heard that very statement. Helva immediately brought the poultice beneath his nose. "That's it, pass out," she said, prompting the first chuckles among the ladies.

"He can't hear you," Daria said.

"Yes, he can," Helva contested. "If he can smell that mix, he can hear us talk. Both go into his brain; we just can't see it. Maybe we should continue talking so he unconsciously registers all of this."

The sound of leaves rustling drowned out what Helva was saying. Wind picked up and trees stirred, stopping the ladies abruptly in their tracks. As they slowly continued to trek along the path, they noticed something that made them cringe. The leaves on the trees dried as soon as they passed them, flowers wilted just as swiftly, as if time was rampaging through them, speeding up their death.

"What's happening?" Leanne asked, astonished. She noticed that once they passed those areas, the flowers and trees came back to life, as if the mere shadow of her and her friends brought a temporary death to the landscape.

"Keep walking, the Lady probably knows we're here. As long as Ezekiola is not attacked, we should be fine," Helva said, coolly. Leanne glanced at the cliffs, and the small cracks visible here and there between the cliffs, wondering if something would emerge from them.

"Where is the Lady of the Mountains exactly?" Leanne asked. Both Daria and Helva looked upwards. "The highest mountain there, right at the top. That's where Yossan said to bring Ezekiola."

"Helva, do you know what she looks like?" Daria asked. Helva shook her head.

"That far uphill?" Leanne asked. Helva nodded. She looked at the mare who was unaffected by any of her questionings.

"Stay confident, the mare can carry him upwards. It's just the peak part that could be difficult. But we should get there safely. Let's keep walking," Helva motioned for everyone to continue.

"I don't want to scare anyone, but we have brown Gemins following us," Daria stated a moment after. Brown Gemins, different from the green ones on Circa, popped their heads in and out of caves, displaying mischievous looks in their eyes. They drew close to the horse but were quickly chased away by Helva.

After a solemn walk, the brown Gemins they had chased a moment ago returned with a larger crowd. They giggled and made sounds that agitated the mare for the first time.

"Little pests! They want to knock the horse down. Shoo, shoo away!" Helva warded them off as best she could. Daria and Leanne helped this time. Birds now flocked above. They circulated above ritualistically, as if readying themselves to swoop down to eat a carcass soon. With the commotion of the Gemins, the mare decided to stop. It neighed, shifting its body left and right.

"This is not good; she's not moving forward. We must calm her down," Helva said. Daria grabbed a stick and scared the Gemins gathering in ever larger numbers. For some reason, Daria's shooing seemed to work. They dispersed quickly, going back into their hiding spots in the caves.

"Wow! Did you see how fast they ran back to their—" as Daria turned around, her face suddenly went white with fear, and the rest happened in an instant. Her body limped, her eyes rolled back, and she fell to the ground. Helva spun around to look in the same direction, and just then the horse reared, Ezekiola, too, fell, and the mare took off. All Leanne caught was a glimpse of Helva getting propelled in the air by a powerful gush of wind, which sent her flying in the air. A moment later, Leanne too fell to the ground, pushed back by an invisible force.

"You bring death into my land!" a voice hissed.

Leanne screamed. Noise that wasn't there before suddenly filled her ears. There was a screeching sound as if the land had been disturbed from a deep slumber. Leanne instinctively crawled towards Ezekiola and grabbed him, pulling him in her arms and off the ground as best she could. She heard the flapping of massive wings. She looked up, horrified at that flying thing. Terror flashed in her eyes. She knew what it was. The seventeen-foot winged being, the few who survived Circa's massacre who scattered off to other worlds. A Surran. It was one thing to see it on a wall, and quite another to come face to face with one. How could it possibly be living here?

"He's not dead! Please don't kill us!" Leanne pleaded, trembling. She screamed again when she saw and heard the land cracked beneath her, as if readying to swallow her.

"He reeks of death! I can smell him mountains away! How dare you foul bodies from Circa enter here!" the Surran scolded. While Leanne was mortified and speechless facing the Surran, Helva crawled next to her. Though she had little space to think in such a nerve-wracking moment, Helva suddenly realized something that could be of help.

"She's not from Circa. She's from Planet Blue," Helva said, hoping this revelation would change the Surran's stance. Upon hearing those words, the Surran looked at Helva, its demeanor changed. The Surran approached Leanne, sniffing the air, as if verifying the origin of her essence.

"Why are you with their kind?" it asked, looking intensely at Leanne.

"They are my friends and he's been poisoned. We were sent here to see the Lady of the Mountains so she can heal him."

"He is from Circa," the Surran said knowingly. "Why should we help and heal those who have slayed us in the past?"

it asked, eyes narrowing. The question took Leanne by surprise. She wasn't asking the Surran for help, but rather the Lady of the Mountains. Leanne stared wide eyed at the Surran, not knowing what to answer.

"You see, those from Circa are unworthy of healing. None of them deserve to live. And this boy too shall perish!" It screeched, once again flapping its wings violently in the air. In desperation, Leanne, remembering something special about the Surrans in her history class, finally said something.

"Please don't! He revived the Fountain of Fire!" she said.

The Surran abruptly stopped beating its wings and looked suspiciously into Leanne's eyes again, as if evaluating the truth of that statement. Holding its monstrous gaze, Leanne wasn't sure if this was going to be her last moment alive.

"The Fountain of Fire?" it asked.

"Yes, the Fountain of Fire," she repeated. "Him and I, we both revived it. Your prophecies speak of it, don't they, of the Fountain of Fire?" Leanne repeated what she learned in her class. It had been something that had sparked her curiosity about their species, at how the Fountain of Fire was spoken of even in their own writings. While the Surran evaluated her under its gaze, Leanne decided to speak some more.

"And, and I give you my Word, that you will share in the glory of the Fountain of Fire," she declared, knowing well she was going over her head with this. She was ready to do whatever it took to keep everyone alive. The Surran tilted its head, whether mocking her or considering her words, Leanne couldn't tell.

"And how will you honor such a Word?" it asked, putting Leanne on the spot. Since she had gone this far, Leanne spoke without thinking.

"I will stay here until my Word to you is fulfilled," she

blurted. "But he must be healed first by the Lady of the Mountains."

The Surran observed her for a while.

"If what you say is true about the Fountain of Fire, I will hold you to your Word. But if you are lying, he will die. Give him to me," it said. Their agreement seemed to be sealed.

The massive body of the Surran picked Ezekiola's body up, surprising Leanne with its gentleness. Like a child in a mother's arms, it first turned to look at the sun, then positioned itself relative to it, so that the sun was behind it. The Surran placed Ezekiola's body back on the ground. Then, in a magnificent display that put to shame any of the painting of the walls in the tavern that day, its wings unfolded majestically, stretching themselves to their maximum. When the light of the sun touched its wings, they became almost translucent, and a spectrum of colors emanated through them, as if the rays of the sun were penetrating its wings. It was a variation of colors Leanne had never seen. Even the most fantastic pattern of colors on the wings of exotic butterflies fell short of its beauty. Like a cascading waterfall, blazing light radiated from them. The Surran shifted its wings, casting a shadow over Ezekiola's body. Upon being touched by that light, Ezekiola's body shook with slight movements as if bathed in it, and his chest rose higher, as if the light penetrated his skin, filling his lungs. To her surprise, under the illumination, Leanne could see a subtle but visible thread of light, radiating a different grade of brightness, connecting her to Ezekiola, as if he were a continuity of her. Realization dawned. There it was, the link between them, the Fountain of Fire, the very one that had been sealed between them by the Emeralds. What was invisible was now visible under the light of the Surran's wings. She could see the flames of the fountain, in motion, as if they were dancing. And so did the Surran who was healing him. Leanne stared at those dancing lights, hypnotized by them. She didn't know how long the healing session lasted, but it was Ezekiola, who suddenly opened his eyes, and snapped her out of her trance.

"Leanne!" he said, recognition awoke in him. His eyes were a lively blue, vivid, and full of spirit. "What happened?" he gasped when he saw the great shadow of a Surran standing in front of him. Leanne grabbed his hand. "It's alright," she said, as he backed away from the Surran, bringing himself closer to her. She observed Ezekiola for a moment and immediately was struck by his skin. There were no more cuts on his face or hands, his cheeks were rosy, full of life, and the back of his neck was whole.

"You spoke truth," the Surran said, folding back its wings. "I stand witness to the Fountain of Fire. And you are witness to his healing and the Word I have been given. You and the boy will stay here until your Word is fulfilled. There are many in my clan who wish to speak to you," it said, then shifted its gaze to Helva and Daria who were standing further away.

"As for you two, you shall go back to Circa and deliver a message to your warriors," it said, in a voice filled with spite. Suddenly, the air filled with Surrans. They came landing one at a time and approached Helva and Daria. There seemed to be some telepathic communications between them as they knew what to do. A tearful Helva helped Daria stand up, still in a semi-conscious state, and without being able to say another word, they were escorted back to Circa through the same portal they had entered.

Upon her friends departing, Leanne found herself in a stillness unlike any other. She looked at Ezekiola with relief and dread.

What have I done? Her first thought emerged. For some reason, her next thought went straight to Gespar. Like a ray of a sun breaking through a crack of stormy clouds, something struck her. It was the sentence Gespar said before they entered the forest: *"Remember, the Lady heals. Don't be afraid."* Gespar had known. The Surrans were the Lady of the Mountains. This was a dwelling of theirs. With the greatest healing abilities, wielding invisible forces, able to give life or bring death. She just hoped that the Emeralds would find a way to honor the Word she gave the Surrans without starting a new war and somehow, some way, bring her and Ezekiola back on Circa.

Chapter 19

The Sacred Spot

"Where are they? Where are the SONS?" Igor Sanza, the leader of the Emerald warriors arrived frantic and breathless, half expecting to be immersed in a monumental battle, half ready to die at the hands of the SONS. His Emerald warriors, however, who had arrived well before him, looked at him with regret. Igor had no inkling of the news he was about to receive.

"The SONS are all gone. Every one of them," one of his warriors said curtly.

"What?" Igor blurted, stupefied.

"Ezekiola is also gone, along with three ladies. They were actually sent away by..."

"Sent away where?" Igor demanded immediately.

"They were sent to the Lady of the Mountains," the warrior answered.

"WHAT?!"

As more details filled his ears, Igor became livid. His face changed several hues just listening to this dreadful briefing in the middle of the forest. His mind was like a bouncing ball, unable to follow the rapidity of the news being delivered to him. As his warriors explained the sequence of events, Igor's head bobbed around turning left and right, up and down, looking at the Watchtower, then at the portal used by the ladies, the strands of rope used to tie the mare, and finally the bloody, purplish-blue cloth on the ground used to stop the bleeding behind Ezekiola's neck.

"And which raving lunatic led them to the Lady of the Mountains?" Igor asked finally.

In the moment of silence that ensued, the crowd parted. As they did, two men stood amid the Emeralds, and all eyes rested on them. Yossan, standing firmly, was ready to confront whatever was coming his way. And right next to him was Gespar, who stood still as a rock as if in the middle of a tempestuous sea, carrying the countenance of a man who had seen many storms in his life. When Igor's eyes landed on Gespar, an old enemy who had caused deep scars in his past, he turned into a furnace ready to consume his foe by fire. He thought he would never see that bastard again in his life. He was clearly wrong.

"Stay calm, just let me explain," Yossan gestured steadily with his hands as he saw Igor stomping towards him.

"Move away!" Igor commanded Yossan through clenched teeth.

Over a hundred Emerald warriors showed up, and more were pouring in, as if a major battle was about to take place. But the SONS were gone, and the show was long over, with Yossan and Gespar having clearly stolen it. As the Emeralds circled the duo, Gespar and Yossan stood as targets in the center.

Igor stared hard into Yossan's eyes as if he was someone who had switched camps. For his part, Yossan deliberately stood in front of Gespar, his body acting as a shield against the weapons about to strike an old enemy.

"This filth has sold his soul!" Igor spat out. "And you, Yossan, just let him put innocent lives in danger! How could you!"

"This was none of his doing, but mine. I led them to the portal to see the Lady," Yossan stated firmly.

"No, that's not true!" Gespar spoke over Yossan's shoulder.

"Shut your mouth! Don't you dare speak in my presence. You should have died ages ago!" Igor was just short of jumping on Gespar. "Move out of the way, Yossan!" he ordered again.

"He saved the boy," Yossan stated without wavering, convinced there was a way to drive reason into the Emerald leader's mind.

"SAVED you say? He sent Ezekiola and three more to their deaths!"

"This was my decision, not his," Yossan argued.

"Again, not true!" Gespar interjected once more. Upon hearing this, Igor pushed Yossan aside, but in an astounding display of disobedience, Yossan refused to give him any space and blocked Igor from reaching Gespar. The Emerald warriors tightly encircled the three combatants, yet hung behind, waiting for a clear order from their leader.

"I will have you killed for this!" Igor glared hard at Yossan, as a final warning.

"Let him through Yossan!" Gespar said from behind, as if he was his superior. "Go ahead, Igor, say it! You want to fight, don't you? Say you want to fight me! You're the child that never grew," Gespar said calmly, escalating Igor's fury to a new level.

"You're a disgrace! You should be rotting in hell! Haven't you shamed yourself enough, entering Circa and walking on our grounds? You think you can waltz back in here and gain honors for what you've done? Our mother should have never given birth to filth like you!" Igor hammered those words out and spat on the ground. Yossan closed his eyes for a moment and sighed. Here was the reason why the Emeralds circling them stayed somewhat behind, giving Igor his space. Everyone knew they were siblings—half-brothers—from the same mother. And they didn't need much convincing to prove their lineage, they carried similar traits. But Gespar and Igor thought they would never see each other again, and now here they were.

"It's a good thing you're not a mother, else you'd be dumping everything that came out of you. We call those kinds of creatures the bottom of the barrel." Gespar said smoothly.

At the utterance of those words, Yossan's body was spectacularly tossed aside and in one swift move, Igor jumped on Gespar. The two hit the ground, rolling. The combustible energy stored in Igor for the battle he had just missed against the SONS, coupled with the deep wrath against his errant brother finally erupted. On the other hand, Gespar, having just brushed aside death at the hands of the SONS, was in an excited state, hovering on the edge of madness. His energy was more of the kind to greet death, just to see if he'd come out of it alive this time around. Within moments, Igor stripped off his Emerald Robe to give himself more space to move, including his belt. As Yossan was about to intervene, several Emeralds held him back.

"Stay back, all of you!" Igor exclaimed. To Yossan's shock, the Emeralds were about to let Igor take his fury out on his brother Gespar, unbelievably pulling him back so he wouldn't interrupt. Instead of performing their duties, the warriors looked eager to watch the spectacle, in anticipation of what would happen next, as if this was the long-awaited fight of the century.

Gespar's arms and upper chest being highly developed, he came in from the right angle, pounding Igor several times using his knuckles and elbows, and within moments, caused lesions on both Igor's cheeks and mouth, knocking him off balance. Igor shaking it off came back up, and struck Gespar hard in the chest, causing his breath to jam. Momentarily, the air got stuck in his chest, and Gespar couldn't breathe. Igor took advantage of this and beat Gespar repeatedly to knock him out. Normally, anyone would have succumbed to Igor's heavy blows, but Gespar, being who he was, took punishment much longer than average. He endured it all and managed to get back up and struck Igor down in turn. Again, they rolled around like wild-cats on the ground, punching each other when the opportunity arose, striking each other's head, slamming elbows into faces, kicking and kneeing. The movements were so swift, there were times that the onlooking Emeralds could not tell who had control. Only when both bodies were on the ground, almost immobile, that everyone realized a little too late that Gespar had been choking Igor with his forearms, his neck held tight in a lock. He maintained his hold, giving no space for counter maneuvers. Gespar could feel the life force slowly leaving Igor's body, and it was at this strange instance where Igor's life rested in his hands that Gespar saw something. A serendipitous image came in his mind, so powerful it was that it brought him to a dead stop.

What happened next could be measured in fleeting moments. Gespar's mind entered into a sort of oblivion. An issue in his life he had never solved until that moment came flashing forth like a lighthouse beckoning him. He retraced the image—it was the one of his hands hovering above the seashore on Voronar, trying to find the sacred spot where air, water and land met, there where it was neither wet nor dry. He let the image guide him, and a part of him became like his hovering hand, glancing at the scene from above. There he could see it, the patterns of his life, how they kept repeating themselves. He saw how that animal soul of his was controlling him in the present moment, the same way that had been controlling his every move all his life. He saw how easily swayed he was by emotions, always reactionary, his inner life continually influenced by outside conditions, and never the other way around. A clarity shone forth. It was not for him to take away Igor's life. This would be a repeat of a pattern he was running every cycle of his life. He let go of Igor.

As he did, Igor ferociously leaped and gripped Gespar's neck in turn, while a flood of Emeralds came down on both. As if watching an event as an observer, none of it mattered to Gespar. It didn't matter if Igor got his revenge, beat him to pieces, nor if he lived. The weight of all the worlds in which he had lived suddenly lifted off his shoulders, and a serenity unlike any he had ever felt settled in him, as if it had been there all along, locked up until now. His mind communed with something greater, experiencing a freedom unlike any he had ever known. Whatever path lay ahead of him, Gespar was willing to follow and submit himself to it and let that superior voice direct his emotions, thoughts, and actions in life.

"What's the meaning of all this?" A powerful voice broke the crowd apart. Several Brown and Blue Robes had just shown up, and at their head was the Count, alongside Nomi.

"Get off of him!" the Count demanded.

Buried beneath Igor and a hoard of Emeralds who had jumped on him, Gespar met the Count's eyes, and in an instant, a wave of emotions washed over him. To the Count, the mere sight of Gespar gave him a long-awaited moment of hope. To Gespar, it proffered atonement not many around him would understand.

Igor stood up, out of breath, his face bloody with purple bruises and one eye bleeding from a cut. He looked as if he had just escaped a pack of wild animals.

"We have traitors on Circa, one new and the other, ancient as our planet!" he lashed out, pointing to Yossan, then Gespar. "And they both sent Ezekiola and several ladies to their death!"

"You're wrong!" Yossan burst. "Gespar saved Ezekiola and brought into play the fountain's power in the girl. I witnessed both," he said, addressing the Count. "We sent the women in the land of the Lady to heal Ezekiola. He was heavily poisoned. We can only hope for his healing and wait for their return."

"Even if they make it out alive, this one act cannot exonerate Gespar for his past wrongs! He has worked, fueled, nourished the evil we see being perpetrated today! His name, his legacy must be ended."

"Mind yourself, Igor! The Count oversees the order of Emeralds. You don't decide his fate like that!" a Blue Robe standing next to the Count spoke out.

"Gespar is a prisoner, not an Emerald! He is unworthy to live!" Igor continued, enraged. The emotional steam produced from his fight with Gespar was nowhere close to being dispersed.

"And what do you know of the times Gespar has lived, or what he's worthy and unworthy of?" the Count responded, addressing Igor. "Gespar has lived many lives just in this one life of his, and died in them as well, whether under the governance of the SONS, the Emeralds before, the salt harvesting striver he was, a seeker in barren lands, a traitor once, a prisoner many times, a hero to some, a sworn enemy to others. You can kill him a thousand times over and it will still not be enough to quench that thirst in you. You speak with a voice coming from a well without a bottom, with an appetite that cannot be satiated. Tell me, who is the prisoner here? What sound decision can come from such a confined mind? And how long will you hold on to your wrath?" The forest seemed to have gone quiet in that instant, not even a rustling of a leaf could be heard.

"Are you saying there will be no justice?" Igor asked, stunned.

"Release from anger does not prevent justice. They are two separate things that play out side by side. And I will add this; you seek also to chastise him but ignore the ways penance can be settled through a variety of acts than can do more good, even for the victim."

Unable to digest any of those words spoken by the Count, Igor tossed everyone out of his way and went off into the woods. As a few Emeralds started following him, the Count intervened.

"Leave him, he needs to have a conversation with himself," he said to the small group of followers. The Count then turned to Yossan and asked: "Where did you say the ladies and Ezekiola went?" A twinkle was perceptible in his eyes. Yossan had just begun relating the events as they transpired when a surprising new voice broke through the crowd.

"WHERE IS HE?!" A woman was walking towards the Emeralds, with someone else almost limping next to her.

"GESPAR!" she screamed next, as if her life depended on it. The Emeralds turned around to see the shadow of a female, struggling to carry someone half-conscious by her side. A crazed look was perceptible on her face even from afar, but as she approached, her expression morphed into repulsion as soon as her eyes landed on Gespar.

"How could YOU!" she yelled.

"Helva? Daria?" Nomi spoke hesitantly, slowly approaching her. Helva could not see her headmaster, nor the Count, or any of the Blue and Brown Robes standing right before her. She had only eyes on Gespar as an outlet for her fury.

"You knew! You knew! How could you have sent us there!" her voice grew steadily louder. Gespar was taken aback not by her presence and Daria's, but by the absence of two other bodies.

"Where are they?" he asked, shaken. Both Leanne and Ezekiola were missing from the crew.

"You fool! They are with the Surrans!" Helva said as her eyes swelled up. Upon hearing the name Surrans, a hum broke out in the crowd as several Emeralds shifted uneasily.

"We were brought back, and they weren't," Helva continued. "Leanne gave them a Word, and they can't leave their world until her Word to them is honored! We could not bring her and Ezekiola back. We had to leave them there," she said and finally collapsed in tears.

"What was the Word?" The Count asked.

"She revealed to them that Ezekiola and she had revived the Fountain of Fire and said that the Surrans shall share in the glory of that sacred fire. They will not let Leanne nor Ezekiola go until Leanne's Word is honored. And they asked us to deliver this special message to you Emeralds," Helva mustered her courage through teary eyes to finish. "Those who have slayed them in the past must come forward and face them in the land of the Lady of the Mountains."

Upon hearing this, the Count gazed at the unsure faces of the Emerald warriors around him, some who he could tell were gripped by horror. They did not expect this kind of battle. It wasn't one that could be waged on the spur of the moment. None present had fought Surrans before. Now, this battle was on their doorstep.

"Prepare yourselves," the Count said and turned to Gespar: "Your fate is tied to the boy and the girl now. What becomes of you will be an act of your will, no one else's. What will you do?"

"Face them," Gespar said, knowing full well that he wouldn't be so lucky with a third brush with death in a single day. "I will go first," he declared, hoping to spare some lives.

Chapter 20

Of Beginnings and Becoming

On the eve of the last day of school, a violent storm struck Cypress School. By morning, it looked like the heavens had waged the greatest war yet against the plant kingdom, wreaking havoc. As Brown Robes walked in the Black Forest through debris of every kind, an uncomfortable silence permeated the air. Not even the main paths were visible. Some Brown Robes even stopped counting dead trees and assessing damages. It was of no use. In every direction, trees had succumbed to the storm. This was unprecedented and the whole school volunteered to clean-up. It was no surprise then that Headmaster Nomi showed up in the Forest Council's quarters. But he didn't show up only to manage the catastrophe. Something new and worrisome started making waves in his school. As much as he never meddled in the affairs of the Forest Council as a rule, a grave line had been crossed. Many of the students at Cypress School started showing symptoms of a respiratory infection, and he had just received confirmation that it was fungi related. Despite previous warnings that the Forest Council received to settle this matter, it remained untreated, so much so that visible mold could now be found inside the Sanctuary. In the aftermath of this natural disaster, notably of the soil disruption, Nomi worried this would further the spread and increase infections.

As such, Nomi's exchange with Falco Rasspan, the head of the Forest Council, was in full swing when Atlas arrived on site. Nomi asked him to be present, with papers in hand, ready to answer questions. Nomi had remained patient with Falco. But with the latest incident, Nomi was about to strike two birds with one stone. He began by presenting Falco with his findings on the voting and election rules.

"This is archaic outdated material!" Falco spat out, waving a hand in the air dismissively, as if brushing away an annoying fly.

"Not so. It's valid, and it's in the Cypress City Archives. Hand me those copies, Atlas," Nomi requested. Atlas soldierly shuffled through a series of documents in front of Falco's blazing eyes, pulling out several pieces of paper, with an elegant stamp on the top of each page. It was the emblem of the City Archives. Indeed, while Atlas was rummaging through ancient books in those archives, he unraveled a most surprising morsel of information that had been forgotten until now.

"Here, take a look. A true copy signed by the Silver Robe, who is the custodian of the Cypress City Archives, stating this to be factual and in effect. This rule has never been nullified. You needed to include one Gemin representative in your election to become Head of the Forest Council, and you did not. You excluded them according to the minutes of your election. In fact, a notice wasn't even sent to the Gemins about this election."

"For ONE Gemin?!" Falco erupted. "This representation is feeble! I still would have been appointed head!"

"It doesn't matter. The procedure wasn't followed, and the

election is invalidated. As you say, it's important to stick to rules and abide by them. We cannot make exceptions to long-standing rules, even if they seem irrelevant to you."

"No one in the past followed such rules! I should not be the one to bear this correction!" Falco challenged, his eyebrows creased so heavily, not a gap was visible between them.

"Unfortunately, since we discovered this just now, it will be applied immediately. We cannot go back in time and annul the past, but we're lucky enough to apply the correction to the present. The present being you," Nomi maintained his stance.

"This is preposterous! Even if you revoke me now, I will hold another election and immediately be reelected by majority vote!"

"To all the members here!" Nomi raised his voice and addressed the Brown Robes who crowded the Sanctuary, eager to follow the heated debate. Even some Gemins approached, hearing the voice of the headmaster. "I would think twice before reappointing Falco Rasspan as your head! Even if you were blindfolded, you could see how things are falling apart here under his care. The Sanctuary is rotting, the vegetation around the Sanctuary is at its worst, and overspreading this flora is a dangerous growth, impacting the health of my very own students. A simple matter such as hygiene has degenerated so quickly under his governance, that now we have the spread of disease knocking on our door."

"What is happening here is not because of us, it's because of those Gemins!" As Falco said those words, additional Gemins approached. "They have made things worse! They are not of our kind! *They* are the pestilence who spread disease!"

Truth was that word of Falco had spread among the Gemins, too. After they found out about Borghis, the Exit Staff, and the treatment of some of their friends, including new rules that Falco sent out even for them to follow, things suspiciously started to fall apart around the Sanctuary. It seemed every time a Gemin passed by their quarters, trees lost their leaves, bushes died overnight, vegetable gardens were razored to the ground by some unknown hoard of insects. And while everything was in dire state around the Sanctuary, the Gemins laid back, almost enjoying the dilemma.

"What is happening here is that you have ignored them while suffocating them with new rules. If *you* don't play by the rules, long-standing rules, they ignore the forest. Simple as that. They can do far more damage by simply neglecting things. Gemins, you should know, are much more skilled than us at caring for life in the plant kingdom," Nomi lectured. "And I should inform you, that all decisions taken from the date you were elected are now invalid, including the expulsion of students rendered under your verdict. I have already advised the city."

"This is foul play! FOUL PLAY I say!" Falco burst, addressing his crowd like a peacock plucked of its feathers. The murmur between the Brown Robes grew louder. "Listen! Listen to me! HUSH! All of you! LISTEN TO ME!! This forest is mine! They're trying to steal it away from me!"

While such tempestuous dialogues took place in the forest, the White Mountains on Circa were about to host an auspicious visit on that day. Bedecked by what looked like gargoyles standing atop every peak, the foothills of the White Mountains were filled with their kind. In Circa's calendar, this would later be marked as a landmark day, one which even the greatest oracles could not have foretold. In a hidden spot in those mountains, a ceremony was about to take place. The Emeralds stood in formation on land, gathered among them were the Purple Robes, who were masters of ceremony, as well as the Silver, White, Brown, Red and Blue Robes among others. Like watchtowers themselves, the Surrans had been invited to attend by none other than Gespar. Indeed, after entering the land of the Lady of the Mountains, Gespar had struck a madman's deal with them. The Surrans were gathered in large numbers, standing on mountain peaks, graced with a spectacular view of the crowd below. It was the first time in ages they had set foot back on Circa. Standing below, the Count and Igor Sanza, the leader of the Emeralds, who despite having settled only half his issues, knew better than not to present himself. Across them were a group of larger Surrans, known as the Elderly. In this inner circle stood Gespar, and next to him were another two his size who he had brought back with him after entering the land of the Lady of the Mountains. Ezekiola and Leanne, now accustomed to seeing so many Surrans, had come home. A Word was about to be spoken, a pact was about to be made. It would include a unique commitment from Gespar—his life to forever be in service of the Surrans, to live with them, to work towards the consummation of the Word given to them, and to be freed only after its fulfillment. Alongside Circa's representatives were eleven other representatives from the veiled planets, making a total of twelve, those who were the original activators of the Fountain of Fire. For what lay ahead of them, this would become a key decision. As for the Surrans, the Fountain of Fire was prophesized in their own writings and had long been awaiting this fateful moment. They were to be the link that would seal and protect the twelve planets and be instrumental in diffusing that sacred fire. The glory of the Fountain of Fire would now be extended to include them. This was the Word they wanted honored.

When the ceremony was over, and everyone made their way back to their homes, Ezekiola seized a moment to speak to the Count alone. There were a few things that had been tormenting him. Although he was physically healed, Ezekiola's memory had undergone trauma. He did not remember most of

Zeke's life, but everything that transpired on the Watchtower with Dakor remained. Even of his own life as Ezekiola, he simply forgot things and could not bring back some memories. But once in a while, there were cracks. Like water that enters through the smallest crevasses, strange memories seeped into his mind. When he finally had the opportunity to speak with the Count in privacy, he didn't shy away.

"Something's been bothering me, and I don't know how to live with this. Zeke, my brother, is often on my mind. Sometimes I feel one with him, as if I'm actually him and what he did and how he lived takes me over," he stated.

The Count paused, assessing him, and answered with compassion.

"When you find yourself in that state, focus not on what you had been. Put your attention on this new beginning. Remember always that guilt is a powerful weapon that they will use against you to interfere with your progress. Be prepared and ready for this. It will come at different times, clothed in new attire, idolizing the past and your wrongdoings, all to arrest what you can become."

Ezekiola shook his head. Even though he understood what the Count said, something else didn't register for him.

"I still don't understand," he paused, uncertain. "How could you still want me in your ranks when you know I've served the SONS?" he asked bluntly, as if he were one and the same as Zeke. The Count looked at him, and Ezekiola could tell he was moved by something, as if the question rekindled memories of his own.

"Your roots may have gone deep down into the darkness of the ground, but above ground, take solace knowing the same tree who knows of dark depths rises tall, producing something far more superior than its lowest parts: fruits that can nourish the many. Those trees are all around you if you only look," he said, a knowing look in his eyes. "And the one thing I would ask you to remind yourself of every day is this: You are never alone." He emphasized those words. They were to be the last words spoken to him by the Count that day. Ezekiola took those loaded words as provisions to be consumed later when he needed them. It would suffice for now. He headed towards the Black Forest, where he was set to meet Leanne. She had told him she had something important to do with an invitee, and to wait for her.

Indeed, in the ladies' division of Cypress School, Leanne was about to cause a surprising stir. Today, something never-before-seen was about to take place. Leanne walked the long stretch of the hallway in her school, while every student within the vicinity parted, to let her and her new invitee through. They didn't exactly have a choice. They stood in rows on each side, wide-eyed, some staring in wonderment, most frozen with fear. Leanne walked and was confident. Confident no one would get hurt. Or killed. As she passed them by, every student gawked at that thing walking by her side. It was tall, imposing, and at any given moment, it could take away someone's life if it so willed. Though Leanne knew it wouldn't. She trusted because they had exchanged words on that. Of all the things that had visited the premises of Cypress School since its inception, no such happening had come to pass. The very same Surran Leanne had given her first Word to was walking beside her, accompanying her on a visit to her school. And she was about to introduce this Surran to her teacher, a Silver Robe, who had just been appointed as her mentor.

"And this is where we hold our history classes, and where I first saw an image of you," she pointed on the side towards an empty grand hall.

When Leanne reached the very end of the hallway, she spotted the three authors of their school paper 'The Eclipse' huddled in a corner, sheltered behind a front line of students. Looking back, she didn't quite get a fair start at Cypress School. Even before she had the chance to properly introduce herself and acclimate to her new surroundings, she had made headlines in the fall issue of The Eclipse, the terrific work of these ladies. She made sure to stop, and curtly whispered to them: "I trust you'll have this in the papers, too?" She left them at that, eager to present her teacher to the Surran.

That afternoon, Ezekiola and Leanne took their longest walk together, off the beaten paths of the Black Forest. Everything and anything that occurred on Circa since Leanne arrived, whether it was with the Emeralds, the SONS, Gespar, the Surrans, all were brought into the daylight. Zeke's life too, was not left out, including the woman and child he had had. Long gaps of silence filled their conversation, but they carried on, nonetheless.

"I never answered one of your questions. I thought this might be a good time," Leanne said at one point, breaking an odd silence. "My answer to you is yes," she said, casting him a nervous glance.

"Yes, to what?" Ezekiola asked, curious. He was unable to recall much of their past conversations. He noticed that several key moments he had spent with his friends were also missing from his memory.

"To a question you had asked, and I never gave you a clear answer. When I first came here, you were back from training with the Emeralds and asked me if I would stay here on Circa, no matter your shade. So, my answer is yes. Yes, to you Ezekiola, or Zek or Zeke, whoever it is," she said.

He stopped and faced her.

"What made you decide this?"

"Well, I just can't see it otherwise. I cannot unsee what I saw and did. And what happened to you. Plus, it's a much better ride than what I'm used to back home," she said, smiling. Yet despite her light expression, Ezekiola looked unsettled by something.

"I heard what I did to you when I got poisoned," he said, his head downcast. "I'm so sorry for that."

"You know, about that, my friends asked me to make you pay for that awful display of behavior. I still haven't decided what to do about that," she said, watching him closely. He nodded in turn.

"Until you decide on that price, can we at least start again? What is your name, where are you from, can I take you to see the sunrise, pluck a dozen sojas and explore portals?" Leanne laughed out loud.

"Maybe, we'll see. But first, you must come with me. We have a surprise for you," she said.

"A surprise? Who's we?" he asked.

"No more questions. Just follow me," Leanne said, wearing a mysterious smile.

Leanne led him back to his dorm, and a curious Ezekiola came face to face with none other than his friends, Atlas and Nohlan. It was the first time he was seeing them since their incident at the tavern. They hugged each other for a long time, and then Atlas pulled a box from a hidden spot and gave it to him.

"What's this?" Ezekiola asked.

"Happy birthday Gemini! This is your first gift from both of us," Nohlan said, while looking at the door, waiting for the second gift bearer to arrive. Leanne stood aside, also keeping an eye on the door.

Ezekiola opened the box and saw two strings of materials. One brown, the other red.

"What are these?" he asked, and looked up at them, a smile forming on his mouth. Then he noticed his friends were only wearing their white tunics, without their belts.

"Are you two giving me your belts?" he chuckled, finding this a bizarrely comical gift. Atlas and Nohlan were trying hard to maintain a straight face, while Nohlan continuously looked out the door.

"Yes and no," Atlas responded. "Actually, there's a second gift we want to—"

"Are we late?" Borghis just dashed in, followed by Keenan and Gordi.

"No, just on time," Atlas said, smiling.

When Ezekiola saw what Borghis, Keenan and Gordi were wearing, that's when he realized something was amiss. The three of them were no longer in their Brown Robes but in white tunics as well.

"Did you all get expelled, downgraded or what?!" Ezekiola asked, worried.

Then he saw what Borghis carried in his hand. A triangular box, one he had seen when he had graduated to the Emerald level. They were the boxes that held the Emerald belts. Borghis opened it immediately.

"Well, I see you've opened your first present. Here's your second birthday surprise. Happy birthday, Zek!" he said and distributed Emerald Belts to his brother, Atlas, Keenan, and Gordi. Ezekiola was momentarily speechless.

"What are you all doing with Emerald Belts? What's going on?" he asked, his voice quivering.

"You can't do this alone, Zek. We can't survive another life and death situation like the one we had in that tavern. We almost died! All of us! I never felt so helpless!" Nohlan blurted out while wrapping the Emerald Belt around his waist. As Ezekiola watched each of his friends wrap their new belts around their waists, a strange emotion crept up inside of him, making his eyes water unexpectedly.

"I'll tell you what's going on," Atlas took over. "What's going on is we're going to become one in this. That's right, we're becoming Emerald Belt students!"

"What? You're giving up your Brown...umm...Red belt, Brown Robes, and—" Ezekiola couldn't speak clearly, nor process what this meant. He looked down at the red and brown belts in his hands.

"Stop it right there," Borghis interjected. "First, you're saving us more than we're saving you here. We escaped the wrath of Falco who we hope never to see again. Who knows if it's possible that the rat gets himself re-elected again. Second, this is not just for you. While it's true that our individual belts and robes are expressions of our desires and what we wish to do with our lives, we're not giving up our powers here. On the contrary, we're empowering all of us by doing this."

"Yes, but still, you can't do this. It's not right that you just—"

"Do you really think we can sit back and watch the Sons of the Night Sky come after you like this and do nothing?" Keenan cut him off this time. "You saw how they infiltrated our world, how close they came to taking not just your life, but almost everyone's here. They won't stop. If we do nothing, not only would we be spectators watching tragedy unfold, but our inaction would make us enablers. It would simply be wrong to think we have no play in this."

"He's right. Your chances, OUR chances of getting through what's coming is if we are behind you on this. It can only strengthen you, and us," Gordi added.

"Even you, Atlas? Your red belt means everything to you." Ezekiola looked intently at his friend.

"Do you have any idea what went on in my mind after what I witnessed? We almost lost you, my sister, Leanne, and

Daria! We will not let this be your fate, nor ours. The SONS are all powerful. We saw what they could do. They won't stop and they'll be back with greater force. They were once Emeralds, weren't they? Then we too can and will become Emeralds. We will find a way to protect ourselves and seal them away for good. This is for all of us, not just one of us. And for the record, I chose the Tavern Surran's Massacre! I guess you can blame part of our decision on what happened there, too," Atlas said, grinning proudly.

"How did they even give you Emerald Belts like that?" Ezekiola asked Borghis last.

"Well, get this. Someone convinced not just Nomi but the High Council to allow for students to progress as Brown Robes and Emeralds, side by side. For any order of belt, actually. This is unprecedented," Borghis answered him with a curious smile.

That last bit of what Borghis said stirred Ezekiola. He recalled the events that day, and as his mind traced them, it came to a quick stop when he thought about the Count, Meredus of Loggia, and the conversation they last had. What struck him now were those last words spoken to him by the Count: "*And the one thing I would ask you to remind yourself of every day is this: You are never alone.*" This surely was no coincidence. He wondered if this wasn't part of the Count's works to forge this new path for students to follow, advancing a new variation of discipline ultimately making warriors out of any type of student. He suspected as much. He smiled, knowing it must have been the Count who orchestrated this.

Dakor brooded long hours over what had happened. He replayed the sequence of events over and over in his mind to figure out how something within arm's reach could have gone so wrong. He had been so close to gaining the fountain's power through his beloved Zeke. He could almost have touched it. Had he succeeded in gaining the fountain's power, Dakor would have moved up in ranks, possibly becoming a Nameless. But in an instant, everything went awry. How did that just happen? Everything was moving seamlessly under his control until that fateful moment when him and his men were propelled in the air by an unknown force. Contemplating long and hard over the scene, one thing kept resurfacing in his mind, as if the answer lay in that one sentence. It was what Gespar said to him, while laughing at him: "*Ha! Dakor, you should've known better than to capture women and expect nothing to result from it.*" Gespar was aware of something, and this bothered Dakor.

He mulled long and hard over that response. Then replayed the events in his mind again. Suddenly, it dawned on him, that blind spot he missed. How could he have overlooked something so essential? How could he not have thought big enough? His vision had been so narrow in the execution of his plan, that he missed a prime element. And that something was a word. That word was a name. Her name. The one who screamed the loudest when Zeke was falling off the cliff along with Gespar. The one who he saw pulling away from one of his men falling to the ground. It was the name Gespar yelled so loud, beckoning her. She was the one who saved their lives. It was Zeke's other half, the one he had linked with, the female, the very one with whom he ignited the Fountain of Fire with: *Leanne.*

He knew now what he had to do.

The End

Acknowledgments

Thank you to my exceptional editor, Gina Roitman for her tedious work, and brilliant editorial eye. And thank you for cutting all my darlings. My deep appreciation goes to my family who provided steadfast support throughout my writing journey. To my husband Eric, who infuses life's journey with meaning, and to our children Diana and Jesse, who manage to somehow distract me from writing, always reminding me that I'm a mother first. The joys they provide ultimately surpass any I could ever imagine. I extend a heartfelt gratitude to my sister Annie, who provided support countless times. To my friends: thank you for championing me and my books at every opportunity and for being such fun critics.

And lastly, to all the readers out there who picked up my book: thank you. I'm honored to have you as my readers. This story has lived in my heart and mind for quite some time now. There's something wonderful about sharing a story that's meant to be told.

About the Author

Through an obsession with pirates, Lucy Kyan first began creating fantasy worlds and characters in her early teens. She spent endless hours writing poems, drawing maps, memorizing flags and imagining sword fights. Later on in life, she took up fencing, and nourished her fantasy world by dream journaling for many years. In her quest to explore more worlds, she studied mythology, history and political science, and graduated from law school. She then entered the world of corporate law where she practiced as an attorney for over a decade. She lives in Canada with her family and their adorable doodle named Louis.

You can find out more about Lucy at www.lucykyan.com.

Also by Lucy Kyan